SHOW ME

EXTRACURRICULAR ACTIVITIES #3

NEVE WILDER

Copyright © 2021 by Neve Wilder

Cover design: Neve Wilder

Editing: One Love Editing

Proofreading: Janine Cloud

Professional Beta Reading: Blue Beta Reading

This book is a work of fiction. Names, characters, places, and incidents are products of the author's imagination, or are used fictitiously.

References to real people, events, organizations, establishments, or locations are intended to provide a sense of authenticity and are used fictitiously. Any resemblance to actual events, locations, organizations, or persons living or dead, is entirely coincidental.

All song titles, songs, and lyrics mentioned in the novel are the property of the respective songwriters and copyright holders.

All rights reserved.

No part of this book may be reproduced in any form or by any electronic or mechanical means, including information storage and retrieval systems, without written permission from the author, except for the use of brief quotations in a book review.

SYNOPSIS

Two Roommates. One Camera. A whole lot of action.

I get crushes the way some people get seasonal allergies.
And sharing a house with four hot roommates is like being stuck in permanent spring.
Too bad I keep getting friend-zoned.

But it's senior year now, and I'm done pining for the impossible.
Time to live it up and go out with a bang.
Or a lot of bangs.

And I'm definitely, *definitely* not getting attached to anyone. Especially not my straight, gym-loving, football-player roommate Sam whose impressively large... *smile* I caught a glimpse of once.
Or several times.

That's why, when Sam asks me for help with a very special, very

NSFW project so he can make a little cash, of course I agree. In the name of *friendship*.

And if it turns out that Sam's more than just muscles—that he's sweet, and smart, and a little bit filthy, and a whole lot less straight than I thought—well, that's neither here nor there, because this time I'm gonna be smart. This time, I'm friend-zoning *myself*.

We've got a list of deliciously hot scenarios, a camera, and Sam's huge... *smile*. What could possibly go wrong?

From the author of **Want Me** *comes the third new adult college romance in the Extracurricular Activities series. Expect low angst, high heat, plenty of laughs, a flustered redhead, a gentle giant of a football player, and enough BDE to power a mid-size city.*

AUTHOR'S NOTE

As always, I owe a huge debt of gratitude to my beta readers: Caroline, Janine, May, and Megan.

Thanks to those I consulted about various things, but especially Janine. Any football mistakes are my own or things I've taken liberties with.

Silver Ridge, where the story takes place, is a fictional city a few hours south of DC.

PROLOGUE: JESSE

I wasn't going to make it. I tried, I really did. I loved nineteenth-century literature and all, but there was a specially ordered precision-molded hunk of lifelike silicone singing a filthy siren song in my backpack, and the semi in my pants was quickly winning out over examining symbolism in *Sense and Sensibility*.

I wiggled impatiently at my desk as time moved like my grandma down a shuffleboard lane. When Prof. Carter turned back to the whiteboard, I bolted from my seat, ducked out of the lecture hall, and raced toward the dorms, my backpack hammering against the small of my back with the additional weight of the new toy I'd all but torn from its Amazon box at the student post office an hour ago.

I'd grown up in a three-bedroom, two-bathroom house with seven brothers and sisters and two extremely tired and overworked parents. I didn't know what the fuck privacy was until I got to college. I'd heard jokes in high school about guys and socks that took me way too long to get because I didn't have the luxury of a crusty sock tossed under a bed. I slept on the bottom bunk in a room I'd shared with three younger brothers, a hamster, and approximately nine billion unmatched socks that had only ever gone on feet.

Since the day I'd figured out how my dick worked, I'd had 2.5 minutes in a lukewarm shower to jerk off before the water turned cold or Armageddon broke out in the hallway. I could knock one out in forty-five seconds if I had to, but it wasn't pretty. I had to blow the smoke off my palm afterward, gunslinger-style.

I'd had blue balls since puberty, basically.

So a college dorm room, even with a roommate, felt like living in the lap of luxury. I swear I spent the first three weeks busting nuts in the room whenever my roommate Nate left for class just because I totally could. I wouldn't even be horny, but I'd learned to live by hobo code of never wasting an opportunity.

But I had something even better now. My very own personal teenage dream. And all the things I'd missed out on in high school? Well, I'd more than made up for lost time. I'd known college would be better than high school, even if the only improvement was privacy, but I never imagined that not even a full year in I'd be so...content. Not bad for a kid whose moments of triumph had previously included fixing six peanut butter and jelly sandwiches in under five minutes *and* cutting them into perfectly equilateral triangles.

I sighed happily as I caught the door on the backswing and hoofed it up the stairs of Hamlin Hall. I waved to Chet, my boyfriend's roommate, as he strode toward me from the opposite end of the hallway. I grinned shamelessly as he approached. "Yeah, I'm gonna need you to disappear for a while."

"I know. I just got the text. I was going—"

"What text?" I frowned.

"From Reid, saying to steer clear."

"Reid sent you a text saying to steer clear?"

Chet's brows drew together. "I feel like we're having communication error, and yet I literally can't think of how to express myself any clearer. Reid messaged me and—"

Thunk. We both swiveled toward the door at the same time. A groan followed, then came another quiet sound that was definitely not someone in pain.

"Well, shit," Chet swore softly, and the sudden sympathy in his gaze made a muscle in my jaw flutter until I clenched it.

I lifted my chin resolutely. "Open the door."

"Mm, nope. I don't think that's a good idea."

I narrowed my eyes at Chet, ignored my churning stomach and focused solely on the facts. "Did you know?"

He gave me an incredulous look. "What? No. I don't know jack. I only see him with you."

"When's the last time you got another text like that one he just sent?"

Chet winced as he looked down at his messages. "Two days ago at 3:00. Monday at 1:00. Um...last Thursday at 4:00." Reluctance was thick in his voice. "Should I keep going?"

I shook my head. My skin vibrated with electricity. I'd probably zap anything I touched. "Open the fucking door, or I'll kick it in." I wouldn't, because I had weak ankles, but I'd cross that bridge when I got to it. I had other options. My shoulders were plenty strong.

"I think—" Chet began, and I reached for the keys in his hand.

He put his palms up in a sign of surrender before fitting the key in the door, turning it, and stepping back. He gestured with a pained flourish.

I pushed the door open wordlessly.

Taylor Swift's voice poured out of a Bluetooth speaker, disconcertingly peppy. Reid's back was to me, bare ass pistoning as he swiveled his hips in time to the beat. Or attempted to. Until five seconds ago, I'd found his lack of rhythm endearing. I caught a flash of wavy blond hair and the pink gleam of manicured nails as the girl on her knees in front of him smacked his ass abruptly.

"Fuck yeah," he growled enthusiastically.

"*Reid*!" She and I both shouted over the music in awkward unison.

I glared at her for the unwanted solidarity.

Reid looked over his shoulder at me, the glazed cast to his eyes sobering. "Shit," he muttered. "But you have class right now!" As if I was the one who'd fucked up.

For a second it worked, and I was thrown into confusion that cleared when the girl looked between us, her eyes narrowing. "Is this your—"

"My tutor!" Reid covered his junk and shot me a pointed look as Chet groaned behind me.

I mustered my sweetest, most patient smile, honed over too many years of siblings' birthday parties, the countless number of times I'd been sneezed or vomited upon, the numerous repetitive birthday and Christmas gifts from extended family who couldn't keep me and my siblings straight, and the single time I'd lied for my brother Jack when he'd come home hammered after junior prom.

I nodded as the girl looked at me for confirmation. "We've been working together for a few months. I'm so sorry about his rhythm. We're still workshopping that, but it looks like he gets a gold star for sneaking in extra practice. Mind your eyes. His aim's not exactly on point either, which is kind of funny given his accuracy with a football."

"Jesse." The resigned plea in Reid's expression was worse than walking in on him had been.

I put up my hand. "Nope. You've found another *study partner*. It's cool."

I flinched at the touch on my elbow but allowed Chet to steer me from the room.

"That was a dick move. *He's* a dick," he grumbled, guiding me down the hallway. "C'mon, I'll walk you to...wherever."

"I'm fine," I insisted, shaking free of Chet's grasp. "Really. I'll see you around." I jetted toward the stairwell before he could say anything else.

I'd always hoped that if I found myself in this situation, I would be smooth and impervious. That I would simply cock a brow, then turn around and walk out, haughty and confident, cool as David Gandy in a Dolce and Gabbana commercial. Except I looked nothing like David Gandy. People seemed to want to ruffle my hair a lot, and I had suffered excessive cheek pinching as a kid. But I liked to think that over the last year, I'd really outgrown my extended gawky phase and blossomed into the kind of stylish twink I'd always hoped to be.

Eyes stinging, I raced across the quad to my dorm, saying a silent prayer that Nate would be gone so I could fling myself dramatically onto my bed and sob into my pillow. Then I'd regroup and immediately begin formulating my phoenix moment. I would definitely need hair dye.

Possibly scissors.

But of course I wasn't that lucky. When I opened the door, Nate was sitting at his computer chuckling at something on the screen. A vaguely recognizable blond hunk stood next to him tossing a football in the air.

God, even the sight of that pigskin made my stomach lurch. How the fuck did people manage this with finesse? *Be Meryl Streep*, I told myself. Calm, cool, and with that badass bitch swoopy hairdo she'd owned in *The Devil Wears Prada*. Hmm, maybe I should go for that kind of coif. Would it look good with my cheekbones? Did the attitude come with it?

Strangely, as Nate and Blondie's gazes swung in my direction, it was then that the heat in my cheeks rose to my eyes and spilled over.

Nate's half-smile slid from his face. "Whoa. Jesse. Everything okay, man?"

I nodded rapidly. "Totally fine. It was just a little hot outside and…and I walked in on my boyfriend's cock so far down a girl's throat he could charge an endoscopy fee. She had really nice boobs." Somehow that was the thing that burned the most. As a gay guy, I knew I wasn't supposed to judge my brethren, that bisexuals were just as valid as I was and not a damn one of us could help who we were attracted to, but damn, I kept hearing Reid's voice in my ear the week prior. *Nothing else feels as good as you. Nothing.*

"Oh shit, that blows. Errr, sucks." Nate winced. "I mean, that's awful. I'm sorry, dude."

Needing a distraction from their sympathetic stares, I tossed my backpack onto the floor by my desk and squatted, unzipping it and yanking out my books and laptop. The silence that descended was pregnant with the awkwardness of three people who didn't know what to say—two of whom were probably desperately trying to figure out how to politely extricate themselves. Too bad. Usually I was accommodating like that. I picked up on that shit. I liked people to feel comfortable. Not today. They could figure it out for themselves.

I pulled out the giant rubber dildo from my bag and looked up when Blondie made a choked noise. He wasn't smiling, thank fuck, or I might've heave beaned him with the thing, but his eyes were wide as saucers as I waved it around.

"Any takers? Clearly I won't be needing it." I'd intended to sound joking, but it came out forlorn.

Surprise, no takers. I winged it toward the wall next to my bed, where it smacked into the plaster with a satisfyingly heavy—but also depressing—thud.

"I have that one actually."

"What? Really?" I swerved my head sharply toward Nate. He'd never struck me as anything but straight heterosexual vanilla, and he sucked as an impromptu grief counselor, but I latched onto the distraction for the lifesaver it was.

"Well, maybe not that exact one. But they look similar. In size, I mean. Big." His expression turned sheepish. "I got it for a costume party and umm…" He gestured awkwardly. "That sounds dumb now."

"Yeah, well, I'd hoped to actually use mine for its intended purpose." I sighed at my glum tone. Perhaps I could also add in how quickly global warming was going to kill the human race.

"You still could, technically speaking."

Nate and I both stared at Blondie for a beat; then Nate gave an aggrieved shake of his head.

"It's tainted now, obviously," I told him.

"Did you smack him in the side of the face with it?" Blondie added. "Also a good use of it."

I sighed again. "I wish I'd thought of that."

"It's never too late." The impassioned words came accompanied by such an emphatic sword fighting gesture that I cracked a tiny smile in spite of myself.

Through the haze of my humiliation and sadness, I could *almost* appreciate the sincerity I detected in the furrow of the guy's brow. He was cute. The kind of cute I'd thought Reid was, too. The kind of cute that would disappoint you by cheating on you or being straight in the first place. God, I was truly spiraling now. "Thank you both for trying to make me feel better, but could you maybe just go?"

"You sure?"

I nodded, and apparently Nate read the deep plea in my eyes and took pity on me. "C'mon, bro," he said to Blondie as he hitched his backpack on his shoulder.

"Side of the face," Blondie reiterated with another gesture. "It'd leave a mark for sure."

Nate groaned. "You're making it worse."

"I have that habit. Sorry your boyfriend is an idiot," Blondie said to me, then fist-bumped Nate. "Catch you after Chem." He bolted from the room like his ass was on fire. Who could blame him?

Nate lingered in the doorway. He was a great roommate, and considering some of the stories I'd heard from my other friends, I'd gotten lucky. He was considerate and easy to talk to and not judgy at all, especially for a preppy guy rushing one of the bigger frats on campus.

But I hated the pitying expression he'd aimed at me.

"Unless you're about to offer to make out with me, please stop looking at me like that," I joked half-heartedly.

"Shit. Sorry. I'm not always good at knowing what to say. That dude is an asshole for real, though. Fuck him."

"I'll be fine." I nodded woodenly. "Who's the blonde?"

"Sam. Pledge brother. He means well, he's just a dope sometimes."

Actually, I'd preferred his cluelessness to Nate's pity. I forced a wan smile. "It's cool."

"A bunch of us are gonna go to this keg party at Kappa tonight. Why don't you come?"

"Meh." I wrinkled my nose. "Maybe."

But I did.

I went and got absolutely blitzed at that party, made out with some rando whose name and face I never, in three years, ever recovered, aside from a vague impression of soft lips. But what I *did* vaguely remember, through the haze of tequila shots, was stumbling into Reid's dorm at three in the morning and duct-taping the dildo to his door, along with a strongly worded message that Chet told me later consisted primarily of gibberish and the word "fuck" written over and over.

What could I say? It'd been satisfying at the time.

1
JESSE

"Whoa..." I froze in the doorway of the kitchen in the off-campus house I shared with three other guys, gaze bouncing between my roommate Mark and my semi-sorta friend Chet while I tried to mentally assemble the extremely confounding variables of this equation. Math wasn't my strong suit to begin with unless we were talking cups, quarts, and teaspoons, but I registered the bare chests and how Chet was glued to Mark's side. "What the fuck? Chet?" This could not be the correct answer. What kind of math was this? Was it too late to drop the class?

Chet lifted a hand in my direction with a droll smile that was only the slightest bit sheepish. "Hi."

Oh my god, they were *together*. Wait. *Were* they together? How could that be?

I whirled in Mark's direction. "But you...I thought...*Fuck me fucking sideways*," I spluttered. When Mark had come to me a month ago asking me vague questions about a guy potentially asking him out, I'd thought he'd meant someone at his summer internship. Not Chet-fucking-Pynchon who, yes, I'd had a teeny tiny rebound crush on since breaking up with Reid freshman year. Just like I'd had a minuscule, momentary crush on my former roommate Eric before he fell head over fucking balls for Nate. There'd also been the nanosecond crush I'd had on Nate after he brought me chicken soup once when I was sick, even if it'd been an awful store-bought brand.

"It's just...I don't understand why all the hot ones keep picking these baby bi's." I really didn't. It happened that I was prone to crushes the way some people were prone to heartburn after eating onions. It was also true that my crush-to-sexual-partner ratio was weighted on the side of crushes by...plenty lately, but there was nothing wrong with me. I was a little neurotic, but I was also an out-and-proud ginger who could actually tan rather than burn. That factor alone should've conferred unicorn status upon me.

I nudged Chet aside and opened the fridge with a huff. "You friend-zoned me in, like, two seconds flat. True or untrue?"

"True," Chet replied with a grin. "But that's only because—"

I put a hand up. "I swear to fuck, if one more person says I'm too sweet, or something about boyish charm, I'm going to lose my shit. Yes, I had a boyfriend freshman year. Yes, I very much enjoyed holding hands with him and...and, cuddling in the quad and giving him heart eyes or whatever." I'd had many of them after Reid. One every two weeks that I'd done all of these things with, and when it inevitably fizzled, I mourned briefly and then moved on to the next like a fiend. I'd gone through boyfriends the way some people went through Lay's potato chips—because you truly couldn't eat just one. "But Jesus, a guy's allowed to change. I'm not about that life anymore. I just want the hard-core action now, *thank you very much*. No relationships, no strings. I just want a guy with a big dick—because yes I'm a size queen and—"

"I have a big dick." Sam wandered in and inserted himself effortlessly into the conversation with a shameless grin. He was our newest roommate and one of Nate and Mark's fraternity brothers. Just in case his massive size and charmingly crooked smile weren't enough, he also happened to be one of the U's best tight ends. And let's just say the position designation was fitting. Once I'd gotten past the embarrassment of him bearing witness to my dildo-flinging meltdown freshman year, I'd decided I liked him. Not right now, though.

"Anyone who has a big dick doesn't walk around claiming it, you know."

Sam shrugged, attention shifting to Mark and Chet. "I know you." He narrowed his eyes at Chet, taking in his naked torso, then gestured between them. "Wasn't he the guy who—"

"Yes," Mark answered resignedly.

A couple of months back, Chet and Mark had gotten into a fistfight at our friend Nate's party, which made it all the more annoying that they were bare-chested canoodling in the kitchen right now. I mean, I couldn't even move out of the friend zone with anyone lately, and these guys had legitimate beef with each other and still ended up suckered to each other's sides like barnacles on a pier.

"Why's he in our kitchen?"

"He slept over."

"He slept—" I threw my hands up in exasperation. "Does anyone else want to come out? First Nate. Now Mark. Is someone running some fucking crazy effective psy-ops experiment in that frat? Sam?" Though, when I thought about it, that was the only possible enticement I could think of about a frat. I'd never been tempted to join one and knew little about them.

I suspected they were a little different from the vids I'd jacked off to on Pornhub with a twinky little pledge being taken by a big oafish dude. Now that was something I could actually get behind. The reverse, too, because size differences were fun. But when I'd once asked Mark what went on during the chapter meetings, he'd said, "Well, we vote on various things and plan mixers and community service projects."

What a waste. I'd lost interest immediately.

Sam reached around me, one big-ass bicep that probably came from lifting Mini Coopers brushing my shoulder as he grabbed a juice from the fridge and twisted off the cap. "I'm all set. I sucked a guy's dick once on a dare," he said as amiably as if he was sharing that his favorite color was yellow. "Haven't been inclined to do it again." We all stared at Sam as he chugged his juice and then wiped the back of his mouth. "What, did I fuck up? Break some sort of code?"

"You sucked a guy's dick on a dare?" No fucking way. Sam looked like the kind of guy who'd fist-bump his bro after he banged a hot girl and probably took pride in the decibel level of his burps. But shit, I had to ask out of professional curiosity. "To completion?"

"Rimshot!" Sam pumped a fist in the air as his empty juice bottle arced into the trash can, and then he turned back to me, nodding guilelessly. "Yeah, turned me into a manscaping convert. And I also make sure to eat a lot of pineapple now, too, if I know I'm gonna get some action." He leaned back against the counter and eyed me. "So are you making breakfast today?"

Unbelievable.

"Not for you. Not for any of you. *Ugh!*" If I'd had a cooking utensil handy, I'd have thrown it at him.

"So these are my roommates," Mark said to Chet with a mock flourish, continuing their get-to-know-you lovefest. I wished they'd just disappear back into Mark's room with their sexy naked chests and palpable...*feelings* for each other.

Gross.

Mark bumped me to one side. "Move over. I'm making eggs."

Now we were talking. I scooted to one side, gladly ceding the stove to him. I was usually the one cooking because I was actually good at it, opposed to the other guys who thought stir-fry qualified as a feat of cuisine. And, okay, secretly I didn't actually mind being the resident chef. I took pride in seeing my roomies' eyes roll back in their head when I made something tasty. I could elevate a fucking grilled cheese to art. I could make hipster avocado toast with goat cheese that'd put stars in your eyes. And my roommates appreciated it. Except maybe Sam. The way he wolfed things down, I wasn't sure he tasted anything.

"That's what I'm talking about." Sam grinned. "I've got practice in an hour. Make enough for me?"

"And me, too." I batted my lashes at Mark. "I'm grabbing a shower." Otherwise I'd have taken over, because Mark always did his eggs a little too runny for my tastes. But beggars and choosers and all. I needed the shower more; all that true love unfolding in the kitchen clung to my skin like stink.

I kept pondering Sam's confession as I undressed and stepped in the shower. I mean, was it even true, and if so, who the hell sucked a dick on a dare? Even I would hesitate at that. For at least a handful of seconds.

I shampooed my hair, scrubbed it vigorously, then soaped up my shoulders.

Objectively speaking, Sam was pretty cute. Sexy, even. But if I was being soul-deep-level honest—the kind of honest that made me feel a little shitty—I'd always pegged him as a bit of an airhead. No one that happy-go-lucky was sparing a brain cell for global warming or the difference between an adverb and adjective.

So I was a little perturbed to find myself with a boner and my sudsy hand gliding over it absently as his name floated around my head.

Go away, I told it silently as I shifted gears and washed between my toes. I was done with crushes in general, but especially on anyone who was my roommate. Or straight. Anyone would agree that was a doomed combo, far worse than Selena Gomez and Justin Bieber. And no way was Sam crush material anyway. He was a straight football player, after all, pretty much the antithesis of me.

My dick was responding purely to stimulus. To the vision of beefy pecs and big round shoulders. Shoulder blades that could crush beer cans. Quads like sequoias that would cinch around me and an ass that would—*goddammit*. I growled in frustration and sucked in a breath. Okay, if I was going to do this, I'd keep it general. Big guy fantasy. It could be *any* dude.

I thought of a random meathead I'd spotted in the gym a week ago when I was doing cardio and focused on him as hard as I could while I poured more body wash on my hand and lathered up my cock.

That...wasn't too shabby. I tugged on my balls, imagining sitting on the edge of a weight bench, nameless Big Boy towering over me with a sexy smile before he dropped to his knees and pulled down my shorts.

Fuck yeah, this would do nicely. I'd always been told I'd had a vivid imagination. My teachers probably hadn't anticipated what I'd use it for most frequently.

I bit my lower lip, and fantasy dude stared up at me from

beneath hooded eyes as he slowly sucked me into his mouth, the bulge in his gym shorts hinting at a sizable cock.

I jerked faster, close to orgasm, big fantasy dude working me like a champ, eager and slurpy, his head bobbing wildly. Sliding my fingers in his hair, I tugged his head back just as I was about to come.

In that inconvenient moment, Sam's face flickered into view in place of Big Gym Boy, his brown eyes hot and earnest, cheeks flushed, lips swollen and shiny from sucking me.

I growled with a mixture of frustration and pleasure as I shot.

A minute later, I stumbled out of the shower, wobbly and defeated. I was gonna have to work on my willpower. Stealth face exchanges in the midst of a jerk session weren't cool. *Hmm.* Maybe I should start going back to yoga to clear my mind, find my center again.

Knotting the towel around my waist, I flung open the door and stepped into a massive wall of firm flesh.

"Oof." Sam jumped back with a laugh. "Sorry. Maybe we need one of those blind-spot mirrors in the hallway. "

I stared at him, irrationally annoyed that he'd interrupted my fantasy. He wore an unperturbed grin that my brain had supplied a pretty perfect rendition of mere moments ago in the shower, which made me wonder how often I'd stared at him before without noticing I was doing so. I thought I'd mastered not paying attention to the straight boys at least a year ago.

Okay, that was a total lie. I'd registered Sam and dismissed him in the same breath because I didn't mess with straight guys or curious types. They weren't worth the orgasm or potential drama when watching them on Pornhub served just fine.

"Mirrors?" I blinked, and then it gelled. "Oh. Yeah. Or we

could both just be more aware of where we're going. Fancy that."

I focused very hard on his face and not the front of his boxers, because I was absolutely not going to attempt to verify his earlier claim by scoping out his dick print.

Stepping to one side, I gestured into the bathroom. "All yours."

"Um." Sam flicked a finger toward the Dopp kit under my arm. "Looks like you're about to lose something important."

I knew without looking what it was—because that was always my luck—and sure enough, I glanced down to see the fleshy head of my favorite shower dildo had popped out. I patted his plump crown and grinned. "Not to worry. The real thing is still firmly attached. This is Mike. He's a bit of a wanderer, but he always comes back." I canted my head, observing the delightful and surprisingly flattering shade of pink blooming in Sam's cheeks. "Wow. You actually blush. Who knew?"

"That answers my curiosity about the rings on the shower wall I've noticed before." Sam tilted his head in perfect mimicry of me as heat flooded my face. "Wow. You blush, too." He grinned, and the piquant wink he flashed me hit me like a fucking stun gun, mentally knocking me back a few paces. It should've come with a warning.

He squinted down at the dildo. "Is his last name…Hawk, by chance?"

I groaned. "C'mon, gimme more credit than that. No last name." Its last name was totally Hawk.

"Is that the same one from…?"

"Oh god no." I flapped my hand. "I got rid of that one. It was *unused!*" I tacked on for his horrified expression, then patted him lightly on the chest and stepped around him.

I floated to my bedroom in a stupor, then pulled on some shorts and a tee and stuffed my laptop and books into my backpack. There were two weeks left of summer, and I'd decided to take a few summer courses just so I could have a lighter course load come fall. All part of my grand plan to make senior year the best one. To go out with a bang. Or many bangs, if I had my way.

I hitched my backpack over my shoulder, tossed my towel onto the back of my chair, and closed the bedroom door behind me.

"Jesse? Jessseeeeeeeeeee. *Jesse*, yo, that you?"

I stopped at the top of the stairs. I could've keep going. Sam wouldn't know the difference. I *should've* kept going.

Then I sighed. I still hadn't mastered being a total asshole, but I kept trying. "Yeah?" I hollered toward the bathroom.

"Got a new bottle of conditioner and forgot to bring it with. Can you grab it for me? It's on top of the Target bag on my desk."

"Sure," I grumbled, then repeated it louder and dropped my backpack to the floor.

Sam had taken over Eric's room when he and Nate had moved out at the beginning of summer so they could shack up together. Read: have their own apartment to bone in without worrying about how noisy they were being. I'd had the misfortune of sharing a wall with Eric previously. I knew way more about Eric and Nate's sexual preferences than I should have. And okay, fine, I may have jerked off to the noises a couple of times because I was a perv for a good sex soundtrack and, wow, were they vocal.

I toed the bedroom door open, spotted the bag on Sam's desk, and headed toward it. I bent to read some scrawl on a postcard peeking from beneath the shopping bag, then tried to angle it toward me so I didn't have to look at it sideways, because I was a nosey ass and I didn't even know people still sent postcards.

In the process, I knocked into the bottle of conditioner and blurted out a curse as it in turn fell like a domino against an uncapped water bottle.

"*Shitshitshit.*" I flailed and managed to snag the water bottle before it tipped, but at the expense of the conditioner, which rolled off the desk and dropped onto my big toe. Water sloshed all over the front of my shirt as I hopped back with another vicious curse and bumped into the bed. I wanted to throw that damn water bottle across the room—who the hell left an open container next to their computer?

Composing myself, I rubbed my foot and then hobbled back over to the desk, wiping up a few stray drops of water.

Crisis averted, though; nothing had landed on his keyboard.

Then I froze, my mouth dropping open. In the midst of all that commotion, Sam's laptop had woken up.

I recognized the site immediately. It was one I visited frequently, myself. I started to back away, because taking a peek at a postcard was one thing, but checking out someone's open spank bank account and staring at all their deposits felt a little intrusive.

That was my intention, at least.

Except I couldn't help what I'd already glimpsed, and since I'd already accidentally seen it anyway…shouldn't I just verify?

Because Sam had a Pornhub page opened to what looked like a bunch of videos of solo jacking sessions by some dude named spankit4u. Interesting. I wasn't actually sure what to make of that. Did straight dudes typically watch other guys jerk off? I sure as shit couldn't ask Sam. Who did that leave among my coterie?

"Jesse? Did you find it?" Sam hollered.

I nearly dropped the conditioner on my foot again. I tapped the trackpad to put the computer to sleep again, reluctantly returned the water bottle to the danger zone, and rushed into the bathroom.

"Sorry," I said breathlessly. "I couldn't find any shampoo, just the conditioner."

"I said just conditioner."

"Oh, right."

Sam pulled back the shower curtain, extending his hand and giving me a peek of...skin. Lots and lots of skin and very solid, very wet gleaming muscle.

I almost dropped the conditioner for a third fucking time due to sudden loss of coordination.

I all but flung the bottle at his extended hand. "Who buys conditioner only, though, really?" I joked.

Sam pulled the shower curtain wider, his face popping into view, delightfully wet, dappled with drops of water, and garnished with a charming smile. He looked like a happy Viking. "I still have plenty of shampoo."

"Wait, you actually run out of conditioner first? That's, like...anathema to accepted hair product wisdom. I'm pretty sure it defies at least one law of physics." I'd never met a human on earth who didn't have to replace shampoo before conditioner. "It's not like you've got a huge mane of hair."

Sam's grin widened.

"Oh my god." I was an idiot.

"Conditioner is a little silkier and..."

"Yep. Got it. Okay. Bye. I have to go." I needed to find somewhere quiet to die, which would definitely make me late for class.

"I feel like we've reached a new level of intimacy in our friendship." Sam's laughter chased me out.

I hitched my backpack over my shoulders and thundered down the stairs. In a span of minutes, I'd learned more about my new roommate's sexual habits than...actually, no, I knew way too fucking much about *all* of my former and current roommates' sexual habits, because all of them were fucking heathens.

2

JESSE

Whatever hopes I'd had of spotting the perfect Mr. Right Now at a campaign party for Mark's dad's two weeks later were dashed almost as soon as we'd walked through the doors of the Farrow mansion. The primary demographic was middle-aged professionals with a healthy helping of grandparent-types on top.

I sat at a table with Nate and Eric, who kept leaning their heads together, no doubt cooking up a scheme to wander off and fuck somewhere soon, and Mark and Chet, who were obviously infatuated with each other and demonstrating the *grrrrr* kind of possessive that made me horny. If envy boners were a thing, I'd have popped one a half hour ago.

I gulped a second glass of champagne from a fancy flute, because the likelihood of me getting laid tonight grew slimmer with every blue hair that walked by and gave me the kind of look that said they'd like to pinch my cheek.

Incidentally, the more buzzed I got, the more my gaze

strayed toward Sam. Specifically, his crotch where his supposed lapbeast made its lair.

I was in desperate need of another kind of distraction.

"Does anyone see anything remotely approaching an eligible bachelor under the age of sixty-five? I'm not too picky. Even sixty-five-and-a-half is acceptable, but I'm getting laid tonight." I scanned the crowd glumly.

"I see lots of cougars, for sure." Sam glanced around with a grin.

"I don't want a cougar. I'll definitely accept a... What's the male version of a cougar? How do I not know this?"

"A manther." Sam didn't miss a beat.

"How do you even know that?" Ever since the shower incident, I'd been more curious about him, noticed myself actually listening to the conversations he had with our other roommates, tucking away any tidbit of information, no matter how pointless it seemed. Like his preference for Miller Lite over Natty Lite or that he didn't like apple pie or cinnamon. That he didn't mind the early morning football practices because he'd always been a morning person, which led to me scoping him out for a gearbox because no human college student I'd ever met was a morning person. It had absolutely nothing to do with providing a flimsy excuse to ogle him more.

Sam shrugged. "I pick up on things. I'm not an idiot." He patted my armrest. "I can be your wingman if you want. I'm a great wingman."

"You're not the kind of wingman I need."

"Why not? I can wingman for guys just as well as I can wingman for girls."

"I look like a dwarf next to you. Trust me when I say you're not the ideal wingman when one's hunting *manthers*. I'd be better off—" I blinked my eyes wide, the debate with Sam forgotten. "—hold on. *Hold. On.* Target acquired. Well dressed, definitely under sixty-five. Nothing in his teeth and not wearing loafers or Dockers. I might be hallucinating."

Mark glanced over his shoulder and waved to the approaching Adonis before turning back to me. "I worked with John this summer. Want me to introduce you? He's awesome."

"Fuck yes," I hissed in a tone that I hoped was not too desperate. Nate's amused glance suggested it was. Easy for him to be smug, though, with his own personal sexual Svengali sitting at his side.

Mark made introductions, and John took the seat next to me when Mark got up. Turned out he was a third-year law student, which ticked one more of my boxes. He wasn't too big, wasn't too small. Wasn't too arrogant or shy either, and he had a nice, easy laugh.

"So you're a third-year, huh?" I said. "Do you think you'll join the law firm where you and Mark are interning… What's it called?"

"Preston, Beasley, and Waring." John smiled. "I hope so. That's the plan."

Sam snapped his fingers suddenly and pointed at John, startling me. "I just figured out who you are!" He said it like he was about to pull John's face off, Scooby-Doo-style, and reveal him to be the crooked innkeeper haunting the overdecorated estate. "You're a Sigma Alpha. Class of…" Sam squinted. "2014. No…2012."

"I am, indeed." John grinned. "Good call."

They proceeded to exchange their stupid frat handshake.

"I've been playing a lot of pool recently. I thought your face was familiar," Sam said.

"Ahh yeah. I spent many hours in that library. So they've still got all the class portraits on the wall?"

"Yep. You need to come by again soon."

"I should. It's been a while."

They toasted each other, instant chums, and a prickle of jealousy ran through me. I supposed that was one benefit of being a frat rat.

"Have you ever really looked at the portrait of class of '68?" John's brow lifted in a mischievous arch, one that was supposed to result from me saying something witty.

Sam busted up laughing. "Yes! Every single one of them have the same exact mustache. It's hilarious."

I folded my arms over my chest and stared meaningfully at Sam. Wingman, my ass. "Should we switch seats so it'll be easier for you two to talk?"

"Nah." Sam grinned cheerily at me. "We're good." He turned his attention back to John. "So...wait, were you also the class that nailed all of the chapter room chairs to the ceiling?"

This was fine. I totally enjoyed being a net over which conversation was volleyed back and forth.

John grinned. "Guilty."

"Oh man, that was awesome."

They droned on while I moved on to a mojito, and finally Sam wandered off and it was just me and John again.

Go time. I fixed him with my most winsome smile. "So I imagine you must spend a lot of time at the firm, then. Mark makes it sound pretty cutthroat." I tilted my head to show I was invested in his response and angled slightly toward him to demonstrate I was interested in him as a person. People skills. I had them.

"It's competitive, yeah, but not all the bad. There are plenty of late nights, though, and more ahead." John then launched into a good three-minute soliloquy about the cases he was working on and some of the complexities of employment law until my eyes started glazing over.

That was okay, though. I wasn't trying to marry him or anything, just see what he had on under those khakis. Probably boxer briefs, if I had to guess. Probably a decently sized cock that he used decently in bed. Both were totally acceptable for a night or two of fun.

"Hopefully some of those are the fun kind of late nights?" I gave him a slow once-over, and the corner of his mouth quirked. "Do you have anyone who brings you dinner up there?" The twinkle in his eyes suggested he enjoyed my lack of subtlety. *Hook, line, and sinker.* Now I just had to get him in my metaphorical bucket. Or, more likely, his literal car, since I hadn't driven. Hopefully he had. Otherwise maybe there was somewhere on the premises we could—

"Jesse's a great cook. Er, chef." I gave Sam a flat stare that he failed to properly interpret. He cocked his head, wrinkling his nose in thought. "Chef? Or cook? Whatever. His food's good." He handed John another beer and then passed me something peach colored.

"What's this?"

"Bellini. Isn't that what you were drinking? It looked similar."

That hadn't been the question I was actually asking, but in my confusion over being brought a drink in the first place, I answered, "It was a peach mojito."

"Oh, well, hang on." He snatched the Bellini back.

"Wait—" I blurted, but he'd already set off toward the bar again.

John and I watched as he navigated the crowd.

"He seems nice. Roommate, yeah?" John asked, and I could tell by the way he was studying Sam's ass exactly what calculations were taking place.

I settled back in my chair and laced my fingers over my belt. Fuck me, it was hard being a nice guy sometimes. Too hard. I opened my mouth to pick up our earlier conversation, but my brain-mouth connection malfunctioned. "If you dare him to suck your dick, he'll probably do it, because he's pretty competitive. But he's otherwise straight. On the other hand, I don't require dares. I'll suck a dick because I enjoy it. And Sam's correct. I'm a really good cook. I'm even better at sucking cock."

John choked on a mouthful of beer. "Was not expecting that. Alrighty, then."

I handed him a napkin. "You learn all sorts of fascinating things living in a house with four other guys," I offered chastely.

"Apparently so." John burst into a laugh that tapered off when Sam returned with a different glass.

He held it out to me. "Taste it because I'm not sure he mixed it right. Doesn't a mojito have way more sugar in it?"

I took a sip and closed my eyes in appreciation. "Nope, it's perfect. Thank you."

"Did I miss anything?" Sam took his seat.

John's gaze slid over to mine, a smile quirking his lips. "Not a thing."

"So did you know James Hoffstra when you were at the U?"

John squinted. "Guy who started Sanibel Capital. Yeah, actually I did."

And they were off again.

I tipped my glass back with a sigh.

Eric eyed me thoughtfully when Sam and John went to the

bar together, which I supposed was the frat boy version of going to a bathroom together. "You know, I worked with a guy this summer who might be your type."

I blinked at him. "Oh, were you talking to me? Are you done astrally projecting your dick into Nate's ass?"

Nate put a hand over his mouth, but I saw the fucker's smile. Nate and Eric were…interesting company to be alone with. They'd perfected having an entire obscene conversation without even opening their mouths. It was annoying. And, sure, a little aspirational. It was okay to be jealous of your friends even though you were happy for them, too, right? I ached to know what that was like to have such a vehement and all-consuming attraction returned.

"I'm actually still in there, it's just that I'm excellent at multi-tasking."

"Ease up on the prostate, please," Nate deadpanned, and they chortled merrily like the happily in-love fuckers they were.

"As I was saying, I know a guy—"

"Yeah, yeah." I waved a hand. "Everyone knows a guy. I'm good. Really. I'm just going to sit here and drink this mojito and not be at all bitter that Sam can spark up a bromance faster than I can get a dick in my mouth. I mean, have you seen these lips?" I Vanna White flourished my hand under my mouth, which was in fact a nice mouth. I also thought maybe I should skip the rest of the mojito because I was feeling a bit effervescent in the head.

"You do have a nice mouth." Nate kept his gaze focused on me, though his lips twitched up wickedly as Eric stared at his profile.

"Look at Jesse's mouth often, do you?"

Nate shrugged mock casually. "I'm observant."

"Ugh. Fuck you both. Do not make me some tool of your fucked-up foreplay. Go find a tour bus to fuck in front of."

Eric raked his teeth over his lower lip. "You know you could join us sometime if you wanted."

"What?" Nate whipped his head to the side, and Eric cracked up.

"Stop looking at his mouth, then."

I snorted softly and stood. "I believe my work is done here. You're welcome. I hope you enjoy yourselves. Think of your good friend Jesse while you're…actually, don't. I don't want any part of that."

"Well, if you change your mind, you—"

Nate clapped his hand over Eric's mouth, and I walked off chuckling.

Setting my glass on a silver tray in passing, I asked the server where the bathroom was and was pointed toward a set of french doors.

I ended up in a long hallway filled with fancy oil paintings and elegant family photographs. I strolled along, eyeing them. Mark had been an adorable kid with a cowlick and a smattering of freckles over his nose. There was a great photo of him and his mom all snuggled up as she read to him, and then some of him on the basketball court during high school. I found myself smiling as I walked down the line of them. I knew Mark's life wasn't perfect by any means, and his dad, from what I understood, was a real ass, but they seemed genuinely invested in him, if I went by the photos. Envy cut through me.

My family was great, don't get me wrong. But there were a *lot* of us, so a pic like Mark and his mom all snuggled up? Undivided attention? Yeah, we didn't have any of that. Our version would've resembled a puppy pileup with me on the bottom. By the time I was ten, I was in charge of packing all lunches and shepherding all my siblings to school. I wouldn't give any of them away for the world, but sometimes I wondered what it'd have been like to grow up in a house that wasn't a live-action version of a pinball machine, or with parents who didn't run through three to five names before hitting on the right one when they were trying to get your attention.

As I walked, I opened every door I passed, discovering a linen closet, a small library, a laundry room.

I twisted another knob, pegging it for a guest bedroom and, for the second time in a month, crashed into a flesh mountain when the door swung wide. More accurately, the door banged into my head and I smacked into Sam on the rebound.

He caught me by the arms and righted me.

"We've got to stop meeting like this," he joked.

"I was looking for the bathroom." I blinked up at him. "Your chest has somehow gotten even harder since the last time I ran into it. Are you wearing chainmail underneath there or what?"

"Thank you?" Sam swooped down to pick up the phone he'd dropped and tucked it in his pocket as I rubbed my head. Concern flickered through his eyes. "Shit, did I hurt you?"

"Nah, just my frontal lobe. But I don't need it. I hear that's where personality comes from and with this face"—I waggled my brows—"who needs personality?" Huh. Maybe I'd hit my head harder than I thought.

"You've got plenty of personality to spare, anyway." Sam shrugged affably and gestured through the open door. "It's all yours."

I thanked him, then shut the door behind me and unzipped my pants, staring at the red patterned wallpaper and zoning out as I took a whizz. *You've got personality to spare.* Had that been a compliment or subtle shade? Did Sam even throw subtle shade?

When I rejoined the party, Nate and Eric had vanished, as well as Chet and Mark. I searched the crowd for John and internally pouted when I didn't see him.

"Want something else?" Sam offered, as I approached him and Ansel at the bar with a heavy sigh.

"I think I might actually head back home in a few minutes. By the way, you need to ask for a refund from whatever wingman school you went to. Or at least request a remedial course. What the hell was all of that, earlier?"

Ansel laughed and flashed a peace sign. "I'm dipping out of this one."

"Defend me, Ansel!" Sam protested. "I've been a wingman for you before!"

I slid my gaze across to Ansel as he wrinkled his nose. "The last time you wingmanned for me, I left alone. Remember?" He finger gunned me and walked off.

"I told him you were a good cook," Sam countered. "Everyone loves a good cook. How was that a wingman failure?"

"But then you sat there and talked to him about draft picks for ten minutes solid."

Sam pointed the mouth of his beer at me. "And the second you hopped in, I was going to fade into the background. You didn't hop in!"

"I can't hop in on draft picks because I care fuck all about draft picks."

"Hmmm." Sam stroked his chin consideringly. "Sounds like the two of you might not have much in common, then, because John seemed really into draft picks."

"Great, you date him, then."

"I'm not interested in him," Sam said blithely, and I threw up my hands.

"You had *one* job."

Sam deflated. His shoulders slumped, he hung his head, and for a second I thought he might actually feel bad, which in turn made me feel like an asshole. Then he cut his eyes smugly up at me from beneath his tousled blond curls and thick brown lashes. Except my dick misread it as coyness and *wow*, I really wished he hadn't popped up in that shower fantasy because it'd somehow created an unintentional trigger point between him and my dick.

"I'm a good wingman," he insisted in a rumbly voice that didn't help matters.

Just when I was about to protest, he scrounged in his pocket and retrieved a folded bar napkin. He held it out to me between two fingers.

I started to grin and reached for it, but he snatched it back. "Say I'm a good wingman." He waved the napkin in front of me tauntingly.

"What, exactly, do you think you did as my wingman? I'm missing something."

He gestured with the napkin again. "I'm giving you this. John had to leave and was looking for you, and when he couldn't find you, he left this."

I snatched the napkin out of his hand, glanced at the number, and then carefully folded the napkin and tucked it into my pocket. Okay, so the night wasn't a total wash after all.

Sam cleared his throat and stared me down until my lips twitched with a reluctant smile. Damn my cute roommates. Why was I such a sucker? "Fine, fine. Here's your damn wingman cookie. But just for the record, I'm going to pass the next time you offer."

Satisfied, Sam pushed off the post he was leaning against and dropped an arm around my shoulder. His casual affection caught me off guard sometimes. It was so different from the harried pats and quick hugs I'd grown up with. "C'mon, wanna go mess with Ansel? He looks like he might need at least two excellent wingmen."

Ansel actually looked like he was considering taking a nap on the shoulder of the girl he was talking to. "I think you should keep your mouth shut, though, and let me do the talking."

Sam shrugged. "I can do that."

He couldn't.

ONCE I GOT HOME, I STRIPPED OUT OF MY CLOTHES AND ENTERED John's contact info into my phone, considered sending him a message for all of five seconds, then decided it could wait. I didn't want to look too eager, after all.

After locking my door, I crawled into bed with my laptop for some solo action. Sam might suck as a wingman, but I expressed silent gratitude that he'd accidentally turned me on to spankit4u. The dude's videos were hot, and I'd spent a lot of the past few weeks getting off to him getting off. He made the sexiest little growls and noises as he jacked his meat.

I was in luck, too. A new video had been posted. I reached into my drawer, got my Fleshlight all situated, and gave my dick a few warm-up strokes with it as I cued up the video.

As usual, the quality was amateur, but decent. That was kinda part of the charm for me, though. Spankit focused the camera at a downward angle toward a mirror as he unzipped his trousers and pulled out his behemoth. It was semihard, but still in that floppy stage where it needed some dedicated attention, which was my favorite part because this dude didn't just go after it like some guys, like it was a chore. He luxuriated in the wank. It didn't even bother me that he never showed his face; his massive dick, killer body, and growly little grunts were enough.

My mouth watered, and I groaned when he groaned as I circled the Fleshlight around my swollen crown. The person who'd invented this thing deserved every penny they'd earned.

Spankit flipped the camera, and the angle went wonky as he shifted, resituating himself. He sat and spread his knees, then spat into his palm, the sound filthy and raw. He started jacking himself while tugging on his balls. Another soft groan melted me as he unbuttoned his shirt partway, sliding a hand behind the fabric to pinch his nipples. I loved a guy who gave himself a lot of attention, and Spankit was good for that, too, always pinching or caressing some other part of his body and making a lot of delightfully obscene sounds of pleasure when he did it.

A shiver of pleasure rolled through me as I instinctively stroked faster, then forced myself to slow down so I didn't come too soon. Spankit wasn't one to hurry either, which made us a perfect match. I snorted softly at the thought.

He adjusted the angle again, and I froze with my dick throbbing in my grip as something onscreen caught my eye. I swiped my hand on the covers and paused the video, then backed it up ten seconds and hit Pause again.

With the back of my neck heating and my heart sprinting in my chest, I clicked forward through the video in ten-second intervals. Red patterned wallpaper. A light blue oxford shirt. Massive quads.

No fucking way. It couldn't be.

But it was.

I scanned the caption underneath: "Mid-party jerk. Enjoy!"

Just before the video ended, while his chest heaved from the force of his orgasm, slick with sweat and the massive load he'd just spewed over it, the camera tilted as he went to hit the Stop Recording button, and I caught a glimpse of the back of the toilet I'd been standing in front of hours earlier, complete with the gold-filigree tissue box on top.

It was definitely Sam.

3

SAM

Attending the palm prom. Beating the meat. Playing one-handed baseball. Tug-of-war with the Cyclops. Firing off knuckle children.

Whatever you wanted to call it, I had approximately twelve minutes to do it.

I speed-walked down one of the sidewalks that wound through campus, darting around disoriented freshmen and slow-moving upperclassmen in no hurry to get anywhere fast on the first day of fall semester.

I hit the Record button on my phone as I walked, keeping the camera angled down so I didn't inadvertently capture any faces. It would be obvious by the shuffle of shoes on the sidewalk that I was out in public, though. Those were, hands down, my most popular videos and earned me the most in tips on my OnlyFans page.

Veering off the path, I headed toward an outbuilding I'd been scouting for the past two weeks as the summer semester had wound down. I always scouted before shooting, because while I was all over the extra cash, I definitely didn't want indecent exposure on my record. All the sprints Coach had us do in practice had come in handy more than once.

The dew-damp grass tickled my ankles as I strode around the side of the little shack. I'd figured out during my covert ops that it housed a couple of riding mowers that campus maintenance usually broke out on Wednesdays. Since it was Thursday, I should be home free.

With one last glance at the sidewalk a few yards behind me, I slipped around to the backside where thick bushes stretched out to either side of the building, probably to make it look prettier.

It was perfect, though. Just enough privacy for me to do my thing while passing traffic remained visible through the tree limbs, giving my viewers the thrill factor they seemed to love. And, okay, maybe I got off on it, too. That had been one of those unexpected self-discoveries that I had absolutely no one to share with.

The rush was similar to what I felt on the football field, but with the added bonus of an orgasm.

Dropping my backpack next to the wall, I pulled my baseball cap down low and leaned my shoulder against the metal siding of the building. Then I shoved the waistband on my gym shorts down.

The first video I'd ever done had been on a whim while sitting at my desk in the dorms, and even though I'd been hard as a rock before starting, the second I'd clicked on the camera, my dick had deflated like a windsock.

Now it was an old pro, and my dick had started rising to the occasion the second I'd strayed into the grass. Hell, the buzz of voices and occasional shouts, yells, and bursts of laughter behind me got me harder. I wouldn't have ever described myself as an exhibitionist or risk taker before, but it was funny what you could get used to—even *into*—after a while.

After pressing the button to start recording, I aimed the camera over my shoulder to give my subscribers a quick, blurry view of passersby through the trees, then aimed the phone down at my crotch as I stroked myself to full hardness.

Was it glamorous? Not particularly, but I couldn't deny that I got a taboo thrill out of quietly getting off when there were masses of people nearby going about their business unaware.

Apparently my subscribers did, too. I'd puttered along doing solo videos in my bedroom or bathroom for a month before the whim had hit to mix it up and I ended up in a stairwell in the engineering building. The fifteen-second snippet I'd posted on Pornhub of me leaning against the stairwell railing, about to come while the door on the floor below swung open and a few students thundered downstairs, had gotten me more subscribers in twenty-four hours than I'd gotten all month with my desk chair jerks.

Closing my eyes briefly, I tried to focus, listening to the sounds behind me as I worked my dick. Sometimes I didn't think about anything. Sometimes I mentally replayed a few trusty porn clips. Today, I queued up an old favorite of two footballers with a cheerleader. Trite, but whatever. It did the trick.

Precum leaked down my shaft, and I fought to keep my camera hand steady as I twisted over my head, spreading all the good stuff around and groaning helplessly as pleasure prickled through me when I rubbed my thumb back and forth over my slit.

Shooting a quick glance over my shoulder just to check all was good, I squinted at a slim-figured strawberry blond walking across the quad and slowed my pace.

Was that Jesse? Yeah, definitely Jesse walking with some

other guy I didn't know. The curly ends of his hair and profile were unmistakable.

I grinned, thinking about how surprised Jesse had been at Mark's dad's party when I'd handed him the napkin with John's number on it. He could kiss my ass. I was a great wingman. Though I couldn't really see him with John. Jesse was better-looking than John, and in my opinion, Jesse should be with someone who appreciated him more. I'd noticed John's eyes straying toward other guys at least five times when he and Jesse had been talking.

Jesse threw his head back, laughing at something his friend said, and I jerked my attention back to my cock as fire spiked through my shaft and raced up my spine.

"Fuck," I moaned out softly as I unloaded all over my fist. Damn, that one had snuck up on me unexpectedly.

I slicked my release all over my shaft and pumped into my fist, riding out the little lightning-bolt tremors that racked my shoulders, while hoping I hadn't messed up the money shot when I'd gotten distracted.

I glanced over my shoulder again, but Jesse had moved out of sight.

Clicking to end the video, I set my phone by my foot and reached into my backpack for the wet wipes I kept stashed there to clean myself up. After almost getting caught over the summer at the U's track and having to outrun one of the coaches hollering at me, I'd come up with a whole system for filming days: I carried wipes, lube if I needed some extra squish, an extra tee, and baseball cap in my bag in case I needed a quick change. And I always kept my backpack right beside me so I could snatch it up fast.

Once I got myself back in order, I raced toward Ryan Hall where my first class was. I'd have to wait until after class to rewatch the video so I could make sure everything was kosher and then upload it.

I pondered a caption as I hoofed it up the stairs.

"Yo, Sam-I-am!" Cam flagged a wave in my direction and sped up to catch up with me when I sent him a wave in return. "Where you heading?"

"Statistics and I'm pushing it. You?"

"I'm free right now." He pulled open the door for me. "Hey, I wanted to ask you about something."

"What's up?" I snuck a glance at the clock on my phone. Shit, his timing was awful, but Cam was a good dude. He'd only recently returned to campus after spending some time in rehab. He'd overdosed on pills sophomore year, been yanked out of school by his parents, and rehab had put him a year behind schedule. I knew he was struggling to figure out how to fit back into college life, and I didn't want to be that guy who ditched him as a friend just because he'd dropped out of the fraternity.

"I was thinking...ah shit, I'm just going to put it out there. It's probably a long shot, but I know you guys have that extra empty room. I've been living by myself, and the rent's pretty steep and—" Cam cringed. "I dunno, seemed like it could be a good solution for everyone?"

I gestured that he should let go of the door and stepped out of the way of traffic. We waited for some people to pass around us. "You think that would be good for your sobriety, though? I mean no one's doing drugs or anything, but there's usually booze in the house."

Cam sucked on his lower lip and puffed out his cheeks. "Yeah, I know, but alcohol's not my drug of choice. I mean, I don't drink now either, but it's not a temptation. I've been sober almost a year now. I go to meetings and shit. Have a sponsor and..." He sank back against the wall, his voice growing quieter.

"It's pretty boring at my place. Lonely, kinda. I just thought maybe…" His gaze flicked up to meet mine. "Fuck, I guess that sounds ridiculous."

His hopeful expression was killing me. "I'd be glad to have you, and I'll bet Jesse and Ansel would be cool with it, too. They're mellow. But Mark—"

Cam nodded, rubbing a hand over his forehead. "Yeah, I know."

Cam had been Mark's roommate in the frat house sophomore year, and Mark had been the one to find him near comatose. On top of that, there was some dicey history between Cam and Mark's boyfriend, Chet, that I didn't fully understand and honestly didn't want to.

"Maybe you should talk to Mark," I suggested.

"Oh yeah, totally. I just figured I'd start at the easiest place." He smiled wanly. "You've always been really cool to me. I really appreciate that."

I punched his shoulder lightly. "How about this: you mention it to Mark yourself first, then message me and let me know, and I'll talk to him, too."

"Really?"

"Yeah."

"Awesome. Damn, thanks, man." His grin about split his face in half. "And if it doesn't work out, that's cool, too. Just…" He shook his head when he trailed off. "Thanks. For real."

I watched him bound happily down the stairs and then flung open the door, racing inside toward the lecture hall and relieved to find a bunch of students still milling around outside it.

4
JESSE

I'd switched from trigonometry to statistics at the last minute for fall semester because it worked better with my schedule to satisfy the one math credit I was missing. But I was totally dreading it. I'd heard Professor Horton was a bore, and statistics wasn't my strong suit in the first place.

As I shuffled toward the door, my mood brightened at all the eye candy milling around. Maybe this class wouldn't be so bad after all. Big, brawny, built guys moved toward the entrance, almost as if a quarter of the football team had...*ah, hell*. It *was* a quarter of the football team.

"Jesse!" Sam lifted his hand and flashed me a huge grin. He had the best grin. Glowing and so sincere in its high wattage that even when I was trying to avoid him, it was hard not to smile back. "You didn't say you were taking this class."

Fuckballs. Okay, look him in the eye. Don't look down. "I wasn't until a half hour ago." The back of my neck heated faster than my Instant Pot as the memory of Sam's big hand shuttling up and down his cock flashed to the forefront of my mind unbidden.

He gestured me through the door, then squeezed past someone else, keeping in step beside me and pausing at the same time I did to survey the seats. "You want to sit with us?"

"Um." My gaze skimmed over Sam's shoulders and landed on another pair I knew far better. Or used to. Reid acknowledged me with a lift of his chin. I shook my head at Sam. "I've actually got some friends up front I'm gonna sit with, but thanks. See you later." I brushed past them and headed toward the front of the hall, doing some quick calculations because I'd been lying through my teeth.

I didn't see a single familiar face, and paranoia convinced me that I was being watched to test the veracity of my tall tale, so I made a hasty decision and plunked down in the seat next to a guy with dark hair and glasses.

"Hi. This is statistics, right?"

"It's written on the board?" He pointed.

"Oh, yeah. Duh. Cool glasses, by the way." I nodded emphatically in punctuation. Surely from afar this looked kind of like friendship rather than a pathetic attempt at avoidance?

"Thanks. They're not exactly a fashion statement. I need them to see?"

"Oh, well yeah, of course." I pulled out my laptop and set it on the table. "But you clearly have good taste."

"Thanks?"

The question marks on the end of this guy's sentences were starting to throw me into an existential crisis. Luckily, the professor capped his dry-erase marker and turned around to face the class.

As he introduced himself, I snuck a quick peek over my shoulder, convinced I was still being watched and judged.

Sam flashed me a smile that seemed slightly apologetic, then jerked his gaze away as the professor started talking about course expectations.

I nibbled on the corner of my thumbnail, wondering if there was any possible way Sam might somehow know that I knew it was him on the videos. No way. That'd require some kind of *Inception*-level physics fuckery.

The back of my neck burned through the entire class, visions of Sam's big hands around his even bigger cock taunting me the whole way through. *You're better than that*, I admonished myself repeatedly.

Except I wasn't. I really, really wasn't, and I should probably go ahead and pay the entry fee to Pervdom, get the lapel pin, and run for president because, try as I might, I couldn't get those videos out of my head. They kept looping through my brain, each neatly correlating itself to one of my own jackoff sessions. So now we were inextricably bound together by virtue of whacking off. Except Sam was completely clueless about our exceptional link. What an especially mean twist of fate.

I had so many questions that were never going to be answered because there was no fucking way I could tell him I knew.

Maybe I should switch back to trig.

When class ended, I hurriedly packed up my laptop, responded to Question Guy's "See ya?" with a "Yeah?" and glanced around for Sam so I could avoid him. He was talking to a cute brunette. Figured.

I had two hours before my next class, which was plenty of time for a sandwich, a mercy jerk, and a power nap.

Breezing out the door with my agenda for the rest of the day firmly set, I almost smacked into Reid, who must have veered into my Dipshit Blind Spot while I was busy avoiding Sam.

He jumped dodged to one side with a chuckle, then fell in step beside me. "I heard this class was kinda hard."

"Mm-hmm. Same. You're a football player, though. They know better than to fail you." Did I want the soup and salad bar from the caf or a footlong meatball sub? *Speaking of footlong.* I begged my brain to please stop.

"Well, that's no guarantee. Hey, maybe—"

I stopped and turned to face him. Damn. Why couldn't he be having a bad face day, at least? But nope, he looked as good as he always had, though I now recognized that what I'd once considered an all-American smile actually more closely resembled a simpering weasel curve. "We're approaching something that resembles conversation, which was not my intention. *At all.* Apologies for following up my acknowledging 'mm-hmm' with something that inadvertently opened that door when what I meant to say was 'fuck off.'"

Reid whistled low. "Okay, wow, still mad at me."

"Yep. Try again in…never. Never would be good." I finger gunned him and then picked up speed to leave him behind.

That night I perched in bed finishing off some homework while downstairs the TV blared in what sounded like a cross between a nature program and *Night of the Living Dead*. Mark, Sam, and Ansel were alternately whooping and cracking up. After another five minutes, I shoved my laptop aside and rolled toward my nightstand, digging around for some headphones.

"Jesse?" Sam rapped his knuckles lightly on the doorframe.

I glanced up, one hand still buried in my drawer, continuing the fruitless search. "Usually the knock comes first."

"I have social dyslexia."

I gave up and closed the drawer, then rolled onto my back, pushing my laptop out of the way. "Is that a real thing?"

"If it's not, it should be. I know a lot of people with it."

I couldn't disagree with him, and for a split second I totally forgot the fifty million compromising positions I'd seen him in. But then he pushed the door wider and leaned against the frame. There was hardly a flat area on him. Everything was sleek, carved rounds. Biceps sloping into triceps. Pillowy pecs, big forearms. Even his hair had a swoop to it that highlighted the varying shades of gold.

"Your doorframe poses are on point. Perfect bulging bicep-to-sleeve ratio there. How long did it take you to perfect it?" I arched a brow.

Sam glanced down at his arm and chuckled. "Guess I got lucky and nailed it on the first try."

Well, that backfired. I wondered what else he nailed on the first try. I cleared my throat and thumbed toward my abandoned laptop. "What's up? I'm kinda in the middle of something." Technically I was in the middle of next week's reading for Advanced Comp and retaining none of it.

"Oh. Yeah. Sorry." He dropped his arm from the frame and shoved one hand in the pocket of his navy track pants, which were almost as good as gray sweats. Almost. Navy's downfall was that it hid more than gray. "I just wanted to say that you should sit with us if you want to. In class I mean. Most of the guys are cool. Don't let Reid run you off."

Get ahold of yourself, man. Stop imagining how his biceps flexed as he jerked himself off at the campaign party. It occurred to me he must have wiped himself down good in there because I'd bumped smack-dab into his chest and didn't even catch a whiff. Oh god, now I'd not only repeatedly watched my roommate jacking off, I'd also literally bumped into his spunk.

"Okay, thanks for the offer. I mean, I know. I just wanted to sit with my... friend today."

"Was that the guy in the glasses next to you?"

Cue internal wince. Had we even exchanged names? I didn't think we had. I nodded. "Yeah, that's him. He's a nice guy. Anyway, thanks for the offer."

"Cool."

I thought we were done, but Sam lingered and, after a couple of beats of silence, went ahead and invited himself in. He stopped at my bookshelf and ran a finger along the spines of the paperbacks I'd brought with me from home. I'd had this lame idea that I'd meet the love of my life and share all my favorites with him. Reid had hated reading, and I'd never been with anyone else long enough to even bother.

"I think I read one of these, maybe." His finger had stopped on an eggplant-colored spine of *Thrice Bound By Oath*. "They were really big back in the day, right?"

"Still are. It's my favorite series. I reread the whole thing at least once a year. Sword fighting, intrigue, romance, betrayal, declarations of fealty." I paused for a wistful sigh. "And all the LGBT rep a starry-eyed little gay boy like me could hope for. I was obsessed when I was a teen. Maybe I still am, but shhh. They lived under my bed for years at home so they wouldn't get lost or destroyed."

Sam's brows flickered together with such overt concern it almost took me aback. "Your parents aren't okay with you being gay?"

"Oh no, nothing like that. I mean, I assume they are. We've honestly never had a sit-down about it, ever. I'm not sure we needed to. I just mean that things tended to vanish with that much constant foot traffic in our house. We hoarded our precious shit like dragons."

Sam tilted the book out from the shelf. "Are there dragons in this? I can't remember."

"Yes, actually."

He studied the book a moment longer with a faint smile and then moved on, pointing to a big leather scrapbook on my dresser. "What's this?"

"My younger sis made it for me before I left for freshman year. She was going through a scrapbooking phase."

He traced a finger over the binding before cutting a look over his shoulder at me and lifting his brows. "Can I look?"

"Sure." Better that than the boner that was forming for the slyness in his expression, like he was about to discover some secret about me by going through my scrapbook. Good luck. I couldn't deny that his undivided attention was flattering, though. I'd never had it before, and I'd underestimated how inviting it was. He was also the first person to ever express any interest in looking through my old photos.

Sam picked up the scrapbook, carried it over, and helped himself to a patch of my bed, flopping onto his stomach and sending up a cloud of laundry detergent and the scent of his deodorant. Old Spice Fresh scent. Not that I'd checked or anything.

"Wow. You were on swim team." He stared down at the photos, transfixed, and I cracked up at the note of wonder in his voice.

"Yes, my limbs are occasionally capable of coordinated movement in a sports-like fashion."

He flashed that same sideways smile that made me feel off balance. "I didn't mean it like that. Well, at least not intentionally. I see it now, though, in your shoulders." He scrutinized the picture again. "You were good, too. Did you get scouted for the U or anything?"

"Nah. I didn't have the times. Maybe I could have, but I wasn't... It was just something I did and was decently good at. I didn't have the passion for it, you know? At least not enough to make my entire college career focused on it."

Sam nodded thoughtfully and flipped the page, asking about the people in the photos. I pointed out my sisters and brothers. Our dog, Daisy. I kept waiting for him to get bored and move on, but he went through the whole damn thing, scrutinizing every photograph and the little quotes and decorations my sister had included.

"So did you ever talk to John?" He fiddled with the edge of a photograph, muttering a *shit* and pressing his thumb back over it and trying to tamp it back down when it came unglued.

"Not yet."

"What? After all that smack talk about my wingman skills, you haven't even put the results to good use?" He closed the scrapbook and folded his arms over the top of it, staring up at me. "Did you get scared?"

"No. I just forgot." Sorta. Why did my laugh sound like it was tinged with guilt? "But now that you've reminded me, I'll do it in a minute."

"What're you gonna say?"

"I dunno. How's it going?"

"And?"

"Ummm. That's as far as I've gotten."

"Fair enough." He chuckled and slid from the bed, taking the photo album with him and placing it back on the dresser. "I can fill you in on football draft picks and stuff if you want me to."

I smiled. "I think I'll be okay. I think Pittman is a bad choice for the Falcons. I'd be Newsom all the way."

Sam's lips parted, and he rocked back on his heels as a smile spread slowly. "Wow. I stand corrected. Wait." He narrowed his eyes. "How long did it take you to perfect that?"

"Guess I got lucky and nailed it on the first try," I parroted, then laughed. "Fine. I looked into it after I got back from the party that night." While trying to distract myself from going back through and watching every single video Sam had ever made.

"Pretty impressive. All right, I'll leave you alone now." At the doorway he angled a look back at me. "See you tomorrow, I guess."

Or sooner if my dreams were mean.

Once he'd gone back downstairs, I opened John's contact info and stared at it, mentally composing different versions of a flirty message, then tossed aside the phone without sending anything.

Tomorrow I'd do it for real. I was really starting to fall behind in Operation Bang My Way Through Senior Year, after all.

5
SAM

My phone vibrated just as statistics let out, and I opened the Craigslist app, quickly skimming the message before deleting it and tucking my phone away. Another creeper, another no from me.

"Hey." I upnodded Jesse as he passed by me toward the exit. He always sat at the front, and not that sitting with me was a requirement at all, but I kept getting the feeling he was avoiding me.

"Hey," he replied and continued toward the door with hardly a pause.

Even in the house he seemed to go out of his way to make himself scarce when I was there lately, and I'd been racking my brain trying to figure out if I'd done something wrong. Maybe I really was a shitty wingman and he was good at holding a grudge? That didn't seem like him, though.

I couldn't remember ever being anything other than polite, and it seemed like a stretch that he'd still be embarrassed or something over me being in the room when he'd run in all flushed and teary three years ago. So I was well and truly stumped.

I scrambled to stuff my books in my backpack and caught up with him outside, falling in step beside him. "Do you want to study for the exam together?"

Surprise crossed Jesse's face, and then he blinked at me dubiously. "Really?"

"Yeah, why not?"

He scrunched his nose. "Actually, you probably don't want to study with me. I bombed the pop quiz last week."

"Oh, I did pretty well on that. So maybe you should study with me." I grinned as surprise crossed his face for the second time. Most people assumed because I was massive, on the football team, and also in a frat, that I was an idiot. Or it might have been that I was generally a pretty happy-go-lucky dude. Mark called me a golden retriever, which was fine with me. Life was way more pleasant with a glass-half-full attitude. At least in my experience. So I didn't sweat the small stuff. Well, except where Jesse was concerned.

"Really? You got an A?"

"I didn't get a single question wrong." I clucked my tongue with a wink. "See, all those hits I take on the football field? They have a reverse effect on my brain cells. I'm actually getting smarter." I tapped my temple. "But it's no skin off my back if you don't want to. Just an offer."

Jesse's gaze strayed absently toward the left, and I followed it to the guy in glasses he usually sat with, who was looking our way. I tipped my chin to him in acknowledgement and turned back to Jesse. "Okay, so no?"

"No, no, actually, I'll take you up on that."

Show Me

IN ADDITION TO ME, THERE MUST HAVE BEEN SOMETHING WRONG with my desk, because Jesse kept glancing over at it.

"You don't like my screensaver?" It was a pic of a golden retriever in a headset and sunglasses. Dumb, maybe, but surely not offensive in any way.

"The screensaver is fine, though a little dorky. Way better than a screensaver of yourself on the football field, though. Or a girl in a tiny bikini sitting on the hood of a car." He cracked a tiny smile.

"That'll be my next one."

"That bottle of water right there is driving me crazy, though. Aren't you afraid of knocking it over and frying your computer?"

I'd totally forgotten about it. "Didn't know you were so fastidious about your tech. The cap's on tight, I'm sure."

"Really, because—" He snapped his mouth shut with a shake of his head. "Never mind. I'm sure it's fine."

I set down my pencil and propped my chin on my fist. "Okay, did I fuck up something recently? Piss you off? Say something dumb? Because you're acting weird, and I'm driving myself crazy trying to figure it out. I know I ate all the Rotel dip last week, but it was really fucking good and I was starving. I threw an extra tenner on the counter for groceries, too." I wouldn't tell my mom, but his Rotel dip had kicked her Rotel's ass, then shoved it in a locker and slammed the door in its face. I'd always thought Rotel was pretty simple, so I hadn't even known it was possible to improve upon the standard recipe, but it was. I'd stood at the kitchen counter and finished it off like a total sloth.

"You do consume massive amounts of food," Jesse agreed. "And it'd be a lot nicer if you asked sometimes because...hmm." He pressed his lips together and rolled his eyes, seemingly at himself. "Fuck, that's not it. It's…" He winced, and I figured it must be pretty bad if he was going to the trouble of that many facial expressions over it. "Nope, never mind. Let's stick to statistics." He thumped a page in his study packet. "What'd you get for number five?"

"A legit answer out of you." I folded my arms over my chest stared Jesse down, unblinking. Accompanied by my size, the blinkless stare was one of my best intimidation tactics on the field, but Jesse canted his head, mouth curving in what seemed like amusement.

"Impressive. Unfortunately for you, the big jock schtick has never worked on me. I cut my teeth outrunning guys your size who thought they were way faster than they actually were."

"Damn, really?" I tried to remember where he was from. I was pretty sure it was a smallish town nearby. I'd grown up in a liberal suburb of Charlotte, and my school had been the same. Around tenth grade everyone had seemed to grow out of caring about someone's sexuality. I knew it wasn't that way everywhere, though, and I kind of hated imagining Jesse being chased down by a bunch of homophobic thugs.

His grin broke wider. "Nah, I'm messing with you. Usually I was the one chasing them back then, hoping for a little *something-something* under the bleachers—top five fantasy, bleachers—" He splayed his hands with cinematic flourish. "But unfulfilled to this day, sadly. Anyway, what I'm saying is, you can't intimidate me. What. Did. You. Get. For. Number. Five?"

I looked down at my paper and blew out a breath. Fine. "Fifty-seven percent."

We moved on through the study guide, went over some of the prep questions, and then ran through a few flash cards he'd made.

Jesse shoved aside his computer. "I think I'm as ready as I'll ever be."

"Agreed," I said and settled back on the bed. Jesse's gaze strayed over my crotch, so I glanced down to make sure everything was where it was supposed to be. Sometimes things went sideways when freeballing.

He pressed his lips together and when our eyes met, blinked quickly away, and squeezed them shut as if he was in enormous pain.

"Are you okay?" I stared at him with growing concern. My first aid skills were a little rusty.

Jesse popped his eyes open. "Goddammit, I know you're *spankit4u* and I can't even look at you now because I know I'm not supposed to know, and your dick is huge—just like you said it was— though I didn't believe you at the time, and—" He covered his face and let out another pained sound that was a cross between a keen and dramatic groan as I felt the blood drain from my face. "I've been jerking off to your solo sessions for weeks, and I feel like a total fucking perv. I'm obviously not doing that anymore, since I found out it was you—the jerking off part, I mean—because that would be totally fucking weird, right? But I was definitely doing it before and I...that's *awkward*. I'm still probably a perv any way you cut it."

I digested all of that in shocked silence. I'd been careful to never show my face. I had few identifying marks on my body. No tattoos or unique birthmarks. Nothing crazy memorable. "What...which...how—?" Now was the moment my brain cells chose to abandon me.

"When I got your conditioner that day, I almost knocked a water bottle over and in the process of trying not to fry your computer, woke it up and saw the Pornhub page. I didn't really think of it until I saw the video you posted from Mark's parents' house. Remember when I ran into you when you were in that bathroom with the red wallpaper and that weird gold tissue box?"

"Shit." I hadn't even been thinking about it. I'd been thinking about Jesse and John and draft picks. I had no recollection of a gold tissue box.

Jesse dragged his hand down one side of his face. "I know, tell me about it. I blush every time I look at you now. I snarked at you about dick size and...you totally weren't lying. Now when I look at you, I think about how I know you like to play with that notch when you—" He put his hands over his bright red face. "See?"

Mortification tried to surge up inside me, but I tamped it down, and an unexpected laugh bubbled out in its place. He was right. I'd never even noticed before, but when I thought about it, I absolutely gravitated to that little divot in my crown when I was getting myself hard.

Jesse peeked at me through a crack in his fingers. "You're laughing?"

"I—yeah." I couldn't seem to stop. I fell back on the bed as it rumbled out of my chest and then scrubbed my hands over my cheeks. "Fuck, okay."

Jesse was still staring at me like I'd confused him. I was a little confused myself. But I figured the hysterical tinge was probably understandable. Jesse was the last person in the world I'd ever imagined I'd be caught by.

I sat up. "Okay, let's sort this shit. You watched my vids before you figured out it was me. That's no big deal. No reason to feel like a perv for that. Right?"

Jesse dropped his hands from his face and chewed the inside of his cheek. "Okay, technically you're correct."

"And I don't feel weird about that, because shit, that's what they're up there for, right?"

"Right." Jesse nodded, still working the inside of his cheek furiously.

"So you know what my dick looks like and how I like to jerk off. No big deal." He made the cringe face again, and I chuckled in spite of myself. "I've seen lots of dicks, and I can always tell when you've jerked off in the shower." I hitched one shoulder casually.

"What?" Jesse blanched. "How?"

"You take at least five minutes longer and come out whistling 'Don't Stop Me Now.'"

"Correlation does not equal causation," he pointed out mock sternly.

"Okay, well, once those two factors were in play and you missed a spot on the shower wall."

"Fine, your case holds a little more water now." He cracked a small smile. "Or other fluids, as it were." He wrinkled his nose at himself. "Too much?"

"It was just a tiny spot," I quipped. "See, no big deal." God, the last thing I wanted was to make Jesse feel awkward around me. I really liked hanging out with him.

He sucked in a huge breath and exhaled it out his nose, nostrils flaring. He did that a lot, and it always made me smile. I mean, Jesse in general was attractive. At least I'd always thought so.

"Okay, yeah. You're right. Everyone jerks off. Well, not everyone, but a large majority of the male population."

"If it'll make you feel better, you can jerk off in front of me and we'll call it even."

Jesse stared at me openmouthed for so long that I burst into laughter again. "I'm joking."

He shook his head. "Wow, you're better at deadpan than I thought."

"There are probably a lot of things I'm better at than you thought." I meant that generally, but Jesse cocked his head at me like I'd said something weird. Wait. Was I flirting with him? I considered. I liked teasing people, but teasing didn't equate to flirting.

Except when it did.

What the fuck? Now I was just getting myself confused.

Jesse nodded slowly after a beat. "I'm sure. Okay, so we'll just move on, then. What's going on with number seven because I'm struggling with that one, too. Also, do I really whistle 'Don't Stop Me Now'? Every single time?"

"Sometimes it's Harry Styles."

Jesse nodded in apparent approval at that.

As we moved through the next section, my curiosity grew. "So..." I cut a sideways look at him. "Did you like them? I mean, objectively speaking. Like, the quality? It doesn't seem too repetitive?" I uploaded shorter compilation clips of my solo sessions onto YouPorn, but the full lengths got posted to my OnlyFans. I had to assume we were talking solely about the Pornhub vids because I wasn't about to ask if he'd subscribed to my OF.

Jesse flopped back on my bed and threw his forearm over his eyes. "God, I can't believe we're having this discussion."

"We don't have to at all. I was just wondering."

"No, no. You're right. This doesn't have to be weird. Lemme think."

He was silent for a handful of seconds, then sat up, using his fingers to tick off his list as he spoke. "Okay, the quality is pretty great, and there's not too much camera shake, which is good. You have a nice dick—don't preen, there are plenty of nice dicks out there. I like that you make noise. A lot of videos the dudes are just quiet. It's ten times hotter when you can hear the moans and the squish and..." He exhaled a noisy breath. "Yeah. Moving on. You're definitely missing opportunities by not having an active Twitter or Instagram account, too, where you can tease people with your hot bod—because I'll grant you this for sure: you're ripped. So you should get on that *stat*. It's not hard. Haha, actually it's very definitely hard." He cackled at his own joke. "But you should set up those, take a pic every day. Try to make it good, but really, just anything kinda sexy-cute would work. Then sit back and watch your kingdom grow." He spangled his fingers through the air. "But to your question, yes, it's a little repetitive? That's also kind of the thrill, though. I mean, your whole schtick is pushing the envelope in terms of where you're getting off, right? That's hot. Takes a while before it gets old. But...you might be approaching that point. I'm talking a lot. I'm going to stop."

Wow. That was a lot of opinion. I absorbed it with a thoughtful nod as he confirmed some of my fears. "That's what I've been thinking. There was a little viewer drop-off last month, so I've been trying to come up with some new ideas. Public bathrooms in recognizable places. I've done a few of those."

Jesse's cheeks reddened again. "Sorry." He reached down and adjusted himself—the movement quick and unobtrusive. Strangely enough, the action sent a prickle of awareness through me. I wrote it off as stimulus response. We were talking about jerking off, and he'd just complimented my dick. Made sense. "I was thinking about that one video you did in what looked like a locker room," he continued.

"Oh yeah." I grinned. "That was a total stealth jerk. I was terrified. The first time I tried it, I couldn't stay hard."

"Well, persistence paid dividends because—" Jesse cut himself off with a self-deprecating laugh. "It was well done.

Anyway, so maybe some of that's helpful. Now can we finish studying so I can go back to my bedroom and die of embarrassment?"

I laughed. "Are you always this dramatic?"

He nodded. "It's kind of my MO. Life's more fun in loud colors than in beige."

"Unless you're trying to sell a house. At least, that's what my mom says. She's a real estate agent."

Jesse framed his face and puckered his lips at me. "This? This will never be beige." He snapped his fingers. "You know what would help you a lot? Maybe a selfie stick or one of the anti-shake things to keep the camera still? Because when you're getting close, sometimes it seems like you go out of your head a little, and it screws up the money shot. And that's what everyone's there for, right?"

I snorted. "That won't work in a public place. I mean, a selfie stick might, but if I need to run, that's one more thing I have to worry about. I could give it a try, at least. You've given this some thought, huh?" I ventured.

"Nah, this is all on the fly." He waved a hand, then tapped our textbooks. "We need to go back to this before I can't function." He pointed a finger at me with a stern frown. "I told you, don't preen. You're a dime a dozen."

Now that part I knew all too well. "I have another question. Why is your Rotel so fucking good?"

Jesse's furrowed brow smoothed out into a pleased smile. "I won't tell you the secret, but I'll show you sometime. Then you can make the next batch for the house and I'll resent you a millimeter less when I open the fridge and it's gone."

"Did you really resent me?"

"Nah. I'm a good fucking cook, like you say. Can't blame you." He smirked.

6

JESSE

"Is anyone sitting here?"

I tensed and turned slowly in Reid's direction, treating him to my best dismissive eye flick despite the pang that echoed hollowly in my chest. Three years later, and the bitterness was like a rind of burned sugar in my chest. Nothing I wanted to eat, but it was still sugar. That I still found him attractive, even if only objectively, was annoying. If it'd been up to me, humans would've come with a built-in overwrite button that you could press after a breakup. "Really?"

"Yeah." Reid's smile wobbled briefly, and from the corner of my eye, I noticed Sam coming through the door with his football cronies.

I shrugged. "It's a free country. Oh, hey, Lee!" I waved to Question Guy, whose name I'd finally gotten, as he shuffled toward the front and swooped some hair from his forehead. "Do you know Reid? He's on the football team." There, Reid could deal with Lee, who actually was all right, aside from the question thing.

"Football?" Lee said as Reid acknowledged him with a nod and shot me a glare.

"Yeah, you know. Helmets and head injuries. That kind of thing. Reid has taken a few hits, but as long as you use words that are two or less syllables, he's totally fine. What?" I smiled sweetly at Reid and then smacked the side of my head dramatically. "Oh, duh. Right, that was sil-lah-buhls. It means—"

"Let's get started!" Professor Horton clapped his hands, and Reid, unbelievably, dropped into the seat beside me.

I started to turn a scathing look on him before deciding the best tactic was just to ignore him. It was difficult, though, because he kept trying to get my attention when the professor turned away. When my phone vibrated in my pocket, I pulled it out and set it on my thigh, angling away from him as I opened the message, relieved for a distraction.

Sam: *Hey.*
Jesse: *Hey.*

Our study session had happened five days ago, and I guess it had cleared the air somewhat, because I didn't feel as awkward around him now. He also hadn't been around that much either, and sure, maybe I'd wondered a couple of times—or 999—if he'd ended up getting a selfie stick and trying it out. But I hadn't looked, and I wasn't going to.

Five minutes passed with no follow-up after his first text. What the fuck? Had my signal dropped? I checked and found five juiced-up bars.

Jesse: *What?*
Sam: *What?*

I tossed a glance over my shoulder toward his seat. He smiled at me. I shook my head and turned back.

He had to be fucking with me.

Jesse: *You texted me.*
Sam: *Yeah. I said hey.*
Jesse: *And?*
Sam: *That's it.*
Jesse: *No. That's never it in texting. That's the fucking signal that something else is incoming. No one just texts a random "hey." That's like waving at someone and just turning around and walking off before they can even respond.*
Sam: *Well I changed my mind.*
Sam: *<smiley face emoji>*
Sam: *<eggplant emoji>*
Jesse: *You're an idiot, you know that?*
Sam: *Maybe. Know what else I know?*
Jesse: *Are you going to actually tell me or is this "hey" the redux?*
Sam: *I got an A on the test.*
Jesse: *Congrats.*
Sam: *What'd you get?*
Jesse: *C+. You happy?*
Sam: *Yeah.*
Sam: *I mean, no, not happy. That was what I was going to ask at first, but then I looked over and you were scowling so I decided not to.*

I glanced over my shoulder at him again, and he pulled a face.

Jesse: *I blame your <eggplant emoji> for distracting me from further studying.*
Sam: *It can be distracting, yeah.*

Jesse: *Not like that. I mean that I went back to my room and couldn't concentrate because I was mortified.*
Sam: *I told you there was no reason to be. It's no big deal.*
Sam: *I mean it's big, haha, but it's not a deal. I made a new video, curious to know what you think.*
Jesse: *I'm not watching any more of your videos.*
Sam: *Ever?*
Sam: *It's a shower vid. But the lens got a little foggy. I'm not sure whether I should post it anyway or if I'll just be opening myself to shade about the quality or getting lazy or something.*

Goddamn him.

Sam: *I'm legit curious. You're a good judge of that stuff.*
Jesse: *What an honor. I wonder if I can put that on my resume.*
Sam: *Probably. I know a guy who put head of landscape design on his resume after mowing his parents' yards all summer.*
Jesse: *Was it you?*

A peal of laughter rang out from the back of the lecture hall. Prof. Horton stopped, then resumed after Sam apologized.

Sam: *No. Fuck. Horton gave me the stink eye.*
Jesse: *I'm not watching my roommate's jerk vids.*
Sam: *You did before.*
Jesse: *Technical error. We've been over this.*
Sam: *Okay, fine. But if you do happen to "accidentally" stumble across it or whatever, and happen to form an opinion on it, you could maybe let me know? You don't even have to say it to my face. You can leave it in the comments or something.*

I burst into a laugh, and Prof. Horton stopped pacing to shoot me a withering glare, next.

Jesse: *That was your fault.*
Sam: *No way. I was being serious. You're the one who laughed.*
Jesse: *I'm done with these texts.*
Sam: *Cold, dude.*

As soon as class let out, I bolted up right, slung my laptop under my arm, and hitched my backpack over my shoulder, speed-walking toward the door and falling in step beside Sam when I spotted Reid closing in behind me.

"Hey," I said breathlessly, keeping an eye on Reid as he slowed down before passing me with a frown.

"Hey." Sam grinned. "So…what exactly about that text cracked you up? I was serious.

"I know." I shrugged. God, his crooked grin was the perfect amalgam of cute and sexy. How had I never noted that before? *Stop it.* Subject change. "You know what would be really hot and a little taboo? Doing a video during class."

"You're crazy. There's no way I could make that happen. It's not logistically possible."

"Not in a lecture class, but maybe in one of the larger classrooms? A lab." Reid disappeared into another building. Great. I could wrap this up and move on now.

"You know, you've got an awful lot of thoughts about this."

"Not really. Anyway, something to consider. You and your selfie stick."

"Wanna go get lunch?" Sam thumbed toward the guys walking alongside him, who were engrossed with their phones. "I'm going with—"

"Nope. Gotta go. See ya later." I patted him on the shoulder and peeled off in the other direction abruptly, feeling a little bad for the confusion I glimpsed in his expression as I turned away. But not bad enough to linger trying to converse with him while simultaneously waging a fierce internal war with a burgeoning erection fueled by images of him jacking off under a desk.

Sam leaned in my doorway later that night, a towel slung around his shoulders, the clean scent of him filling the air as he lived up to sports hero fantasy. He massaged his shoulder idly as he looked me over.

"Was Reid bothering you earlier today? In class, I mean?"

"Nah. I helped him make a new friend." I smiled fondly at the memory of Reid's bewilderment. "What's wrong with your shoulder?"

"Tough practice. Wanna massage it for me?"

In spite of Sam's playful brow waggle, heat poured through me. God, if that wasn't a scenario I'd watched a hundred times on Pornhub. "Sometimes I can't tell when you're joking."

"Same. Here's the trick: I'm rarely ever joking when people think I am. Sometimes it works out for the best, sometimes it doesn't."

"All right." I lifted a brow and shoved my books aside. "C'mere."

He cast me a wary glance but came closer and sat on the bed.

I yanked the towel from his shoulders and dug into his biceps.

"Ow, *fuck*!" He flinched. "You're as bad as Pat, maybe worse."

"Who's Pat?"

"One of our trainers."

"You're a sports dude, so you should know getting the lactic acid out is key." He tensed with a groan as I pushed my thumb against the muscle again until it loosened. "So did you reshoot the shower video?"

"Nah. I'm just going to run with what I've got. I was too lazy to reshoot it."

Sam tipped his head to one side as I gentled my touch on his bicep and worked the bands of muscle on his shoulders.

His eyes fell shut as I rubbed the base of his neck. I hadn't exactly meant to move that far, but it was right there and, well, he was fun to touch. My occasional yoga and half-assed running regime along with a raging metabolism kept me lean, but Sam was sculpture.

I ran my fingers over his back, silently naming the muscles as I went.

A lot of my friends had figured out they were gay because they'd gotten crushes on their friends. Me? One of my first boners came courtesy of an anatomical drawing in sixth grade science class, the peeled-back flesh of the man showing bands of muscle along with his dick, small but visibly rendered between his legs. I mean, I'd known before then. Hell, I'd known in second grade, but seeing a man's body like that for the first time had solidified it.

Sam made a pleased rumbling sound that I imagined would vibrate against my hand if it had been on his chest. "I take back what I said. You're better than Pat."

"Damn straight."

"Oooooof," he groaned as I rolled my knuckles over his spine and then trailed my fingers through his hair. "God, that's good." Goose bumps broke out over his shoulders, and I let my hands fall away reluctantly.

"Fine." I sighed. "Let me see the video."

"You sure?" He blinked, like I'd caught him off guard, but complied when I nodded, pulling his phone from the pocket of his track pants and skimming through it before passing it over to me.

He tucked one big leg on the bed and angled toward me so he could see, too.

I clicked Play. Three seconds in, my eyes were so wide I was certain my eyebrows were touching my hairline. "Good lord," I whispered, though what was going down on screen was far from holy.

7
SAM

My shoulders were looser, and my bicep did feel a little better, even though Jesse had gone after it like a sledgehammer. I'd wrenched it at practice earlier and gritted my teeth through the rest of the drills, not wanting Coach to pick up on it. I'd had to sit out the latter half of spring training and go easy during summer training after I'd wrecked my shoulder in a scrimmage that had effectively crushed my chances of being drafted. Now that I was better, I wanted to make the best of senior year season and my last hurrah.

Warmth lingered over my skin where Jesse had touched the back of my neck.

Those touches had been lighter, softer, but I'd felt them deeper in my stomach, a buzzing sensation I wasn't sure how to interpret.

I studied his profile as he stared down at the screen, his lips opening in a soft part. His pulse thumped steadily and visibly against the side of his throat, and he had these little wavy ends of red-gold hair that moved with the flutter of his heartbeat.

He lifted a hand and touched the hollow of his throat, and for some reason I felt it, too, in that same deep pit in my stomach, like it was me he'd touched.

When my cock gave a twitch of awareness, I frowned and pressed the heel of my palm against it. I was watching myself jack off, after all, so the arousal was probably natural, even if it was my own dick being featured.

But the longer I watched, the more I realized it wasn't necessarily the video that was getting me hard. It was watching Jesse watch it, wondering if it was turning him on, looking for the evidence that it was. Would I feel the same if it was a girl? I squinted inwardly at myself and decided yeah, I probably would. Maybe? Jesse was a little different from everything else I knew, though. Guy or girl.

His fingertips kept moving, rubbing that little dish of skin at the base of his throat as he watched, brows angled down.

I was on the edge of my proverbial seat with anticipation for his critique, like I'd just handed over a shitty student film to Richard Roeper and was awaiting the pain of brutal honesty.

"Jesse?"

He blinked away from the screen, eyes lifting to mine expectantly. For a moment I wasn't sure what I'd been about to say, whether I was checking on him or trying to ask something else. It was the weirdest fucking sensation, and I noticed it more and more lately when I was around him.

I'd never much cared whether someone liked me or not, but for some reason I really wanted Jesse to like me. *Fuck me*, that sounded dumb. Next I'd be asking him if my outfit was okay.

I ticked my chin toward the screen. "What do you think? Is it bad?"

He scrunched his nose thoughtfully. "You're right about the steam. It's a little distracting—the physical steam, not the steam rating, which is through the roof, haha. And there's more camera shake than usual... I mean, from what I remember," he quickly corrected. "It's hot, though. Probably your fans will just be glad to have something new from you. No one's gonna analyze and critique it the way I just did or anything."

"You'd be surprised."

"Probably not, now that I think about it. People can be real jerks. Is it weird to have fans of your cock? Like, that's all they know about you? Just this big massive Kraken cock that—" He waved a hand with a soft snort. "You get my drift."

"Kraken cock," I echoed. "Wasn't that a giant squid, though?"

Jesse shrugged. "Giant is the operative word, regardless."

"Never thought too deeply about it before, but yeah, I guess it's a little strange. Temporary, like everything else, though. When I stop making videos, no one will miss them. They'll just find some other big-cocked dude to watch."

"I'm not sure if that's supposed to be sad or relieving." Jesse chuckled and tucked a strand of hair behind his ear. I glanced away when he licked his lips. "So why do you do it?"

I rested back on my elbows. "My baby sister has an extremely rare blood disorder—"

"Oh my god." Jesse's brow creased with sympathy. "I'm so sorry."

I nodded solemnly. "Yeah, she needs this special medicine made from the powdered hooves of a Scimitar-Horned Oryx."

He narrowed his eyes as my lips started quivering from trying to hold back a grin. "You fucker. You shouldn't joke about stuff like that."

"I know." I tried for a repentant expression but ended up grinning. "She actually does have a rare blood disorder, but it's controlled, and my parents have good insurance." I shrugged. "I do it because..." I'd thought about this plenty of times and had answers both shallow and more introspective. "I don't have a shot at being drafted now, and I mean, I'm not dumb or anything, but I know the stats on health issues for football players long term, and I know the job market is tough right now, too. Graduating with an exercise science degree isn't going to have me rolling in dough any time soon. So I think of it like insurance or a twist on a 401K. I put everything in savings. If my family needs a little extra help, I can provide it, and I'm also socking away money for later in case I need it." I laughed at the face he made. "You look so disappointed right now. Are you? You liked it better when there was a noble cause?"

"Nah. That's...very sensible."

"Ah, surprised, then."

"A little. Are you sad about the draft thing, though? I mean isn't that the ultimate goal? The reason most guys play ball in college?"

The sympathy in Jesse's gaze caught me by surprise and I found myself nodding when I'd meant to just shrug it off. "I was. I still get upset about it sometimes, though it was never a guarantee in the first place. I'm just not that qualified to do anything else and—"

Jesse smacked the comforter. "Don't sell yourself short," he said, wagging his finger so passionately at me that my lips curled into a smile.

"You have to admit being a personal trainer or working in a gym or something isn't the same as sharing a bench with your fellow 49ers."

"What the hell is a 49er anyway? Whatever." He winked.

"I thought about maybe opening my own gym someday." It was the one idea I'd stumbled upon after my injury when I was trying to drag myself away from the month-long pity party I'd thrown myself. It'd worked, though, and I'd held on to it ever since.

"I can *definitely* see that." Jesse cocked his head at me, then nodded emphatically. "Oh yeah. It'd suit you." He fanned his face with a self-deprecating chuckle. "Ignore me. Tangent. Anyway, I'm glad you're not too sad. Did you ever consider using some of this money you're earning to bankroll your gym?"

I nodded. "Yep. It's easy money. I don't know if you saw, but I have an OnlyFans account where people leave tips and—"

"I know. I saw," Jesse whispered. He face-planted on the bed and pulled a pillow over his head, muffling his groan. "I signed up for the first month. Again, *before* I knew it was you. I canceled obvs. You take requests." He groaned again, louder this time. "I was the one who asked you to play with your hole and suggested incorporating toys."

I yanked the pillow from his head. "You were hardluck22? Gah, you were a super-active subscriber. Liked a whole bunch of my posts and—"

"Shut up," he hissed. "I *know*. Believe me, I know."

"Man, I was sad when you unsubscribed. I actually missed you. You had some creative use of emojis. Especially the eggplant." At Jesse's miserable expression, I lost it. "Dude, seriously, please don't feel weird or guilty or awkward or something. It's just a dick, and we've all got to jerk off to something. Also, the video I did after your suggestion? It's one of my most viewed."

"Really?" He perked up when I nodded.

"Yeah, it turned out superhot if I do say so myself." I'd gotten a small bendable tripod and had aimed it at the bed before getting bare-assed naked on all fours. Problem was, again, I couldn't get those close-up shots that people seemed to love without doing a million takes.

"Oh, it was definitely hot. Did you end up doing anything with toys?"

"Ummm, no. But only because I wasn't really sure what to get, and, well, I'm not sure I'm down for penetration yet, even though I know the response would be through the roof."

Jesse was quiet long enough that I suspected he was having an internal debate with himself. "Did you ever consider trying to find a camera guy? A lot of the other guys have them, even the ones doing solo jerks."

"I'll get right on that," I deadpanned. "Of course I've thought about it, but I can't just go out and ask a random person. It's not even something I could ask Mark or Nate to do because they have no idea, and they both have boyfriends anyway, who probably wouldn't be cool with that. Maybe I'll look harder sometime. Find someone local that would sign an NDA and wants a percentage of the profits or something. In the meantime, I've got a selfie stick coming, so I'll just carry on." I flicked the screen. "So about this one...keep it or toss it?"

"What? Oh, yeah. I think you can keep it." Jesse passed the phone back, then raked his teeth over his lower lip, exhaling noisily as he met my eyes again. They were so big, a delicately lashed imperfect blue mottled with bits of brown. I wasn't even sure what the color was called. Hazel?

"I could do the camera stuff for you. If you wanted."

"Really? But I thought it made you feel weird." It wasn't as if it hadn't occurred to me, but I sure as shit wasn't about to ask.

He chuckled, and it was a private sound, like an inside joke only he knew the punchline to. "No, jerking off to videos alone in my room and knowing they're you makes me feel like a perv. Being a helping hand...errr, *cameraman*, is a little different. What's weird is imagining you letting somebody you hardly know help you." He shook his head, setting his jaw. "No, I can definitely do it."

I squinted, looking him over and trying to determine whether he was bullshitting me or not. He looked serious. Sounded serious, too.

Only one way to tell.

"All right, let's do it."

Jesse stared at me. "Really? Just like that?"

"Sure." Shit, had that been a trick question or something, and I'd failed? I liked the idea of Jesse helping me with my videos. My stomach dipped, and I honestly wasn't sure whether it was due to nerves, relief at having found the solution to my predicament, or the weird satisfaction I got out of feeling like I'd finally somehow connected with Jesse. "Good. I'm gonna take my ad off Craigslist, then."

"What?" Jesse's eyes got huge. "Please tell me you're joking."

"Totally joking."

"Oh my god, you're not. *Sam.*" Jesse smacked my arm. "There are crazy people out there."

"Hey, I got some normal-sounding messages. One guy said I could film in his basement apartment anytime and that he had lots of cameras. And also a St. Andrew's Cross, which I'm not sure what that is, but it sounds pretty high-tech."

Jesse's concerned expression broke on a grin. "You're such an idiot." I had no defense. "How do you even know what a St. Andrew's Cross is?"

"Same way you do, I imagine." I winked at him and slid from the bed. "So, want to try the first one tomorrow?"

"Tomorrow?" He cleared his throat. "Tomorrow is great. Sorry. That wasn't a squeak. My vocal cords do this weird thing sometimes."

"Mine do, too." I nodded in mock understanding. "I always thought we just called those words and sentences."

"Yep. Okay, smartass. You can leave now." He gave me a sarcastic wave. "Bye."

It wasn't until I'd gotten back into my room that I pinned down the funny swooping sensation in my stomach.

It was excitement.

8

SAM

"This is it?"

"This is it," Jesse said lightly, stepping around me to close his bedroom door.

I searched the corners of his room, made another visual sweep from the stuffed bookshelves to the artsy black and white photos on his walls, trying to figure out if I was missing something. When he'd said *super-erotic idea*, I was expecting…I don't know. Furry cuffs, or whipped cream, or…some kind of sensual scenery. A sex swing? Yeah, probably not. I'd spent my AM practice and all my classes thinking about it. I'd had a semi through most of my kinesiology class.

But this was just a slightly messy college guy's room.

"Okay."

Jesse chuckled at the disappointment in my voice and thwapped me on the bicep in passing. "Strip and I'll break it down for you. You're just gonna have to trust me on this for second. Let's go! We've got a solid hour, and I don't want to waste any of it just in case."

"Just in case what?"

"I don't know. Just in case I need extra time to..." He waved a hand distractedly. "If I mess something up. I won't, but I'm just saying. Extra time is always good."

I pulled my T-shirt over my head and tossed it aside, attention straying to Jesse as he rested his ass against the arm of an easy chair and pushed it next to the window. The sun glinted off the crown of his head, burnishing the strands a warm golden red. He had a tiny smattering of freckles just under his eyes, too, that I'd never noticed before.

He gathered clothes from the floor in a heap, tossing them onto his bed, and adjusted the blinds so sunlight poured in across the chair. There wasn't anything fancy about the chair either; it was just a standard plaid overstuffed armchair.

He dug through the heap of stuff on his bed and pulled free a white blanket then set about tucking into the chair to cover up the plaid.

"No offense, but this looks a little... basic?"

"It *is* basic, that's the point. This video in particular is going to be hot because of that. Plus, the light's gonna come in at an angle and form all kinds of sexy shadows on your big-ass He-Man chest. Might as well showcase the glorious rewards of all those hours you spend in the gym." Jesse fiddled with the blanket some more, then whipped around and stopped, staring at me. He splayed a hand over his chest. "Wow. God." He shook his head with a teasing smile. "Don't even say 'what.' I can see it forming on your lips, and you know what. No one spends that much time in the gym and doesn't know what they look like shirtless."

I looked down at myself, fighting a laugh. "You just took it from compliment to making me strangely self-conscious." And I was, but there was another feeling wrapped around it, too. A warm sensation woven through the tease that made the hairs on my arm prickle with awareness.

"You're welcome. Leave the underwear on," he said, when I hooked my thumb behind my waistband. "Actually, no, take them off. Boxers are boring. I've got something better." He reached into a drawer, moving with businesslike efficiency, pulled out a pair of briefs, and lobbed them at me before returning to his nip/tuck business with the chair.

I stared down at what looked like a torn-off remnant of someone's biker shorts. "I won't be able to fit these over my thighs."

"They're stretchy. The fit's not the point. We're showcasing, remember?" He cut me a saucy wink. He was kinda cute bustling all round with purpose and energy, and his excitement over the idea, which I still didn't quite understand the allure of, proved infectious.

I dropped the doubts and decided to go along for the ride.

But the briefs were way too fucking tight. "Nothing can breathe, Jesse."

"Fortunately, dicks don't need their own air supply, or they'd have come with gills. Gross image. Here." He started to reach for my crotch, then pulled his hands back and shook his head at himself. "Just, umm, re-tuck." His hands moved comically in the air, like they were controlling the one I wedged behind the skintight briefs. "Angle your shaft up, yeah. That'll give your balls more space, too. Plus, when you get hard, it's gonna make a massive sexy bulge that people are gonna drool all over their screens for. Come over here so I can oil you."

"Oil, too?" I wondered if this was what porn stars felt like. The attention was nice. Aside from the team trainer, I hadn't been touched much lately, and it'd been a while since I hooked up with someone. I'd grown up in an affectionate household, and I missed the casual touches sometimes.

My nipples pebbled and goose bumps erupted over my skin as Jesse smoothed baby oil over me. When a little tremor ran through my shoulders, he stopped and glanced up at me inquisitively.

"Sorry. I'm used to deep tissue massage and feeling like I've been beaten up afterward. This actually feels good. Can't help it."

"I need to go get one. A massage, I mean. I don't think I'll ever be able to afford a personal massage therapist." Jesse laughed, poured another handful of oil on his palm, and caressed it down my biceps and forearms, moving slower.

"I thought about becoming one once."

"Yeah?"

"Mm-hmm." I let my eyes fall shut as he smoothed more oil over my skin. "Maybe if the whole gym thing doesn't work out."

"Trust me when I say you'd be very popular as a gym owner or massage therapist."

I groaned absently as another layer of oil coated my skin, losing track of the conversation because the way Jesse stroked both hands down the length of my arms, one after the other, firm and steady, somehow translated to a tingling sensation in my balls.

I wondered what that same kind of touch would feel like directly on my cock.

Just as I had the thought, Jesse's gaze lowered to my crotch where the stretchy fabric had started to strain. When he lifted it again, humor danced in the warm hazel tones. "Maybe I missed my calling. You know what this makes me think about?"

"What," I asked belatedly, entranced by the quick movements of his hands and the electricity spreading over my skin everywhere he touched. I probably sounded like a dolt. Man, who knew I was such a sucker for being doused in oil and caressed?

"Some of my favorite videos are the straight guy gets a massage trope. Have you ever seen one?"

I shook my head.

"You're missing out. Search for it on Pornhub next time and see what you think." He moved to my back, rubbing more oil on me before giving my shoulder a sharp smack. "I think we're ready. Go sit in the chair, and let's get to it."

"You didn't put any on my ass."

Silence. Then Jesse laughed. "Really?"

I'd kinda been joking, but damn, he'd lubed up everything else on me aside from my cock, and now I was curious whether he'd do it. "Sure, why not?"

"Ohhhhhkay." He hooked his fingers through the waistband of the briefs and inched them down over my ass. His warm palms glided firmly over my cheeks.

"Jesus, they feel like boulders. Do you think you could actually crack a nut between them?"

"Never tried." I laughed and then muffled a groan as he squeezed while simultaneously pressing his thumbs into the dimples above my ass. It was one of those spots that made my knees go weak, and one of the few occasions when getting worked over by the team's trainer that the groan I let out was from pleasure.

Jesse did it again on the other side, and this time a groan did slip free. Jesse swatted my cheek lightly. "Uh-uh, none of that. Not until the camera's on."

And strangely enough? It was the swat combined with the reprimand that took me from semi-hard to full-on engorged.

I adjusted my dick through the spandex, and Jesse shot me

another commanding look that made my dick twitch. "Sam. Chair. Now."

Laughing, I took a seat. "All right. If you're gonna direct, go for it." I figured I'd just pull my dick out and start stroking it, but suddenly the idea of Jesse telling me what to do was more appealing. Less intimidating somehow.

"I was hoping you'd say that. God, that sunlight is perfect. Hang on." He held up his phone, snapped a pic, and then showed me the screen.

I wasn't one to stare in a mirror a lot, but I got what he meant about the light and the shadows. It definitely had a vibe. With the white blanket covering the chair, the pale gray wall in the background, and the sun spilling warm gold all over everything, it looked like one of those artsy Instagram shoots my sister Talia liked to do with her air plants and succulents. Except we were doing it with my dick, and there was no way I could ever show off the artistry to her.

I handed the camera back. "I like it."

"Good. Okay." Jesse tapped his lower lip, and then his brows shot up. "Oh my god, I just had another really good idea. Fuck, this is fun. You're like my own private sex doll." He waved a hand violently through the air. "I mean, not like that, but...you know what I mean."

"Jesse." I tried a different tack, since I could tell he was getting flustered, and kept my voice low and steady as I shifted around in the chair.

"Yeah?"

"Tell me what to do."

He blinked at me and then nodded slowly before handing me the bottle of baby oil he'd been using. "It's a brand-new bottle, by the way, not like...my leftovers."

I didn't care if it was the same bottle he used to jerk off. In fact, my dick kinda liked the idea, too—again to my surprise.

"Jesse?"

"Yeah, I'm focusing. I'm not sure why the fuck I'm getting all shy when you're the one sitting in the chair." He took a deep breath. "So once we get rolling, just start doing your thing, but maybe use the oil, too. Very liberally. Think of it like…treating yourself. Luxuriating in yourself. Slow and sexy and seductive."

Jesse got the camera going and signaled me with a nod. I poured some oil in my hands and rubbed it up and down my arms. At first, I felt ridiculous with him watching, more so than if I'd just been jerking off.

Jesse must have been able to tell because he nodded encouragingly. I bit back a laugh when he did the chef's kiss gesture and waggled his brows.

"Stop," I mouthed, and he rolled his eyes with a grin.

But once I closed my eyes and focused on the oil sliding over my skin, I started to lose myself in the warmth of the late-afternoon sun falling over me, the slippery glide of my hand.

It did feel good.

Really fucking good. Why hadn't I incorporated oil before?

I took my time stroking over my biceps, massaging the liquid into my pecs in languid circles, rolling and pinching my nipples between thumb and forefinger until they were stiff peaks that sent tingling little shock waves radiating outward.

I groaned as my cock twitched when I slid my hands up and down my abs.

"Good. Keep going. Lower," Jesse instructed in a raspy-soft voice that lifted goose bumps on my skin.

I flinched back to groggy awareness when he hissed out a curse and barked, "Cut!" like we were on set.

"What'd I screw up?"

"Nothing. You were perfect. I was talking, though. You'll be able to hear me on the video."

"So? We can cover it with music or..." Fuck, my dick was so hard it hurt. "Or not cover it because it's kind of sexy, don't you think? I mean, don't you think the viewers would think that?" I babbled, my gaze catching on and sticking for way too fucking long to the erection tenting his pants. I mean, it wasn't like I didn't expect it to happen, but the extra kick of heat in my balls from looking at it was unexpected.

Jesse narrowed his eyes and remained silent for a long moment. Then he nodded resolutely. "Yeah, you might be right. Okay, game on." He hit the button on his phone and resumed. "Tease yourself, maybe pull your waistband down a little, give us a peek, but not the full thing yet. *Perfect*," he cooed, and my dick twitched again.

Damn, what was it about his voice?

I slid my hands behind my waistband, gripped the base of my dick with one hand and my balls with the other. The oil made my nuts all slippery, and when I rolled them around and tugged on them, tiny electric sparks shivered up my spine. I stroked my shaft slowly, the fabric constraining my movements and keeping the pressure tight. With a nudge of my wrist, I flipped the waistband down, revealing the glistening precum sliding down my glans.

Jesse muttered a curse, and my gaze flew to his again, worried I'd fucked up. He shook his head quickly. "Keep going. This is insanely hot. It's perfect, actually. So sexy."

Once again, my gaze drifted down to the strained fly of his jeans, and another surge of electricity rolled through me.

"Pull the underwear down now, all the way to your ankles, but leave them on." This time there was no hesitation in his voice. It was demanding and confident.

I hurried to comply and inched the underwear down, exposing myself slowly. On a whim, once they were at my ankles, I picked up the bottle of oil, angled it just under my neck, and squeezed.

Jesse made a noise that sounded almost like a whimper but might have been encouragement, as the liquid cascaded down my chest, funneling down the center of my torso and spreading over my groin.

I reached over my shoulder with one hand, grabbing the back of the chair for leverage, then widened my knees and gripped my cock with the other. Pleasure rolled through me in waves of liquid heat as I stroked, the loud, filthy squish of my oil-coated hand on my shaft ratcheting my arousal higher.

Jesse hadn't moved, but his breathing had quickened, his chest rising and falling noticeably, and that in turn fed my desire. I was turning him on and...*shit*. I was turning him on, and I *liked* it. I really fucking liked it.

"Je—I mean, Josh?" I sputtered, belatedly remembering the codenames Jesse had finally decided on after a long verbal cataloguing of his favorite romantic comedies. I paused on an upstroke and closed my fist around my head. I had to bite back another moan as he lifted his gaze from the screen.

"Yeah?" he rasped.

"Never mind." I floundered and shook my head. I'd been about to suggest he could jerk off, too, which seemed wildly inappropriate when I thought about it. But fuck, I think I actually wanted him to. It could totally be the arousal talking. I mean, it probably was because horniness was weird that way. Why else were there literally search terms for everything under the sun on Pornhub. One time, out of curiosity, I'd typed in 'pie', thinking *no way*. But...way. And I'd nutted over what I'd watched, too.

I resumed stroking myself and then, with my gaze still glued to Jesse, lifted up my sac and slid a finger along my taint and over my hole. A tremor racked my shoulders. I didn't do it often and had forgotten how sensitive that area was on me. But damn, it was doing the trick today. In spite of Jesse's request to keep the underwear on, I freed one leg so I could hitch my foot over the arm of the chair and have easier access to my ass. Jesse trapped his lower lip between his teeth, eyes glassy as I played with the puckered skin.

My gaze ping-ponged back and forth between his plump pink lip in its white cage and the bulge in his pants. Extending my other leg, I braced my heel on the floor. The inside of Jesse's calf pressed against it as he moved closer.

"There. That's perfect." The softness in his tone dragged over my skin like a feather, eliciting the same intoxicating response. "So perfect. You're so big and hard."

"Fuck," I whispered, a fresh surge of desire rolling through me. The tiny patch of skin where his leg touched mine might as well have had the surface area of a continent for how intensely I felt it everywhere. "Je—" *Goddammit*. "I mean, *Josh*," I panted. I'm gonna come. I've *got* to."

Jesse shook his head chidingly and my nuts tightened in response. "Not quite yet. You can hang on just a little longer, can't you?" He purred.

His voice was a full-on caress, velvety and soft rubbing over my skin with a crazy kind of aural friction that made me writhe. Tension wound around my spine, the signal smoke of impending orgasm, but I nodded anyway and tried to keep my focus from blowing apart every time he glanced up from the screen.

9
JESSE

Rule #1 of filming a sexy-as-hell football player jerking off. You do not go into that scenario hot. I'd made sure to take care of myself an hour beforehand and was even wearing an extra-tight set of briefs.

But I had vastly underestimated the nuclear heat level of a living Thor covered in oil and writhing on an armchair as he played with his presumably virgin hole in front of me. Had I been transported to the center of the earth? Because this shit was magmatic.

Whose idea had this been?

Oh. Right.

Scooting closer, I filled the phone's screen with Sam from the neck down as he rested his head back against the cushy chair and closed his eyes. His chest rose and fell with a hypnotic steadiness as he rubbed the heel of his hand up and down his shaft, then deviated up to his pecs, teasing his fingertips over his nipple until it formed a fine point that he rubbed with his thumb.

He arched his back, licked the pad of his thumb, and rolled it over his nipple again, making the tight brown flesh gleam with spit.

I knew right then that nothing short of a straitjacket would've kept my dick in check. I'd never ever watched a guy jerk off in front of me before, not like this. Sure, maybe some of the dudes I'd been with got a head start, but this was the thrill of voyeurism the likes of which I'd never experienced before.

I focused on keeping my own breathing steady and zoomed in on his pecs, then followed his hand back down to his ass where he rimmed himself with the tip of a finger. God, was he going to push it inside? I might come in my pants.

So much saliva flooded my mouth that I had to swallow twice to clear it.

"Fuck," he muttered on a gasp, hips arching into his grip. "I never get to do this when I'm filming it myself. Always have the phone in one hand. This is awesome."

I nodded in mute agreement that it was indeed awesome.

The other hand still played with his nipple, but now his thigh and calf muscles tensed with each slow thrust as he moved his hand up to his massive dick and stroked it.

Fucking hell it was big, like the T-rex of cocks, with a juicy fat mushroom head all shiny and plump with blood flow, so stiff I had to bite back a moan as I imagined how much a dick like that would stretch me. It was some kind of cock. Correction, it wasn't a cock. In the hierarchy of dicks, this one definitely registered as a schlong. I'd made that size queen comment in the kitchen mostly as a joke, but the joke was on me because I was fucking starstruck by his XXL rocket ship and would've tripped over my own feet for the chance to help him achieve liftoff.

Precum oozed from his tip, and Sam smeared it down the

side of his shaft before corkscrewing his fist and concentrating all the action on the head.

He caught my eye, and I gave him the thumbs-up that we were all good. Then he really started working it.

Here's the thing. I mentioned before that I'd seen a lot of porn. Amateur, professional, whatever, and I'd been with my fair share of guys. I'd had some good sex and some not so good sex, and some that I barely remembered, but I couldn't recall *ever* seeing someone enjoy a solo session so much.

As I'd previously noticed when watching Sam's videos—before I knew it was Sam—he seemed to genuinely take pleasure in...pleasuring himself. There were plenty of guys who seemed like they were just getting off because they were bored, and watching them was akin to watching someone yank on a piece of taffy: a lot of mechanical jerking with no enthusiasm.

Not Sam. I thought it was probably why his videos were so popular. He was just so damn into it.

Even with me filming him, I could tell when he started to lose himself in the pleasure. His gaze went distant, and his moans grew increasingly uninhibited, like he'd forgotten I was there.

This was voyeurism in its purest form, and my whole body was on fire with it. My dick might as well have been swinging from the rafters of my best intentions. The tight briefs I was wearing hadn't done jack before, and now they were actively working against me.

Every time I shifted the slightest bit, the waistband rubbed tantalizingly against my leaking head. I bit back moan after moan as Sam fondled his balls, kneading and stroking them while he worked his shaft in patient, luxurious strokes, his slit spitting out thick strings of precum that I'd only seen this close in my wettest of dreams.

"Oh shit." It was a sound that was a cross between a groan, a growl, and some kind of subliminal messaging that whispered directly to my balls to pack up and prepare for launch. *"Oh shit."*

His desperation and arousal transmitted palpably through the air between us. I swallowed back a whimper and clenched my jaw.

I couldn't bust in my pants because I'd jiggle the camera. So I held it steady and stared at a crack near the corner of the ceiling for a few seconds, pondering how long it'd been there and whether I should tell Mark we might need to have it looked at.

When the impending danger of release receded to manageable levels, I looked back at Sam, still going after it like a champ. A very sexy, sweaty, cheek-flushed, ball-twistingly hot champ.

Sucking in some fresh air, I stepped in closer, Sam's leg rubbing against mine crackling over my skin like static.

"Changing the angle," I explained softly, and he gave me a dopey, pleasure-saturated nod.

Jesus, yes, this was the money shot. Framed perfectly within the viewfinder, Sam's gorgeous abs rippled with every breath and stroke as his massive tree trunk of a cock took center stage.

I silently congratulated myself on my excellent cinematography skills and wondered if I'd somehow missed my calling. This wasn't so bad, aside from the fact that my dick felt like it was a sausage casing for the load that was begging for me to unleash it.

But I was a professional, and that wasn't going to happen. At least until I got back into the privacy of my own room and then, yeah, I was pretty sure I'd be painting my palm in under two seconds.

Sam exhaled another throaty, gut-twisting moan, and I fought back a tremble as he arched into his fist, his pace faster now, more relentless, his palm stroking over the head of his cock every few strokes, and taking advantage of nature's lube. His teeth clamped down on his lower lip, and his neck arched, all the veins in his throat straining deliciously with the movement. Then his eyes fluttered open and locked on mine and I nearly gasped out loud.

My stomach tightened as he held the gaze, gasping out another curse. "Shit, I think I really do have an exhibitionist streak. I'm about to come just from you standing over me like that. I don't even know if I need my hand."

"Exhibit away. You're golden," I managed weakly, and even that taxed my brain, which was way too intent on how his balls were visibly tightening up.

"Oh god…" Sam gasped, and the same emphatic, needy words echoed in my head as he gave his dick another hard stroke and then pulled his hand away and clutched the arms of the chair as he shattered. He rode the air through his orgasm, lips peeled back from his teeth in one of the most seriously sexy O faces I'd ever witnessed. Truly, it was the *David* of O faces and it captivated me as thick streamers of jizz shot into the air and spattered his abs before slowing to a glistening flow down his shaft.

His body went limp as he panted with a tired smile plastered on his face.

I kept the camera focused on the glossy kiss of spunk coating his abs until his breathing steadied, then flicked the button to stop recording.

Stepping away, I grabbed a towel lying over the back of his chair and tossed it toward him, anything to distract myself from the throbbing erection in my pants.

Sam eyed it as he wiped himself down. "So I guess that gets the gay roommate seal of approval?"

I nodded, not trusting my mouth at the moment to speak anything other than, "Take me now, stallion."

He sighed. "I kept accidentally almost saying your name."

"Really? I didn't even notice." I laughed when he glared at me, even though at the time those slip-ups had put me through the fucking wringer, and I was pretty sure that had he actually spoken my whole name, I would have instantly busted in my pants. "It's fine. We can fix it."

He extended his hand. "Can I see it?"

"If you're lucky." I smiled. "Oh, did I say that out loud?"

Sam chuckled. "You're a huge flirt, you know that?"

"I'm really not." Well, usually I wasn't. On a scale of one to restraining order, I typically registered in the earnestly-attempted-but-unremarkable range, so maybe it was all the testosterone floating freely in the air. "Flirting's fun anyway, and I figure you're a super-safe bet. You've serviced the merchandise before and declared it not for you." His smile faltered, and I blanched. "I mean, unless me teasing you makes you uncomfortable. Then I would totally stop."

"It doesn't. Or, you don't. I feel really comfortable around you. Which is kinda surprising given what we're doing. But there it is." He flashed me a crooked grin, then took the phone from my hand when I offered it out. He pressed Play on the video, brows pinching together studiously as he watched.

"It'd probably be even better with a legit camera, but for an iPhone, I think it looks pretty good. What do you think?"

One hand had strayed to his chest, and he made a funny little repetitive scratching motion as he watched. "It's...wow. That's really good. I don't mean that in a narcissistic way. I mean you were right about the lighting and the chair and..." He glanced up at me, eyes bright. "It's about fifty million times better than anything I've done before." He looked down at the screen again, shaking his head. "Seriously, thanks."

"Your followers are going to love it."

"Yeah?" God, why was he so cute? Even the way he said it wasn't like he was fishing for a compliment but was genuinely delighted at the prospect.

"Oh yeah. I wore my tightest pair of underwear and...yeah. That was insanely hot."

Sam's gaze strayed toward my crotch as he wiped himself down and cleaned off his hand, then tossed the towel aside and ran a hand over the top of his head, mussing the already messy strands into complete pandemonium. "I had this crazy idea in the middle of filming that I'd tell you you could jerk off if you wanted to, but then I thought maybe that would be weird."

"It would definitely be weird." I paused, thinking. "I mean, wouldn't it?" I had no idea what kind of parameters were supposed to accompany filming your roommate jerking off, but I'd racked up quite the laundry list of events and people that seemed like a good idea when I was all horned up only to become regrets later when the orgasm haze had worn off. This probably fell squarely into that category.

"I guess. Didn't seem weird at all at the time," Sam replied carefully, echoing my thoughts. "But yeah. Whatever." He grinned. "I got nervous for a minute at the start—"

"I couldn't tell at all."

"Okay, good. But after that, it was great. Totally different from trying to do it myself and trying to stay aware of how I'm holding my hand at all times, trying not to shake the camera." His brows flickered together. "Was it too weird for you, though? I understand if you want to renege."

My brain screamed, *Save yourself from a future of blue balls on the regular*. My mouth said, "No way, it was fine."

He seemed relieved, his expression tinged with shyness. "Okay, good, because all kinds of ideas are popping into my head now. Some more risqué stuff, like public restrooms or... okay, maybe not public restrooms, we'll see about that, but like semipublic places."

He chattered on, and I nodded like a bobblehead, completely taken by his open enthusiasm and wondering how he'd slipped under my radar for the past few months. Part of that was just due to summer and his football practices, but dang, Sam was pretty great.

I mentally smacked myself. *No*. No more roommate crushes.

"I think we should make a list," I ventured, and he nodded agreeably.

"A list is a great idea."

A list was probably the worst idea.

10

SAM

Once we'd gotten over the hump, so to speak, of that first scene together, we started down a list of ideas we'd compiled in no particular order in an effort to amass a backlog of scenes. Over the next week and a half, I'd jerked off in the woods at Washburne Park—because Jesse said I'd underutilized outdoors and nature scenes—and also in my car while it was parked near the back of a Target parking lot. It was kind of incredible how fast I got used to him filming me jerk off. And it wasn't just that I got used to it, but it turned me on, too.

Another plus was that Jesse was easy to get along with. He had good ideas, and he wasn't afraid to speak his mind if something wasn't working or looked bad. Sometimes I got the idea that people blew smoke up my ass, either because of football or because of how big I was. Not Jesse, though, and his honesty put me at ease.

"Sure you really want to do this?" Jesse cast me a skeptical glance as we stood outside the door of the hot yoga studio on a Sunday afternoon.

"How many is the number of times you want me to say yes? Just tell me so I can go ahead and get it over with? Is it five? Yesyesyesyesyes. Six?" Except, I wasn't sure I wanted to do this. I'd already done a morning workout, and we'd had a strenuous home game yesterday, but I hadn't been doing anything else that afternoon besides lying on the couch zoning out to *SportsCenter* when Jesse had thundered down the stairs looking purposeful in tight little shorts and a muscle tank that emphasized his lean build.

Yoga seemed like a better way to pass the time than more *SportsCenter*. Also, I liked being around him. I never knew what was going to come out of his mouth.

Jesse cut me off with a slice of his hand through the air. "Just checking, because hot yoga isn't just doing some flexibility stuff in a warm room while watching girls sweat."

I snorted. "Thanks. I'm not sure if you remember, but I'm a *sports ball* player, as you say. I can handle rigorous exercise in the heat."

But I'd never held a ninety-second-long warrior pose at a million degrees Fahrenheit before.

Ten minutes into the class, I was dripping sweat in time to the plinky nature music playing in the background. Compression tights had been the wrong call. Jesse had warned me, but I'd insisted because I worked out in them regularly. My leg hair was a mat of carpet smothering my skin, and I wasn't necessarily an overly hairy dude. My balls rivaled Okefenokee at the height of summer.

Diagonally to me, Jesse maintained the pose with little apparent trouble, eyes closed, his expression peaceful. Even the sweat rolling down his face did so at a sedate pace.

He inhaled and exhaled serenely while my quad tried to peel off the bone.

When the rest of the class deepened the stretch, I shortened mine and wrestled off my soaked T-shirt. It hit the ground with a wet plop that cut through the music. The lady next to me flinched, glancing over at me with flared nostrils and a shake of her head as if I'd committed a major faux pas.

"Sorry," I muttered, which must have been another faux pas because I got more stares, the guy to my left getting in on the action this time with a stern, thin-lipped expression aimed my way.

The instructor, Honora, moved gracefully toward me, laid one hand on my lower back, the other on my stomach, and somehow forced my posture straighter.

From the corner of my eye, I thought I saw Jesse's lips twitch into a smile.

"Breathe from your core," she suggested. The inferno raging in my thigh got worse as she smoothed down over it and urged me deeper into the stretch.

Not wanting to look like an idiot, I complied. Or tried to. "My rib cage is touching my throat," I whispered.

"Because you're not breathing from your belly." She tapped my thigh lightly. "The shaking is normal," she murmured. I wanted to tell her I knew all about muscle exhaustion, thank you very fucking much, but I refrained. She smiled gently. "Find a point of focus. It helps."

What I wanted to find was a massage parlor or an ice bath.

I tried to breathe from my belly and found a place in the mirror to stare at, but my gaze kept drifting toward Jesse.

His movements were poised and smooth as we transitioned from Warrior I into Warrior II. He was lean, hardly what anyone would call muscular, but elegant and taut. A rivulet of sweat fell from a strand of hair to the nape of his neck and funneled down into the gulley of his spine, where it moved in a slow trickle to the curve of his ass. His spandex shorts might as well have been nonexistent the way they cupped his cheeks, perfectly delineating his crack, and the side of one cheek where it shallowed out from the tension in his thighs. It looked rock fucking solid, which was another surprise.

I almost lost my balance when I realized I was getting hard. I couldn't get hard in fucking compression tights. My dick literally had nowhere to go, and if tossing a shirt and talking was a faux pas, I couldn't even imagine what popping wood would qualify as.

After sneaking a furtive glance around, I adjusted myself and thwapped the head of my dick for penance to get it back in line. Then I shifted my gaze resolutely to an elderly man. If he wasn't the safer bet, I had some more questions about myself that would need answering—in addition to the ones popping up with increasing frequency the longer I spent in Jesse's company.

"So?" Jesse drew the question out smugly as class ended.

I rolled upright from Savasana. "I liked the end." Honora had instructed us to lie on our backs and close our eyes, then had gone around the room, offering us a tissue with lavender oil on it to lay over our faces while we focused on our breathing. At the very end, she had a small bell she rang three times, and the sound, along with the lavender and quiet breaths of the people next to me, had given me the good kind of shivers. "That has to be the only reason people put up with the rest." I tried to mop my chest with my soaking T-shirt. I was so drenched I probably needed something that replaced electrolytes.

Jesse laughed. "Too strenuous?"

"It was...challenging." And I didn't necessarily mean challenging to my flexibility. I'd tested my mettle a few times by looking over at Jesse again while we moved through the sun salutations. Downward fucking dog had almost done me in, and crow pose, with Jesse's thighs spread wide apart, his narrow waist, and his asscheeks tense...all of it had been confusing and intriguing.

"But do you think you'd like to come again with me?"

I stared at him for a long second, my head mixing up the sentence to mean something completely different. The cocky half-smile on his face didn't help matters.

"Maybe?" It was possible the heat had gotten to me. "I need ice cream," I said abruptly.

"Ice cream?" His brows shot up, and then he considered and shrugged. "Okay. There's a place right down the street."

We cleaned off our mats and returned them to the shelves, then walked down the street. I went from sweating balls to shivering in the ice cream shop, but once we had our double scoops and found a bench outside, it was the perfect combo of cold and hot.

"Nice man spreading." Jesse fixed me with an accusing stare. "Your DP is out of control, by the way."

"DP is...I thought that was something else." I licked a big hunk of chocolate from my cone. Heaven.

Jesse fought a smile. "I was trying not to say it out loud because..." He gestured around and leaned closer. "Family types." His breath smelled like strawberry ice cream and blew cool over my ear as he spoke. "Dick print. Actually, hang on." He popped off the bench and held up a finger as he dug out his phone. "Lower the cone just in front of your chest. Little to the left. *Perfect.*"

I scooted my legs closer together to make room for him when he dropped back onto the bench next to me, angling the screen so I could see. I checked out the photo he'd taken and laughed, shaking my head. "That's obscene."

Jesse had captured me from the neck down, the chocolate ice cream cone perfectly centered over my chest, legs spread wide, and yeah, he'd been right, the dick print was on full display.

I handed the phone back and nudged my dick around to make it less obvious for innocent passersby.

"Still looks like it's trying to make a jailbreak." Jesse smirked and waved the phone. "It's perfect. Can I put it on your Insta? C'mon. Marketing, remember?"

"Really?" He'd helped me set up an Instagram account and a Twitter and insisted people loved daily updates when I told him I didn't see the point. *It builds community and engenders familiarity*, he'd said, like some marketing specialist. But he'd been right. I'd seen a steady uptick in subscribers for my Only-Fans, and I'd gained a lot of new followers.

"Watch and learn, my friend," Jesse promised, with all the confidence of an expert. "Who doesn't love ice cream and dick prints?" He fiddled with the phone and squished closer to me in a fresh waft of strawberry tinged with the metallic bite of sweat, which was strangely enticing. As we stared at the screen, the likes came flooding in almost instantaneously.

"What the hell?"

Jesse grinned triumphantly. "Told you."

I checked out the caption which read, "Wanna lick?" and cracked up. Then I noticed the wall of hashtags and gave him a stern look. "How do you know all these hashtags and you didn't know what a manther was?"

"My brain has very selective retention." He tilted his chin toward the phone. "Bet you get at least ten new subs out of this. Oh, you know what we should've done? A clothed version and a naked version." He frowned. "We'll do that next time. I should've thought ahead." Jesse was still staring at my crotch thoughtfully, though, and I got a little distracted by him licking his ice cream cone as he did it. "So all the guys wear those tights to practice in? Can anyone come to practices?" He wiggled his brows and laughed when I nudged him with my shoulder.

"We usually wear cups or jocks, too, so it's not the dick buffet you're probably imagining."

Dick buffet, he mouthed, then said aloud, "Let's change the subject. I'm wearing the wrong shorts for it. So how'd you even get into football?"

I told him about my dad being the coach at our high school, all the sports he'd coached when I was growing up, and about my big-ass family. We had that in common. "I was pretty good early on, and it was just one of those things where...I dunno. It was something my dad and I could share together. It's hard to stand out in a big family, you know? So I ran with it. I liked having that with him. My younger brother, Tanner, is a baseball phenom and Cassie, my sis, is awesome at hockey."

"What about the other three? You said there are six of you, yeah?"

"Yeah, they're not into sports, so we don't acknowledge them. It's hard for me to remember their names," I joked, then told him about the rest of my siblings.

Jesse caught a drip of ice cream on his tongue. "I wish I'd had something like that, though. My claim to fame was just keeping everything running smoothly." He wrinkled his nose. "Boring."

"What about cooking? You're good at that."

He snorted. "No one says, meet my son, he's good at cooking."

"They probably do if you're Grant Achatz."

Jesse's mouth fell open. "You know who that is?"

I nodded after a lick of my cone. "And Anthony Bourdain

and a few others. I watched a documentary one time when we were on a bus heading to a game. Sounds cutthroat. But if you love cooking so much, why aren't you doing that?"

"I dunno. I mean, I've thought about going to culinary school next year, and I just started that sous chef job at Fuego that Chet helped me get. We'll see, though."

"What's so funny?"

"I dunno, I guess it's just...if you'd told me I'd be sitting outside Slurpy's eating ice cream with a football player, who happens to be my roommate and who also happens to film jerk vids and knows who Greg Achatz is...it sounds a little crazy."

"You mean because I'm not a one-dimensional football player? I'm a real boy, Gepetto?"

Jesse blanched. "No, I just mean...or maybe a little bit, yeah. But I..." His cheeks flushed. "I just mean I like hanging out with you, even if you created a lake of sweat in yoga class, threw your shirt on the floor and—"

"You didn't mention the no-talking thing," I reminded him. "I felt like an idiot."

"I figured that was a given. No one talks. Ever. Even if someone accidentally farts, you don't acknowledge it."

"Are you shitting me?"

"That would be extremely frowned upon, too." Jesse snorted at his own joke. "But yeah, I guess it is kinda weird, actually, now that I think about it."

He pulled out his phone and scrolled through it while I polished off my cone and then stretched my arms out, closing my eyes and letting the sun beat down on my face.

I was enjoying the nice day until Jesse blurted out, "Holy shit!"

My eyes flew open in time to catch a lady glare at him as he thrust the screen at me.

At some point he'd navigated over to my OnlyFans page. I stared down at the display and had to fight to keep my jaw from gaping.

I'd posted the first video we'd shot in his bedroom before AM practice and had then gone about business as usual. I typically checked at the end of the day to see how things were doing. It wasn't even noon and there were a hundred comments on the video and…"$185 in tips?" I balked as Jesse grinned.

"Read some of the comments."

I was still bowled over by the $185 in tips. At max, I'd gotten $50 once when I slid the tip of my pinky in my hole. I clicked down through the comments.

Somebody got a camera guy!!!! Loving it.
Hottest one yet. Keep 'em coming. Can't get enough.
You have the sexiest cock I've ever seen.
Blew my load before you did. Nice.

I laughed at that one.

Whoever's holding the camera was clearly enjoying it, too. Extra hot.

I glanced up at Jesse, and he buffed his nails conspicuously against his collar with a smug smile. I wondered if he'd read that last comment.

"You know what this means?"

"What?"

He had a little dimple on his left cheek with a freckle on the border that kept snagging my gaze. "It's time to step up your jerk game even more," he said, lowering his voice ominously.

"I've noticed that despite initial protests, you seem to be settling comfortably into this role," I pointed out.

Jesse wiggled his shoulders in a preening fashion and blew me a kiss as his gaze strayed to my crotch. "I love a project, baby, and this is *definitely* a project."

"Are we talking about videos or my dick?" I teased.

"Does it matter?"

We both cracked up, then stood and tossed our trash into a nearby bin. I nudged Jesse's shoulder with my upper arm as we ambled lazily down the sidewalk. "So since I did yoga with you this time, does that mean you'll be running sprints with me next time?"

"No, no, *Jake*. That's not how this is going to work," Jesse reprimanded me, but as we turned into the parking lot and headed for his car, he exhaled noisily. "Okay, fine. I might be persuaded to attempt some sprint training in the interest of not being left behind if we ever find ourselves in a situation where we have to run."

"I'll go easy on you the first time, I promise."

Jesse folded his arms over the top of his car and stared across at me, lips pursing before he shook his head. "Nope, not gonna. I'll be a good boy."

And though I knew he was teasing, the innuendo hung there between us, searing through my gut and speeding up my pulse when I realized exactly how curious I'd become about him.

11

JESSE

Sam had a death grip on one of the shelves of the bookcase he stood in front of as he worked himself. Judging by the way he'd clamped down on his lower lip, he was close, and fighting it, too, trying to make his expression appear as normal as possible.

He kept glancing over at me as if to make sure I was holding up my end of the bargain as both lookout and camera operator.

I gave him what I hoped was an encouraging nod and tried to keep my expression blank, doing what I hoped was a believable couple-of-guys-browsing-the-anthropology-section-of-the-campus-bookstore look. It wasn't easy, but I was starting to get used to the perennial blue balls these sessions brought on.

Yanking the bill on my ball cap lower, I sent my gaze over the students milling nearby. Tactically speaking, we were sitting pretty. Sam and I had both scouted this location multiple times at different times of the day all the previous week, figured out where the cameras were and the best place to position ourselves.

"Slow down," I told him, keeping my voice low. "We've got time. We're good. I promise."

Sam nodded and squeezed the head of his dick, letting out a quiet sound that wrecked me, a muted whimpery moan that would inevitably replay in my head when I jerked off later, despite my best efforts.

I thought I knew edging? I'd been naive. Filming Sam was the biggest edge of my life, a guaranteed twenty to thirty minutes during which my cock swelled and throbbed in my pants and every subtle shift and movement became torturous pleasure I couldn't capitalize on. Sam would shoot me imploring glances on occasion, like he wanted to make sure I thought what he was doing was hot, and it only ratcheted my pulse that much higher. I'd thought he was cute before. Now I found him off-the-charts sexy.

I kept my voice quiet as I adjusted the camera. "Good. So fucking good."

"Yeah?"

"Mm." I nodded. "Do that thing." He shot me a questioning look, and I glanced around before leaning closer. "The thing where you twist over your head and stroke your balls."

He did the thing—my favorite thing—which made his eyelashes flutter with ecstasy, and I fought to keep from drooling. "That one?"

"That's it." God help me, I should get some sort of pervert's medal of honor for not busting in my pants. Sam, bless his clever heart, had on a pair of shorts he'd cut the bottom half of the pockets out of, so he could fish his johnson out with ease whenever he needed to. They were a pair I'd seen on him many times before, and knowing what I knew now was the ripe cherry on top of my blue ball sundae.

His dick was leaking all over the place, and his strokes took on a frenetic edge, telling me he was close to shattering. Fuck me, I knew his jerk habits as well as I knew my own now.

Two rows to the left, a guy and a girl browsed the bookshelves together. A few rows to the right, several other people strolled the aisles slowly. We were near the rear of the shop, with Sam angled toward the back wall. The front of the aisle was partially obscured by an endcap display with a bunch of Silver Ridge U stuffed rhinos. I stepped in closer as the guy and the girl moved.

"What now? Tell me what to do."

My nuts almost exploded with joy at the lusty timbre of his voice. It took a few seconds for my brain to reach them with the memo that directive had—sadly—not been for their benefit. They were so persistently optimistic in that regard. Sam had started doing this with increasing frequency lately, though, asking for direction. I wasn't sure if it was because he was so keyed up and turned on that he forgot all but the basics, or because he wanted to make sure he wasn't repetitive in his videos or something.

But telling Sam what to do? It wasn't exactly a hardship. "Slow down a little."

Sam's gaze flicked toward me, his eyes tight with need as he complied, murmuring a soft, needy curse when he did that almost wrecked me. *Good goddamn.*

I'd resolutely avoided watching his videos aside from when we were checking them before uploading them, but right now I would've killed to have clicked on his page and gotten to see this as a first-time observer on a bigger screen than the one I was currently positioning over his crotch. The noise of the bookstore around us, his thick cock protruding from a nest of pastel plaid fabric.

"Good. So good," I encouraged. "Keep doing it just like that.

Nice and easy so when you come, it gushes down your knuckles. *Perfect.*"

"Oh fuck. Oh *shit*," Sam whispered, tightening his hand around his shaft. "Ready?"

"Fuck yeah, go for it." I made sure the camera was trained for the money shot and checked on the two dudes who had started down the aisle perpendicular to ours. "You're perfect."

"I like when you talk to me." His strained voice tapered off into a moan.

Wait. What? I wasn't sure what kind of face I made for that revelation, but it didn't stop the gush of cream from his slit.

And fuck, there was a lot of it.

Sam's head drooped, and a tremor of pleasure ran through his shoulders. His breath puffed out of his flared nostrils in sexy little bursts of sound. He made a cap of his palm, keeping his release from spraying the bookshelves. Instead, it streamed down the sides of his shaft, and he rubbed it in as he chased his orgasm to its finish. Just in time, too, because the pair of guys I'd been watching swung around into our aisle.

I stuffed the camera in my pocket and hooked an elbow through Sam's.

"Hey!" he protested.

"Incoming. Walk slowly and get that kielbasa back in your pants."

"I'm drenched."

"Too bad." I guided us to the opposite end of the aisle as Sam managed to tuck himself away and swiped his hand on his shirt.

He glanced over his shoulder as we turned down another aisle. "Do you think they saw?"

"Nah, probably not. They were talking to each other. Let's get the fuck out of here, though. You smell like bukkake."

Sam cracked up and cut right in front of me so that I bumped into him.

I shoved him through the front door of the bookstore. "Seriously, you need a shower. Maybe two."

We both froze as the anti-theft sensors shrilled around us. My eyes widened in panic as one of the cashiers walked briskly toward us with a grim expression on his face.

"Fuck me," I muttered. "Run!"

"Jesse." Sam caught me by my upper arm before I achieved liftoff and laughed as he squeezed it. "Relax."

"What if they saw something?" My heart thundered at the prospect.

"They didn't. It's just the sensor alarm. Did you pick something up?"

"When would I have done that? Are you asking if I shoplifted school supplies with one hand while the other was filming you jacking off and you somehow missed that?"

He grinned, but the cashier stopping in front of us prevented his reply.

The guy was around our age and wore a no-nonsense scowl on his face and a nametag on his shirt that read Dave. "I'll need to see your backpacks."

Sam shrugged. "Okay, we didn't take anything."

"How many times do you think I've heard that before?"

We handed our backpacks over, and the cashier pawed through them. "Lift up your shirts please."

This time Sam looked slightly stricken, and I was the one fighting back a snicker. "Isn't that something security is supposed to do and not a cashier?"

"Sure, yeah." Dave rolled his eyes. "Would you like to wait here for the next half hour while I make the call, or would you like to lift your damn shirt up and let's get on with it?"

Sam shot a glance at me, then pressed his lips together and lifted up his shirt while I did the same.

Dave walked around us. "You can lower them," he said, then made a clucking noise and peeled something from my shirt before holding his finger up. On it was a puffy little sensor-embedded sticker. No clue how it'd gotten there. Guess I'd rubbed against a book or shelf the wrong way.

"Now, aren't you glad we didn't wait for security?" He cocked his head at Sam. "Hey, you're on the football team, yeah?"

"Yup." Sam smoothed his hand over his stomach with a curt nod. "Are we free to go?"

The guy's face fell, and he nodded. "Yeah, sure."

We hitched our packs back on our shoulders. I nudged Sam in the ribs. "What was that? You're usually way nicer. Wait, did *you* take something?"

"No! You psyched me out! I kept thinking that guy was probably smelling me or that I'd lift up my shirt and have flakes of dried cum all over my stomach and he'd judge me."

"What exactly would he be judging?"

"My aim?"

I snorted. "You caught it in your hand."

"I guess, yeah, but I wasn't paying much attention where I wiped it when you were dragging me toward the front."

"I was, and it wasn't on your stomach."

His bewildered expression morphed into a smile. "Should've known that, as detail oriented as you are. Hey, thank goodness you didn't have a dildo in your backpack this time, right?"

"Ugh, please stop reminding me that you were there to witness my abject humiliation." I handed him a pack of baby wipes so he could clean up better and glanced at my watch. "I've got ten minutes until class. You?"

"Same." We headed in the direction of a stand of trees, intent on the shade beneath it. Sam cut me a sidelong look. "What I said back in the bookstore about liking when you talked to me, I—" He scratched his jaw, hesitating. "I just meant the direction you give me is helpful."

"Oh, I know. All kinds of random stuff slips out when people are circling the big O. I can't tell you how many orgasm-induced I-love-yous I've heard. They're like little bugs, skittering away when you try to get a closer look. I didn't think you meant anything by it." I rushed to fill in his pause so he wouldn't feel compelled to explain. "Want to see if there are any new comments on your SM?"

Sam nodded in assent, wiped himself down, leaving a pile of wipes beside him, and then stretched out on the fluffy grass, lacing his fingers behind his head.

I sat with my back to the tree and opened the last thirty-second teaser clip I'd posted to his Twitter account. "Wow, you've got a lot of likes and retweets on this one."

"Yeah?" He didn't sound as enthused as I'd expected.

I mm-hmmed as I scrolled through the comments, chuffed when I saw a few complimenting the camera work. I passed the phone over to Sam. "You've got a special request."

"Wow. This is…intricate. Rope. Handcuffs. I'm okay with that. No to a ball gag, though." He angled the screen and squinted at it. "Man, the requests for seeing me with another guy are really ramping up lately, too."

"Yeah, just ignore those. They'll keep watching. They're just throwing it out to see if you'll bite."

Sam's brow furrowed. "I've considered it."

"Really?" My stomach flip-flopped on itself as I imagined Sam with another guy, which was totally ridiculous for multiple reasons—though the part where it was ridiculous because I thought Sam would never do that was starting to sound like less of an issue. "You'd do gay for pay?"

He sawed at his lower lip in thought. "Another guy I was chatting with early on who has an OnlyFans says it's the way to go, that his subscribers really love it. And it's not like it's a hardship getting your dick sucked or jacked off I mean, unless you're really homophobic or just very, very straight. I'm definitely not homophobic, and I wouldn't be skeeved out by a guy touching me or vice versa."

His gaze on me seemed careful, but he should've known I'd be the last person to judge him for confessing something like that. "I'd imagine not since you claim to have sucked a guy's dick before. Didn't you hate it, though?"

Sam shrugged. "It was just a thing I did. I feel ambivalent about it now, I guess. I didn't really feel anything back then either. It was freshman year. Or maybe sophomore. We were both pretty drunk. Standard, right? There were a bunch of us, so it wasn't like it was an intimate moment between the two of us. It earned the same level of enthusiasm as if I'd chugged a beer, except the aftertaste was definitely different." His smile was wry, and he hesitated a beat, shading his eyes against the sun and peering over at me. "That's just how it goes for me sometimes, even with girls."

"Like...you're not into it?"

"I'm just not very into stuff that's only casual." His expression was almost sheepish. "Ironic, right? Football dude with plenty of opportunities? Sometimes I do it just because. Other times, meh. It's sexier to me when it's someone you've known for more than five minutes. I guess I'm a little traditional that way."

"Do you know what demisexual is?"

Sam waved a hand. "No, I definitely have a libido. And I get horny and like jerking off. I like watching porn and stuff, but when it comes to an actual human, I like it more if I know them."

I laughed and shook my head when his brows pinched together. "You can be and do all those things and be demi. Or, whatever. You don't even have to claim a label at all. You just said all of that like you felt guilty for *not* wanting to sleep with people sometimes, and you shouldn't. Like being good at football, or liking pineapple, it's an aspect of you, but it doesn't have to define you. I mean, unless you want it to. Sometimes people do."

Sam passed the phone back to me and laced his fingers over his stomach with a thoughtful nod. His shirt had ridden up over his abs, and I tried to ignore the light fuzz of his treasure trail, a slightly darker mimic of the fur on his legs. It didn't look wiry like some body hair, but like it'd be really soft to the touch.

He was quiet for a stretch, then shrugged. "Okay, yeah, maybe." He angled a look at me. "Subject change. So did you ever hear back from John?"

"Yeah. We text a little here and there. We're trying to find a date to get together that works with his crazy-ass schedule." I wasn't as excited as I thought I should be about it, though.

"Cool." Sam rolled upright and dusted bits of grass off his shoulders. "I need to get to class, I guess."

"Hang on." I reached out and plucked a few stray pieces from his shoulders. "Hm?" I said when I noticed him studying me with an amused quirk of his lips.

"You're pretty nice."

"Oh god, lower your voice," I hissed. "Don't even speak it into existence. That's the fucking kiss of death right there." *Nice.* Nice was for kittens rolling around in baskets of yarn and grandmas who shared their Werther's with you. Nice was undoubtedly how I kept getting shoved into the friend zone, even though I didn't actually think I was all that nice, and even though the way Sam said it in conjunction with the sincerity in his expression made it actually feel like a compliment for once. A genuine one that buzzed in my stomach and made me warm all over.

Sam chuckled. "I don't think so. I like nice people. Nice is underrated." He rose to standing and extended his hand to pull me up, too, then shouldered his backpack. "So if I wanted to do this gay for pay, is it really as easy as going to a club or getting on Grindr and finding a guy?"

I dusted my hands off on my shorts. "Yeah. I'd stick with a club, though, so you can vet in person," I said, even as my stomach sank. The thought honestly made me nauseated. "There'd be guys lining up for you in a New York minute. You'd just need them to agree to filming and sign an NDA. But trust me, when they see you, that's not going to be a problem."

Sam did something that I thought was supposed to be some kind of fashion pose. "You think I'm cute?"

"Maybe I was talking about your dangling accessory parts. Don't get smug." I thwapped him on the shoulder.

"Okay, great, so when are we going to the club?"

"*We?*" I sputtered.

"Well yeah, I don't know what the fuck I'm doing. So this time you get to wingman for me."

12

JESSE

"Well, isn't he taking to it like a duck to water," my friend Tazla shouted over the thumping base at Hype.

I could only stare. Sam was generally easygoing, but I'd expected some sort of initial tentativeness upon his first introduction to one of the gayest of gay clubs in town. But by the time we spilled from the long hallway into the ballroom, Sam already had glitter on his cheeks courtesy of a cute little twink bopping around with sticks of the stuff.

An hour in? He was bouncing in the middle of the dance floor to a juiced-up remix of The Weeknd's "Blinding Lights" like he'd been born with confetti in his veins.

I shook my head in wonder. "He's a unique one."

"A *hot* one." Tazla tossed back a shot. "Think he'd flex his sexuality for a night with me?"

I nudged him with a laugh. "No. Stop."

Tazla waggled his brows and flashed me a lascivious grin. "Coming back out?"

"In a minute." I held up my water, and Tazla headed toward the dance floor with a dramatic eye roll.

I found Sam again, a smile hooking my lips as he threw a hand in the air and did some sort of Chippendale-style hip swivel. I'd noticed that though he seemed at ease, he wasn't dancing with anyone per se, and it wasn't for lack of people trying. The second we'd hit the dance floor, he'd been mobbed like the second coming of David Bowie, but anyone grinding up on him didn't last for more than a few seconds before he bounced away.

Mark smacked into me with a sloppy grin and followed my gaze to Sam. "This is hilarious. You dared him to come?"

I returned Chet's wave as he leaned over the bar top to order drinks. "Nah. I think he just didn't want to be at home by himself tonight. He asked to tag along," I lied.

Mark arched a brow. "Interesting."

In a perfect world, Sam and I would've come alone, but Mark had asked my plans earlier and when I'd told him he'd gotten all excited and invited himself and Chet along, too. Tazla was almost always here Wednesday nights anyway, so my best-laid plans of keeping it low-key between me and Sam had exploded. Sam had taken that perfectly in stride, too.

I tore my eyes from his bebopping form and nudged Mark. "Did you think any more about Cam moving in?"

Mark shot a look over his shoulder at Chet and then shrugged. "A little, yeah. What do you think?"

"It's an extra hundred bucks a month in all of our pockets, and I don't have a problem with him. He seems cool. But I don't know him as well as you and Sam."

"Know who?" Chet handed Mark a tall glass.

"Cam."

"Oh."

Mark set his glass down and eyed Chet. "Oh? See, what does that mean? Cam moving in would make you jealous?"

"This sounds like a convo I don't want to be a part of." I finished off my water, but Mark nudged me with a laugh.

"No, stay, we're just...uh...exercising communication skills."

"It means I was thinking about it." Chet blew out a breath. "Fuck, I do feel bad for him, honestly. He seems really...solitary, don't you think?" Chet edged closer to Mark and ran a finger along his collarbone, and thankfully, when I darted a look elsewhere, I spied Sam moving toward us.

I held out a bottle of water for him, and he guzzled half before swiping his mouth. "Thanks. I'm burning up. The music is great here, though. I mean, a little gay, but good." He gave me a jokey wink. "I don't think I've ever been so bumped and grinded in my life."

"Told you you wouldn't have any trouble here."

"This is crazy for a Wednesday night."

I scooted closer and raised my voice to be heard. "That's because of the drag show earlier. Gets people all amped up."

"How can you possibly complain about not being able to get laid?" Sam scanned the dance floor. "It seems like the greater challenge here would be walking out without actually getting laid. I'm pretty sure at least two guys that I saw were getting handies near a table, and there was one girl with her hand definitely in the other's skirt." He nudged me when I didn't say anything. "I was waiting for something more along the lines of an answer. C'mon, I'm genuinely curious." He leaned against the bar and swept the crowd again. "What about that guy?"

I followed Sam's gaze to a brunet guy about my height and shrugged unenthusiastically. "He's okay. I see him here a lot. Kind of skeezy."

"Okay, ummm." Sam swung a look in another direction.

"Guy with the hipster glasses. He looks intellectual and not skeezy. Seems like something you'd be into."

"The hipster or intellectual part? He'll probably want to talk about feelings while I blow him." I wrinkled my nose.

Sam balked, then barked out a laugh. "If he's talking about how good it feels, that's not necessarily a bad thing?"

"You know what I mean."

"You're just making shit up. Okay, dude in the backwards ball cap, white T-shirt. Built." Sam tried to subtly point with his elbow. I eyed the guy assessingly.

"Maybe."

"Weeks ago you were ready to bang anyone under sixty-five."

"It was a low moment. Besides, we're not here looking for me. We're looking for you, right? So how about any of those guys you just pointed out?"

Sam wrinkled his nose.

"Ha! See?"

"My issues are different." He shook his head. "I've got a theory about you, though. You know what I think? I think you're not actually that interested in hooking up. I think you want something meaningful."

"Ewww, gross. You keep that kink to yourself."

He shoved my shoulder as I laughed.

Tazla bumped into me from behind, and Sam caught hold of my waist as Tazla rested his chin on my shoulder and grinned at us. "Can we switch so I'm the sandwich filling?"

I bumped my ass back against him. "No."

"Fine," he pouted, then grabbed us both by the wrist. "Back on the floor."

Tazla instantly Velcroed himself to my back while Sam once

again bobbed in a sea of eager partners. We lost ourselves in the music for a couple of songs, and when I blinked open my eyes again, Sam was dancing with Sawyer Harker.

"Oh my god," Tazla laughed. "You'd better go save him."

I elbowed my way over and cut in when Sawyer did a flashy spin, trying to impress Sam.

I grinned cheerfully at his resulting scowl and twisted around, resting my back against Sam's chest and grinding against him as I tipped my mouth toward his ear. "You don't want him. That's Sawyer, and he has a big mouth. Not the fun kind, but the kind that's gonna share *all* your business with the whole world and any neighboring planet within range. If you're trying to keep things quiet, he's not your guy."

"Shit. He seemed cool."

"Yeah, that's his MO. He seems like the sweetest, most harmless little thing in the world, and you'll spill all your secrets to him. Next thing you know, he's telling everyone within a five-foot radius about the time you got crabs from trying on your stepbrother's jock strap."

Sam's chest rumbled against my back with laughter. "Speaking from experience there?"

"No! He did that to my friend. Anyway, he's not your guy."

I spun around and looped my arms around Sam's neck, curious to see whether he'd let me linger or put distance between us like he'd done with everyone else. "You said your issues were different. What'd you mean?"

"It makes me feel weird. I don't..." Sam shook his head again. "I've been thinking about it all night, and I don't know if I can mess around with a stranger like that. Kinda per our conversation the other day." He hitched one shoulder in a shrug, and I tried not to react in surprise as he dropped his hands around my waist and anchored them to my low back. When he splayed them, they covered the entire surface area halfway up my spine. I quelled the tremor of delight that wanted to race through me imagining them on other parts of me. He could probably palm my ass in one hand. I craned my head up at him as he spoke again, hoping he would ignore my burgeoning erection. "I just don't see this working. I'm not going to be able to find someone here."

"Don't give up yet." I tried to inject the level of enthusiasm I suspected I was supposed to have versus what currently existed and was quickly ebbing the longer I was in Sam's arms. "I could talk to some guys. Anyone you see as even a remote possibility, I can go talk to him. Vet him. I'm not shy. I could maybe get a better sense of who would be down and who might be a good match." I scanned the crowd again. I'd been coming here since freshman year and was accustomed to the crowd. I knew a lot of the staff by name, and there were plenty of regulars. Surely among them would be a low-key, discreet guy Sam would vibe with. I had that thought even as Parson, a third-year fashion student, flipped a fan open dramatically and used it to scythe his way through the crowd toward the dance floor. Hmm. Maybe we should've gone to one of the leather bars.

I was pretty sure a leather daddy wasn't what Sam had in mind either, though. Fuck, this was harder than it seemed. And I still didn't want to be doing it at all.

Feeling Sam's gaze on the side of my face, I tipped him a querying look.

He glanced away and over the crowd again, then finally looked down to meet my eyes, his grip on me tightening. "It has to be you. You have to do it."

"Do what now?" I was surely hearing things.

Sam grabbed me by the elbow and guided me off the dance floor where it was quieter. "I need you to do the videos with me. I mean, if you're willing. Or want to. Or…willing, yeah. Just willing is good enough."

Oh god, was I screwed.

13

SAM

I'd had a fun night dancing at Hype, don't get me wrong. I loved to dance, and it made no difference to me whether I was surrounded by girls in crop tops or guys in the same while I was doing it. But every time some guy danced up on me or drifted into my field of vision, I tried to imagine hooking up with them and couldn't. When I tried to mentally chart the logical path forward, I arrived at a lot of missteps and awkwardness. Because even if some guy did sign an NDA, could I truly trust them?

The closest I'd gotten to interest had been Sawyer, and that was because he'd made me feel at ease almost immediately, the same way Jesse did. But when Jesse put the kibosh on that and pressed against me, doing some kind of inhumanly hypnotic undulation with his spine that made his ass thump steadily against my groin, I forgot everything else. It got me going, and I made an instinctive grab for his hips to keep the pressure focused and intense before the rest of me could catch up to what was happening.

Then he'd swiveled, canting his head back toward me as I looped my arms around him the way I hadn't been able to—nor had any desire to do—with any other guy in the club, and I knew.

It has to be you.

Still, I didn't mean for it to come tumbling out of my mouth the way it had, like some sprawling awkward octopus of a statement that was technically supposed to be a request.

Now Jesse was giving me one of those gape-mouthed stares that suggested I'd lost it.

I wasn't going to pretend that just because I was offering and Jesse was a gay guy that I expected him to leap at the prospect. Still, given all our activities over the last couple of weeks, I'd expected something a little more diplomatic than his face twisting up like I'd just told him I'd punched his grandma.

I took a step back to put some distance between us. "Okay, I'll take that as a no, and let's just keep doing what we were doing."

Jesse grabbed my arm when I tried to push past him. "Wait a minute, do you really think that's a good idea, though? I mean, we're…we're…friends and roommates."

"Exactly, we're friends. I'm reasonable, you're reasonable. The other stuff has gone really well…" I waved a hand. "But never mind. I totally understand. Let's just pretend I never said anything."

"That's probably for the best."

The craziest thing, though, was that as I headed toward the bar to get another bottle of water, I was pretty sure the feeling in my stomach wasn't the sting of rejection, but disappointment.

THE NEXT MORNING, I SLOWED ON THE SIDEWALK AS I SPOTTED Jesse speed-walking across the quad toward me, jaw tightly set. I wondered if he was hungover. We'd stayed another hour at the club before all piling into an Uber. I hadn't had too much to drink, but getting up so early for weight training had still sucked on so little sleep.

My smile faded the closer he got. Damn, was he coming to tell me he didn't want to film my videos anymore after what I'd said last night? That would suck, too.

I'd woken up this morning and immediately inwardly groaned at everything that had transpired last night. I shouldn't have said anything. I'd probably made him feel weird. "Hey, Jesse, listen," I started. "I've been thinking more about last night. I wanted to say it's fi—"

"I'll do it." His nostrils flared and his eyes burned fierce with determination like he was answering a call to a duel or something, not agreeing to get busy with me.

I forgot what I'd been about to say. *Something-something* apology for making things weird last night. But apparently, I hadn't made things weird after all. This guy confused me. And that I liked it also confused me. "You will?"

He fell in step beside me with a nod. "Yeah, but I think we should have some ground rules and discuss things first."

"Definitely." I nodded emphatically. Fuck, this was great, though. This was *perfect*. Jesse would have some idea what he was doing since he'd obviously had more experience than me. We were friends. Or...increasingly friendlyish, so it wouldn't be too weird. I felt comfortable with him, and I didn't have to worry about him being a crazy stalker or running off at the mouth.

There was something else, too. A seed of...excitement almost, or curiosity, dancing in my stomach. Something I didn't have a word or label for yet. "I was just about to go get something to eat."

"Your default. Do you do anything else?"

"Many things." I let a meaningful pause stretch between us before cracking a grin. "Between eating."

Jesse rolled his eyes and told me to lead the way.

We got my usual booth at Cafe on Main, and I sent a wave over to Cam once we sat. Jesse twisted around to see who I'd waved to.

"Oh yeah, I forgot he worked here." He waved, too. "So," he started, leaning in, then pausing as Cam came over with menus.

Cam held a fist out for a bump, which I gave, and then he smiled at Jesse, looking him up and down thoughtfully. "I haven't seen you in a while."

"Hi. I still exist."

"Very much so," Cam said, and Jesse's gaze went as suddenly sharp as I was sure mine did when Cam's smile turned almost coquettish.

"Do I remember you mentioning you've had Applebaum for a class?" Cam rested a hand on the back of the booth near Jesse, and my gaze kept straying to the distance between his fingertips and the back of Jesse's neck.

"Oh yeah." Jesse frowned in sympathy. "Superhard."

"Ugh." Cam groaned. "I hoped you would tell me he gets easier as the semester goes on."

"Sadly, no, but as long as you do all the assignments, it's okay. I got out of there with a B and without being called out like he loves doing."

"I already got called out. It was brutal."

"But you survived. Hey, I still have my notes, I think, if you want them?"

Cam perked. "That'd be great."

Silence fell for a beat, and they exchanged a glance before Jesse promised to get the notes to him.

I looked between them, unsure if there was another conversation taking place that I wasn't privy to. After Cam left, I planted my forearms on the table. "He was flirting with you."

Jesse looked up from his menu with a laugh. "Maybe, and?"

"Just another example of how you're constantly talking about how you can't get laid, and yet since I've been around you, I've seen countless dudes make a pass. Just saying."

Jesse rolled his eyes, then lifted the menu like a divider between us, which I stared at resolutely. There was a smile in his eyes when he lowered it a couple of inches again, though. "You're still there."

"Shocking, right?"

He tossed the menu aside. "Fine. I can get laid. Getting laid is easy—"

"But—"

Jesse lifted a finger. "I said getting laid is easy. Meeting someone I want to do it with on a consistent basis is the hard part. I have certain...standards. A mental checklist of sorts."

"Oh?" I cocked a brow. "And what might these standards be?"

"Uh-uh." Jesse shook his head. "A lot of them are too embarrassing to admit. Suffice it to say, I doubt Cam or any of the other guys you're thinking of would meet them, so I've shelved them until after this year."

"What about John?" I asked, and Jesse pressed his lips together. Bullseye.

"John meets a lot of the criteria, but he's also really busy, so we'll see."

"What about that date you were supposed to go on with him?"

"He had to cancel last Thursday because of work. He said something about next week, but who knows."

I felt kind of bad for hoping John got tied up. But seriously, if he hadn't made time for Jesse already, was he really a good match for him?

We paused our conversation again when Cam returned to take our orders. Jesse shook his head at me when he walked away. "Stop looking at me like you expect me to tear off my clothes and run after him."

"That wasn't how I was looking at you. But would you bang him?" I had to admit, given all Jesse's talk of lists and stuff, I was curious what interested him, and the little prickle that ran through me, well, that was just *awareness*. Or conscientiousness. I mean, I was about to embark upon a sexual adventure with him. It was probably only natural to feel a little...protective.

Jesse bopped me on the head with his menu. "We're here to discuss our...our *business endeavor*. But in point of fact, no, I wouldn't bang Cam. He's cute, but there's too much history. It'd be trouble. Now, let's get down to business." He pulled out a small notepad and flipped it open on the table, then dug in the pocket of his backpack for a pen. "So I began a small list of ideas..."

"A new list? What a surprise," I teased.

"Duh. You can't just go into this haphazard. No one wants to see two guys fumbling around tripping over their underwear trying to take it off, or doing a dry jerk if someone absolutely hates a dry jerk."

"Do you hate a dry jerk?"

"Not if it's done right, which is exactly what we need to figure out. First, we talk scenarios. Second, we talk likes and dislikes." Jesse spoke matter-of-factly, blessedly oblivious to the fact that just the mention of a dry jerk made my dick twitch. The only good dry jerk I'd ever had had been the one I'd given myself, because he was right, there was an art to it for sure. That wasn't a requirement or anything; I'd had plenty of great hand jobs with spit as lube and actual lube, but now I was curious about Jesse's technique.

Concentrate.

"Let's start with scenarios." Jesse rapped the pen lightly on the top of his pad like we were about to write out the world's filthiest grocery list.

"Okay, you start," I said. "Name the sexiest things you've ever watched on Pornhub. Anddddd go."

"Wait, I need parameters."

"There are none. We're talking fantasies, right? Why are you looking at me like that?"

Jesse was unrelenting. "I need parameters, trust me. Like, how freaky can I get here?"

My cock gave another little twitch. Interesting. I was starting to feel like a scientist of sex lately, and what I was uncovering definitely needed more observation. "Umm, exactly how freaky are you? Never mind. Okay, parameters. "

"Take furries, for example. Is that a hard no?"

"Yeah. I mean, no? Or maybe? But I don't want to wear a furry costume because I'd get too hot. I mean, I sweat when I eat sometimes," I admitted. I wasn't proud of it.

Jesse's mouth hooked up, and I could tell he was fighting a laugh as he nodded. "Fair point. Although we wouldn't have to worry about anyone recognizing us."

"Not our target market, though, I don't think."

He did that thing that happened on occasion where he seemed surprised by something I'd said. "True. Okay, furry is out for multiple reasons, then." He fixed me with a gimlet-eyed stare I wasn't sure how to interpret. "Coach and player, coach and cheerleader, coach and coach, coach and…"

I cracked up. "Got a thing for coaches?"

"Baby, this is just the warm-up to ease you in. Sports is your thing, right? Players in a locker room, players in a shower. Teacher and student. In a classroom. On a desk. Under a desk. In a locker room under a desk with a shower pouring down on top of it. In a box with a fox—except we said no furries. Laundry room." He rattled them off one after another like a machine gun of porn premises. "Guy gets head stuck in dryer and is taken advantage of. Don't make that face. Search it on Pornhub and see for yourself. It's incredibly common."

"It is literally impossible to get stuck in a dryer."

"Shhh." Jesse waved a hand dismissively. "*Literally* no one cares."

"The laundry room thing could actually work if we time the schedule right. But that's still fucking ridiculous."

"*Oh!*" I jumped at Jesse's exclamation. "The straight guy gets a massage." He waggled his brows "That's *such* a classic."

"Yeah, okay, but is it overdone?" I pondered.

"All right, Roeper, maybe it's a little overdone. Will I click on every one that comes across my screen? Yes, I will, so it goes on the list."

"Okay, well, you're the target market, so." All this talk of sucking and jerking scenarios had me uncomfortably hard. I wondered if Jesse was, too.

We both fell quiet as Cam brought out our food, but as soon as we'd scarfed half down, we went right back to the subject at hand, adding to our list, which mostly meant Jesse barking out ideas as they came to him and me shushing him when he got too loud and nearby patrons stared.

"We could just shoot it in a bed."

Jesse stared at me aghast, as if I'd suggested tying him to a pole and flogging him. No, actually, he might have liked that.

"Mm-hmm," he hummed blandly. "That sounds great. We'll just get naked and get under the covers and I'll jack you off. How titillating. I'm nodding off already." He rested his head against the back of the booth and started snoring. I was just about to throw something at him when he popped his eyes open. "That's boring and beds are for couples."

"Seems to work pretty well for Max and Tomás." I'd subscribed to their OnlyFans recently to see what kind of content they produced after they'd left a comment on one of my videos. "They have a ton of subscribers, and they're always getting tips."

"Yeah, but they show their faces, and they're a real couple. That's the thrill, see? A peek inside someone's actual bedroom. We've got to deliver fantasy. But don't worry, I think we'll have enough. Now it's just a matter of choosing which one to start with first." He set aside the notepad and leaned forward, taking a long suck from his shake, wincing at the brain freeze, and then fixing me with a sober expression. "Something you should know…"

"STI's, yeah, for sure. I'm good. I was checked recently." I'd thought of that immediately.

"Okay, yeah, that. And same." He chuckled. "Just a warning: I'm pretty good at sex. All forms. So, like, don't go getting attached or anything."

I stared at him, trying to determine whether he was serious or not. "Anyone who's good at sex doesn't need to advertise it," I said, echoing what he'd said to me in the kitchen about dick size weeks before.

Jesse threw his head back and laughed. "God, okay. Well done."

An hour later as we strolled through the aisles of Food Mart tossing items in our cart, I was still trying to determine whether or not he'd been serious about his sexual prowess. "What makes you think you're so good at sex? Has someone told you that? Scored you on a scale I've never heard of? Or is it just a gut instinct?" Also, why couldn't I get it out of my head?

Jesse chuckled. "I was messing with you. I mean, I think I'm pretty decent in the sack and have been told as much—though sometimes it's hard to determine what's genuine and what's just someone babbling while their brains are being sucked out. But the getting attached part was just me teasing you."

He grabbed a package of Oreos off the shelf and tossed them in the air. "Catch!" he cried with a grin.

I scrambled to snatch the package before it hit the floor, then flourished it in his direction. "Reflexes, baby. Are we actually getting this?"

"Yep." Jesse whipped out his phone and scrolled as I tossed the Oreos into the cart. A pensive frown tugged his brows together. "Tomorrow through Friday all work for me."

It took me a second to catch up to the conversation. Fuck, we were really going to do this. "Okay, ummm, how about Thursday, then." I probably needed a day to mentally prep myself.

"Good idea."

Jesse hedged. "I do think having a loose plan or script would probably be better than just trying to jump in. How're your acting skills?"

"Shitty. When you hear people say they were assigned to play the tree in the school play? I was that kid. Yours?"

Jesse seesawed his hand. "They're decent. I was a flying monkey in our high school play of *Wizard of Oz*, which is basically a step above a tree, but you better believe I worked it."

I tossed a bag of bread in the cart. "Okay, so a scene from our list. Maybe we should start with something easy to set up?" I racked my brain. "Maybe we should try the roommates who help each other out in the bathroom one." I cleared my throat awkwardly and wished the action would reset my misfiring libido. "And then..." I spangled my fingers. "Stuff."

Jesse nodded with conviction. "That's perfect."

14

JESSE

I sat through every class Thursday with a nervous stomach, like I was going on a first date. Actually, there'd probably be more foreplay involved than some of the first—and often last—dates I'd been on. I reminded myself this was a transaction with a definitive goal on both our parts. It would be a hot and enjoyable way to spend an afternoon, but I didn't want to give it more weight than it warranted. No-strings-attached hedonism was, after all, what my senior year was supposed to be about, after all.

Still, when I stepped through the front door and caught sight of Sam's huge-ass Nikes abandoned near the couch, I forgot to be irritated that he'd left them out, and instead an electric thrill shot through me at what was to come. I liked sex, who didn't? And sex with someone you cared about was awesome and fantastic but also? Sex for sex's sake could be just as dandy. Even more so when it came with a few dollar signs after it and a big, fat cock.

Freshman-year Jesse would've been horrified. Freshman-year Jesse had believed in hearts, flowers, and unicorns. Senior-year Jesse knew that unicorns took shits just like any other horse.

I snickered to myself as I climbed the stairs.

"Sam?" Ew. Why did my voice sound so reedy? I glanced at my watch. Right on time.

"Yup," he called out. His bedroom door was open, and the bathroom door was cracked, too. I dropped my backpack off in my bedroom and allowed myself a quiet, two-minute freak-out.

"Tell me if you think this is dumb, but I was thinking about how we ran into each other that time, when you were coming out of the shower, and then how you came back in with my conditioner..." God, when Sam had said that in the grocery store, I went semi just like that. And then he kept going as I nodded slowly, having to work hard to keep my shit together because I'd had fantasies that ran along these lines about all of my roommates at one time or another. Which was what I got for living with a bunch of hunks, I guess.

My nod seemed to fortify Sam's conviction, thank fuck, because he'd soldiered on, and we'd cobbled together a loose scene breakdown between his King Slayer and my eager hand. In an effort to babystep toward the bigger stuff, a handjob was a natural beginning point, after all.

I checked my hair one last time, kicked off my shoes, and pressed my palm to my chest. If my heart didn't try to kick through my sternum, I wasn't sure my dick wouldn't go rogue next. "Everybody needs to settle the fuck down," I admonished my anatomy quietly. Strangely, it helped, and I headed toward the bathroom with the gravitas of someone walking into battle.

Steam billowed over the threshold and enveloped me in the scent of woodsy body wash as I pushed open the bathroom door and stepped inside. Sam was whistling a catchy Miley

Cyrus remix that had been playing in the club the other night, and I caught myself grinning before I tamped it down. Remembering the objective, I aimed the camera at the drawn shower curtain, where only the frosted liner remained after we'd depersonalized the bathroom. It created a sexy peekaboo silhouette of Sam's big body.

"That you, Josh?" Sam used the code name I'd chosen in honor of my favorite nice-guy hero from *Clueless* as my gaze dropped lower to the obvious bulge in his silhouette.

"Yeah," I chirped. Not a good sign that I was already having trouble with voice modulation. "Found your conditioner."

"Awesome, thanks." He whipped back the curtain, and I didn't even have to force myself to hold the camera still because I was transfixed as the screen filled with his massive body, water droplets hugging every round curve of his shoulders and biceps, funneling down the trough between his ripped abs, and cruising along a vee so fucking defined that it'd make gay and straight dudes alike weep.

I hadn't even gotten to his cock yet. It hung heavy and swollen, flushed with enough blood that it was already an impressive display of manhood, telling me he must have done a little pre-stroking to get it ready for its close-up.

I almost dropped the conditioner handing it over, proving that me, conditioner, and Sam were never going to be a good combination.

Glancing up, I noticed Sam was staring at me expectantly and realized I'd forgotten my line. What the fuck was my line?

What the fuck was my name?

Oh, right. "Here you go," I said woodenly and then shook my head to try to clear the fog. I was supposed to be the drama savant, after all.

Sam's shoulders shook as he tried to stifle a laugh when I

glared at him. *Laugh it up, chucklehead.* Maybe when he saw the video, he'd understand what had happened to my brain.

"You going to that party tonight?" Sam's attempt at our terrible script was equally stilted. He was right; he wasn't the best actor. No one would care, though, not with all that wet, dappled skin I would've happily licked clean. Crap, we hadn't fine-tuned, exactly, what was fair game. Could I lick his nipples?

"Not sure. You?" I said belatedly.

"Thinking about it."

I kept the camera trained on him as he opened the bottle and squirted conditioner on his palms. Sucking in a breath, I tried to focus my role and not how hard my dick was. "Mind if I shave in here while you finish up?"

"Sure, it's all good." Sam scrubbed his scalp, then dropped one slippery hand to his cock, giving it an incidental stroke that made it twitch. The thing looked like an elephant trunk, and I didn't even have to fake the envious sigh I let out.

"Damn, your dick is *so* big." I was pleased with how natural that sounded, probably because it was true.

"Ha. Thanks. I've been so horny all day, too, I couldn't wait to get home to jerk off." Two-second pause. Also, somehow stilted. "Actually, is it going to skeez you out if I rub one out while you're shaving? I'll try to be quiet."

"Nah, man, go for it."

Just two guys awkwardly trying to sound sexy. Maybe we should've done a trial run.

No, we *definitely* should've.

I aimed the camera at an angle toward the mirror, showing my hand removing a razor and shaving cream from the drawer, pausing when the first lusty groan came from behind the curtain

"Fuck," Sam moaned again.

That was my cue. I swiveled the camera back toward the shower, where Sam had left the curtain about a foot and a half open, giving me a convenient view of his hand shuttling leisurely up and down his shaft. He groaned again, bracing his free hand on the tile as he started fucking his tight grip.

"Shit, dude, you're really going after it." Goddammit, that sounded...not at all sexy.

Sam's hand slowed, then stopped. He let out a sigh that I echoed.

"This isn't working, is it?" I set down the razor.

"Think we're in our heads." He peeked around the curtain with an apologetic smile. "I'm having trouble concentrating."

"Everything we're saying sounds really obviously fake. I mean, not that that's any different from a regular porn, but it's throwing us off, I guess."

Sam pulled the curtain back farther, and I glued my gaze to his face and not the naked glory of his body, his sequoia quads, giant arms, and flagging Cocktimus Prime.

He raked a hand through his hair, skimming the water from his golden crown. "What if we try something different? We're trying to make something sound natural that's just... not. What if we just lean into it? Go full fucking force into the fantasy. We sound like we're afraid of the other person making fun of us. What if we embrace the ridiculous premise? Go into it full throttle. Say some ridiculous shit to me, who cares? If we crack each other up or screw this up, whatever."

I nodded slowly and swallowed. "Okay, I'm game to try." I let my gaze drift lower to his semi and licked my lips. "I really want to touch you," I confessed.

Sam's gaze jerked to mine, his expression bewildered, as if

I'd caught him off guard. Maybe we were supposed to count down or something?

"You do?"

Sam wanted full throttle? He was going to get it. I nodded. "Can I?"

He gave me another one of those slow, glaze-eyed nods.

Closing my eyes, I steadied my breath, then blinked them open and pressed forward resolutely, wrapping my hand around his dick. *Oh Jesus*, it was huge. Huge and silky and wet and so very fucking warm in my hand that my mouth watered.

I squeezed it, and Sam's eyes fell shut for a second as he grimaced with the pleasure, then seemed to remember himself. "I'm not...I'm not...are...*goddamn*."

I bit back a smile.

"It's okay," I said softly, soothingly. "Just let me help you out. Roommate to roommate. It's no big deal. It feels good, right? That's all this is about, making you feel good. It doesn't have to mean anything else."

"Jesus Christ," Sam whispered, eyes burning into mine, confusion crossing into his expression again. It was obvious he was waffling on whether this was some part of the script he'd forgotten or if this was me going with the flow. He pursed his lips like he was about to say something, then blew out a slow breath instead, gaze dropping to my hand on him. "You're sure?"

"I've been thinking about it all fucking day, trust me." I didn't even have to pretend about that either.

I danced my fingertips over the head of his cock and teased my thumb over Sam's tight slit until I was gifted with a slippery dollop of precum and a slow, carefully measured exhale from him. I knew he leaked like a motherfucker. Now that it was game on? I couldn't wait to have him dripping.

"Shit," he whispered as I began pumping his shaft. "*Oh shit, that's so fucking good, Jes—I mean Josh.*" He wet his lips absently and fumbled for the towel bar in the shower, gripping it hard, knuckles pulsing in time to my strokes. The other hand fisted the shower curtain. I bet he didn't even notice, but I did. I reveled in the small signs of him coming undone, soaking myself in them while I grew harder.

I had to focus to keep the camera aimed at the right place with my free hand, mesmerized as I was by the forward-and-back surge of his hips, how the powerful muscles of his quads, ass, and thighs flexed and contracted as he fucked into my fist.

I kept flickering gauging glances up at Sam's face to make sure it felt good and that he was okay, though it was shortly apparent that I didn't need to. I was pretty A-1 whether it came to jerking a guy or blowing him, and Sam's blissful expression reflected that. I didn't really have anything to prove to him either. I couldn't change his sexuality and, in a way, that added an element of liberation to this experience when I thought about it.

I was free to indulge every underlying straight-boy fantasy I'd ever had, and I was hell-bent on enjoying the hell out of ticking this box off by showing him the best damn time he'd ever have with a guy.

Plus, it wasn't every day I had a cock the size of Maryland asserting states' rights on my hand. I couldn't fucking wait to get it in my mouth, eventually. The fun would really start then.

15

SAM

I hadn't worried about staying hard with Jesse because I didn't find Jesse repugnant in the least, and a hand on my cock was a hand on my cock. But I also hadn't worried about coming too soon either, and it was quickly becoming clear I should've.

Because despite being a seasoned meat slapper and consummate self-edger, I'd underestimated just how fucking good Jesse's touch would feel and how into it I'd be. The guy was talented, seemed to know instinctively when to ease up and when to go harder. His brows furrowed with concentration as he worked over my head, delicate little fingers twisting and rubbing, expertly gathering up all the precum dripping from my slit and spreading it around. I had trouble keeping my body in check. All kinds of things were trying to quiver or twitch or wiggle or shake with the pleasure rocketing through me at every expert glide of his fist. My quads firmed with tension as I tried to tamp down the instinct to buck wildly into his perfect, velvety grip.

"You like my hand on your dick?" Jesse lifted his eyes to meet mine, the flare of heat in them causing an unexpected spike of desire in me.

I nodded openmouthed like an imbecile.

That…was not in the script. Actually, I didn't know if it was in the script or not. I'd forgotten the script entirely aside from the fact that Jesse was going to jerk me off and that the reality of this scenario was completely different than what I'd imagined in my head.

But in the best way possible.

I couldn't stop staring at his fingers on my shaft. Every time they spread apart and closed together again, tightening around me and then twisting over my head, I was afraid I was going to lose my shit.

He was watching, too, one corner of his lower lip caught between his teeth in concentration. When he glanced up and caught me staring, he let go of his lip and smiled, a twinkle in his eye and a short jump of his brows that I translated as *See? Told you I was good at this.*

I figured my dick was doing a good enough job confirming that without me having to say it aloud.

"*Shit.*" I gasped one of the few words remaining in my vocabulary as my orgasm surged to the foreground so suddenly it staggered me. I shook my head fervently so Jesse would slow down.

"Face me fully," he murmured.

I scrambled to comply, taking over the filming when he indicated the phone with a nudge of his chin.

Sighing with what seemed like relief, Jesse squeezed the bulge in his jeans. "It's about to get really fun. You ready?"

"Uh, will there be balloon animals? What kind of fun are we talking here?" It was already fun, if by fun he meant the kind of pleasure that made my knees weak and severed the link between higher consciousness and primal consciousness. I was a little concerned about staying upright if there was more to come, and we were definitely off script now, but I couldn't make myself care. I was intrigued, especially by the knowing gleam in his eyes I didn't think I'd ever seen aimed my way. Or at anyone, really. It was like witnessing a different, wilder side of Jesse.

And I really fucking liked it.

Jesse put a finger to his lips, the glint in his eyes shading into mischievous territory as he reached lower and took my balls in his hand. He gave them a firm tug before circling his thumb around them at the same time he wrapped his fist around my crown and did something with his fingers that made my mouth drop open and my eyelids flutter as pleasure rocketed through me.

I made a sound I'd never made before, some kind of cross between a grunt and a howl that probably closely replicated what was issued by the first man to discover fire.

Jesse wasn't even doing the standard up-and-down jerk anymore. No, somehow it was a multidimensional assault of pleasure from all sides.

"*Oh god.*"

My hips swiveled trying to keep up with it, and when Jesse spoke in a soft, cajoling coo, "Shhhh, relax and just let me"—which I was pretty sure *had* been in the script but sounded exponentially hotter in the heat of the moment—I lost it.

It took all my reserves to keep one hand gripping the phone.

"*Fuck. Oh fuck.*" I meant to grab the towel bar with my other hand but ended up digging my fingers into Jesse's shoulder instead as I blew apart in hot, thick spurts that nailed my chest and ran over his knuckles like a lava flow.

Jesse tightened his grip on my balls and stroked me from

base to tip in long, slow pulls until I was utterly and completely spent. All that was left were a few twitches and shudders as Jesse wrung every last drop of ecstasy from that orgasm.

"Holy...hell," I panted. The urge to return the favor was overwhelming, and I figured the orgasm must have knocked me a little delirious. But I didn't question it; I went with it.

I stepped out of the tub, dripping all over the floor as I reached for the waistband of Jesse's pants. He shot a look askance at me but let me haul his pants down to his thighs.

When he took the camera from my hand, I hesitated.

"You're sure you want to?" The skepticism in his expression only strengthened my determination to give him even a sliver of what he'd just given me.

I nodded and swiped my hand through the mess on my abs. I wasn't about to have my dry jerk skills judged by a supposed master, and after his recent performance, I had zero doubts about his claims or any future ones. That was easily the best hand job I'd ever received in my life.

I passed my hand lightly, ineffectively over his shaft, which made me look like I didn't know what the fuck I was doing. Getting ahold of myself and focusing, I squeezed my fingers around him. I was a pretty big dude, and while Jesse wasn't a small guy in the dick department, my hand enveloped his cock like an oversized glove.

He let me take the phone back and then shuddered as the heat of my palm met the warmth of his skin.

A tiny thrust of his hips made the skin of his shaft slide deliciously in my grip. He bit down on his lower lip as he moaned. "That's it. *Fuck*."

"I want it to feel good for you." I thought that had been in our script somewhere. One of Jesse's lines, maybe. Guess I'd stolen it, but I meant it. Part of it was some weird sense of tit for tat, and part of it was sheer curiosity mixed with competitive spirit over whether I'd be any good at getting him off.

"It does. It really fucking does. It feels so good just like that. Your hand is so fucking *big*." Jesse sucked in a breath as I sped up the tempo, placing one hand on my waist. He rested his forehead against my collarbone for a beat as he gave another little press of his hips, then straightened. "Right now you could exhale six feet away from me and I'd probably bust. *Oh god, just...*"

I took that to mean *please continue*. I was good at endurance after all, so I kept the pace steady, the pressure exact, the camera in my hand as immobile as I could while he started to go wild.

Was I supposed to be filming him? Who fucking cared.

My nerve endings buzzed with leftover adrenaline from busting a load along with the newfound zing of electricity at pushing Jesse closer to the edge. The erotic juggling act between the camera and his dick got tougher to maintain, but I didn't want to give up either. On a whim, I let go of him, slicked my hand over the mess on my stomach again, and returned, sandwiching his hard rod between my hand and my slick, soft cock.

Once again, I'd underestimated the impact this would have on me because suddenly it wasn't just the alien sensation of another guy's dick in my hand. Now it was pressed against me, sliding against my own, hot and slippery. Jesse's fingertips dug into my shoulders with every practiced roll of his hips, his panting breaths mingling with mine. Briefly, his temple brushed along my jaw, and I had this crazy idea that he might turn his head and kiss me. I would've done it, too.

Instead, a second later, Jesse let his head fall back, a sultry curse falling from his lips as he gave himself over to the moment and pumped against me furiously. He managed to shove his shirt up higher just before he spattered his chest in an echo of my earlier orgasm.

"Fuck, that's so hot." The admission slipped out of me before I could stop it, but Jesse seemed lost to his own pleasure anyway.

He rested his forehead against my shoulder, chest heaving, and I hit the button to end the recording and tossed the phone carelessly onto the counter.

Jesse's panting morphed into laughter that hit my skin in warm puffs. "Ahhh fuck, that was definitely not in the script."

"I forgot the script almost immediately," I admitted.

"Mmmm," came a sexy rumble of sound that vibrated against my skin, and then Jesse straightened, taking a step back from me just as I'd been about to pull him closer. Probably a good move. Cuddling him could've gotten awkward, but shit, I kinda missed the weight of him the second it was gone.

He sank against the counter and we eyed each other's torsos with matching grins. Twin Rorschachs of spunk. Wow, I was getting weirder by the second.

"Maybe we should've practiced first or something. Perfected it. I definitely didn't mean to become part of the scene at the end. The whole point was me getting you off."

"Seemed pretty perfect to me." Jesse's gaze shot to mine, and I stumbled over my words. "I mean, you know, cinematically speaking and stuff. I might've shaken a little when I blew." *Since it felt so insanely good I forgot my own name.* Jesus, if this was a hand job, what was Jesse's version of a blowjob like? "I guess we could practice before the next one, sure, but maybe we should just cover the basics and let it ride. Isn't it hotter when people get carried away, anyway? I mean, I've always thought that...or like to think I can tell when someone's actually into it, versus just…" I snapped my mouth shut. What the fuck was I saying? Was I talking about him or myself?

Jesse regarded me carefully, then shrugged. "Yeah, sure. That works." His attention shifted to his still-rucked-up shirt and glistening stomach, and he laughed. "God, I'm a mess, and look at you. Wow."

"I didn't jerk off for two days because I wanted it to be impressive." I turned on the shower. "I'll just rinse off real quick if you want to hop in after."

"Okay, sure."

I stepped under the spray and pulled the shower curtain. Through the frosted liner, I watched the movements of him removing his clothes, while I tried to think through everything that had just happened logically. I'd responded to stimulus, no problem there, and I couldn't imagine I was the only one in the history of gay for pay to get turned on by my partner beyond just the stimulus response. Hormones and pheromones were weird fucking shit. But whatever this was? I was more than happy to continue with the experiment.

I stepped out of the shower to find Jesse holding out a towel for me. I grabbed it and toweled off my hair, sneaking a gaze at his ass as he tugged free the one wrapped around his waist and stepped into the shower. "If I order pizza or something, you want some?"

"Nah. I'll probably just make something."

"Ramen?" I grinned, waiting for it.

And there it was. Jesse poked his head around the curtain and fixed me with a disapproving scowl. "As if. Gross. I've got a study group in a little while anyway."

"That's what I thought you'd say." I picked up his towel and draped it over the towel bar so it wouldn't get soaking wet on the floor. On second thought, I reached into the cabinet and got him a fresh towel altogether. "Lemme know if you change your mind about that pizza." I lingered a minute longer, though I wasn't sure what the fuck for, then dipped when I could no longer justify staring at him through the curtain as he adjusted the shower tap.

An hour later, after I was stuffed with pizza and Jesse had gone, I locked myself in my room, flopped on the bed, and queued up the video we'd made. The beginning was stiff and awkward as fuck as we'd both suspected, and then, somewhere in the middle, it shifted.

I settled back on my pillows, staring at the screen. Jesse's ragged breaths underlay mine as he stroked me, and I caught something I'd missed earlier: Jesse grabbing his dick through his pants at one point, like he was trying to hold himself back from coming while I unloaded all over my abs and the floor.

I sucked on my lower lip and rewound that part, then watched it again, my dick hardening along my thigh as Jesse squeezed the base of his cock. Then I skipped forward to the part where I started jerking him off. Sliding a hand down my track pants, I fisted my shaft, moving in time to his strokes, each ripple of his stomach as it flexed and contracted making mine do the same. I clicked to turn the volume up and came to the sound of the quiet moan he'd released when he shattered.

As I stared down at the mess on my stomach, courtesy of my roommate, I realized I needed backup.

I clicked away from the video, waiting five until the endorphins freewheeling through my system had settled down, and then called my brother Joel. He was only three years younger than me, but he was also fifty times smarter. On the other hand, he couldn't catch a football even if I put it in his hand. Mom and Dad had held him back from starting kindergarten for an extra year, and sometimes I regretted that we didn't get to experience at least a year of college together.

"What's wrong?" he answered immediately, concern in his voice.

"Nothing. I mean, nothing dangerous. I'm not hurt or anything. You busy?"

"In theory I'm on a date right now."

"Shit, you can call me ba—"

"Nah, he didn't show. What's up?"

I decided to go in full bore. "I guess I'm gay. Or bi. Whatever. Not straight."

There was a long silence before Joel said hesitantly, "Okay, I'm going to need to know some details, but understand I don't want to know *detailed* details. Catch my drift here?"

"No anatomy discussion. Got it. Believe me, likewise. Okay, I'm about to lay a lot of stuff on you that I need you to just keep to yourself. Swear?"

Once my brother leerily swore himself to secrecy, I sketched a rough picture of the situation with Jesse. And when I say rough, it was as rough as all my other attempts at art, meaning hardly more than a stick figure outline. I didn't mention the videos.

When Joel *hmmm'd*, I could hear his frown through the phone. "Some of this doesn't make sense. Actually, a lot of it. So you two decided to start hooking up just because. But now you think you like it, and you're not sure what to do about it? I think the obvious answer would be to continue doing what you enjoy and maybe not jump the gun on dissecting it too much just yet. Honestly? I'm more concerned about this other guy." Joel huffed out a breath. "You said he's out, right? I'm not sure why any self-respecting out guy would mess around with someone who claims to be straight. No offense, because I love you and think you're great, but really."

Now I was the one frowning into the phone. That made Jesse sound bad, and I didn't like that I'd painted him in a bad light that he didn't deserve. "Uhhh no, back up. J...this *guy* is definitely self-respecting. In fact, he's the one—" I cut myself off with a swear. There really was no way to give Joel the full picture without...giving him the full picture. *Pure brilliance, Sam.* I rolled my eyes at myself. "Anyway, like I was saying. He's very self-respecting."

"So he's just indulging himself in some good ol'-fashioned straight-boy kink? All right, respect. Fine. Can't blame him, aside from the fact that you're my brother. So, gross."

"Straight-boy kink? Is that real?"

"Uh, yeah. It comes factory installed on plenty of us. Not all, but plenty. Sits parallel to the lesbian fantasy of the same and is kissing cousins to the straight-guy fantasy of two girls making out. The common thread? All of us are *really* hoping it works out in our favor in the end. But most of us know it won't. Unless it's happening in a porno." He chuckled, and I frowned harder at the phone. I decided I needed out of this conversation.

"Still there?" Joel asked a second later.

"Yeah."

He swore softly. "Man, I'm messing this up. Okay, shit, hang on. I'm so used to you being the big brother that it's weird to hear you asking me for advice. Or whatever it is we're doing here." He cleared his throat. "Okay, remember when I came to you in eighth grade because I kissed that guy on the baseball team, and then flipped my shit because it was my first kiss, and even though I was sure I was gay it was still a little scary? I was worried about him saying something at the same time I was panicking over whether I should immediately announce that I was gay."

I smiled. Joel had been so flustered it'd taken me a few minutes to figure out that he was ecstatic, not injured, but also panicky. "I remember."

"And you told me to just take it easy and that I didn't have to figure out everything all at once or blast my business right that second." He paused. "So maybe you could take the same advice. If you're into this guy, see how it goes." His next pause was longer. "I will say, though, that if at any point you get an idea that you're just using him and that maybe he's into you? You should cut it off then, because that wouldn't be fair to him."

"I wouldn't do that," I promised, and meant it. I didn't ever want to hurt Jesse. "Actually, I think the danger is more the reverse."

"Oh, well, if that's the case, I'll kick his ass. How big is he?"

I laughed. "About your size. He's really cute."

"Oh god, my brother likes twinks. Of course you do, you big lunk. God, I'm sorry I asked. Okay, I'm ending this call now." He groaned, but I could hear the smile in it. "Don't keep me posted. Or do, but minimally."

I wasn't sure I'd solved anything, but just talking about it with my brother had made me feel better. And I mean, he'd basically given me permission—no, *insisted*—that it was best for me to continue to experiment. Who was I to deny the sage wisdom of my younger gay brother?

16

JESSE

"Hey." Reid helped himself to a chair next to me in the cafeteria. "Can I join?"

"Usually you ask the question before you take the seat." What was with people lately?

He chuckled as he unwrapped a sub. "Right. Gah, I forgot how funny you are. What are you looking at?" he asked as I made a point of glancing around.

"Listening for your invitation to join me." I cupped my hand to my ear. "Nope. Nothing. Hmmm. Doesn't sound promising. Goodbye. Table for cheaters is over that way. You don't need an invitation for it. You just help yourself to whatever you want, like all the rest."

Reid blew out a breath. "Jesse…"

The unfortunate thing I'd learned over the past three years about love and relationships was that nothing was ever finite and nothing was ever truly done. I could say I was over Reid breaking my heart, and I could believe it was true because it was in the most important sense. On a cerebral level I was done with him. But emotions didn't work exactly the same. Those assholes had no concept of logic. They left little remnants that could activate over and over again, and I still felt a twinge of embarrassment and shame when I looked at him, because I'd been such a fool for him.

I made a shooing motion. "Off you go."

"I was an idiot, Jesse, and I'm sorry." Reid's expression had all the right ingredients for somber and sincere, but I wasn't sure I was buying it.

I put my hand up to ward off the apology. "You were definitely an idiot. It's over and done now, though. No need to detail the many ways in which you were."

"I don't think I gave you a proper apology, though."

"You gave me sunflowers. Believe me, that was enough."

He sighed loudly. "You hate sunflowers. I know that. I knew that back then, too. I just wasn't thinking straight and grabbed the first thing I saw."

"Yeah, that seemed to be a theme." I shook my head and started wrapping my sandwich to take with me when Reid's hand shot out and covered mine.

"Don't. Just listen to me for one minute. *Please.*"

The note of plea got me, hitting a trigger leftover from growing up in a house where we each had to fight to be heard. I'd hated the feeling and tried never to provoke it in someone else. Even when that someone else probably deserved it.

Reid leaned forward at my prompting expression. "I have no excuse. I was an asshole. You didn't deserve that. You were nothing but good to me, and if I could take it back, I would, believe me." He pulled his hand away from mine and dropped it in his lap. "Every time we cross paths, I can feel the…the distaste coming off of you—it's potent as hell—so I just wanted to reiterate, in case it would help. I'd rather not leave this year behind with you hating me, if I can help it. I got caught up in trying to be a badass freshman year, suddenly having access to a bunch of things I hadn't before." He pressed his lips together. "Never mind. My explanation doesn't matter. The apology does."

It was the apology that should've been given the first time. Maybe I was a sucker, but the regret I read in his eyes softened me toward him. Not enough to fling an arm around his shoulder and tell him it was okay, but enough for me to nod and say, "Apology accepted. Thank you," just as Sam stopped in front of the table.

"Y'all almost done eating, or can I join?"

"You can join us," I offered just as Reid shot him a pointed we're-in-the-middle-of-something look.

Sam glanced between us curiously. "Um, actually, I just remembered…"

I made a grab for his wrist. "We're supposed to go over that statistics stuff, remember?"

He shot another look at Reid before nodding and dropping into the seat next to me.

"I had a little trouble understanding that one, too. Great. We can all go through it together," Reid said decisively.

What followed was the most awkward impromptu study session I'd experienced in all my years at the U. It topped even the time I was in a group of six and Charlie Denham had a big piece of spinach between her teeth, and the rest of us spent a half hour pinging each other with our gazes and silently arguing over who was going to be the one to tell her until I finally did it. Then she'd glared at us all for the rest of the study session like we'd betrayed her. Which, to be honest, we kinda had.

"Well, that was enlightening, but I've got another class," I said as we limped to a finish. I tossed my books in my bag, grabbed my lunch trash, and pushed my chair back, jetting while Sam and Reid were still in the midst of zipping their backpacks.

Sam caught up with me on the quad. Damn my short legs. "Was he bothering you?"

"No more than usual."

"I can talk to him."

"What? No." I didn't want Sam stuck in the middle. Despite not knowing all that much about sports, I did know that the teammate bond was a real thing and could affect a game. I had no desire to cause strife between Sam and Reid. "I've got it under control."

Sam wanted to say something else. I could tell by the way he chewed on his lower lip. He nodded reluctantly. "Okay. I mean, I know you can handle your shit. I didn't mean to imply you couldn't or anything. I mean, if I did."

I stopped and turned toward him. The sunlight hit one side of his face, and instead of his usual smile, I read something that looked closer to worry. I didn't like that expression on him. Or that I had caused it. I preferred his smile. "He wanted to apologize again for freshman year, that's all. So he did that."

"Good. He should've." Sam's gaze strayed over my shoulder as he paused a beat, then returned to my face. "Does he want you back?"

I burst into laughter. "I don't think so."

"Then he's still an idiot."

The relief that the return of his smile brought me was kind of ridiculous. "Even if he did, I don't want *him* back. But you're right. I deserved that apology, so I'm taking it. Where are you heading?"

"Biology. Wanna walk me there?"

I nodded a yes, and we started walking again. "I've got another scene idea I want to run by you. For next time our schedules align." I knew he had an away game coming up, and I'd be working until close at the restaurant both nights of the weekend anyway, but was I dying to get my hands—and hopefully my mouth—all over him again? You bet your ass I was.

Sam laughed as he stuffed his hands in his pockets. "All right, hit me. No, wait, let me guess. Is it a variation on the coach-player theme?"

"You think you know me so well."

He bumped me with his shoulder, wearing a playful expression that shouldn't have lassoed my heart and tugged as much as it did. "I think I'm starting to figure out what you like, yeah. Which seems only fair considering that you seem to have ninja-level skills at getting a guy off."

"Is that so?" Free floating praise? Don't mind if I do. And it was true that I'd gotten him off with a dry jerk in under five minutes when we'd filmed the other day in the LGBT Studies section of the library. We apparently had a thing for both books and irony.

Sam's cheeks took on a precious pink hue, which he rubbed at as he shook his head chidingly. "Don't get all cocky about it."

"You like it when I get cocky, too." I snapped my teeth at him playfully, and that he only gave me another shove in response confirmed I was right.

17

SAM

Reid glanced at me over his shoulder as he whipped the towel from around his neck.

Puckering his lips in a kissy face, he flexed one asscheek, then the other. "I can give you my glute routine if you want it?"

"I'm good." I flipped him off. "I was just checking out what I can expect when middle age sag hits. You should try some more squats. That'll give you a little lift." I *had* been staring. Not the way he thought, though. I'd been trying to imagine him and Jesse together. It unsettled my stomach a little, though Reid's ass was on point. No denying that. I made a mental note to add more squats to my lifting days.

Reid snorted and flipped me off in return. I turned away, running a towel over my hair as Coach barged in, rapping a rolled-up magazine against one of the lockers for our attention. "All right, clowns. A reporter from *Collegiate Athlete* is here to do a profile of the team. He'll talk to you in groups, then he'll be back in a few weeks for the homecoming game. Don't act like idiots." He stared pointedly at me and Jansen, while Ackerman snickered on the bench beside me.

"No clue what you're talking about, Coach." I pasted on an angelic expression.

"Put some pants on over your jockstrap this time, or I'll bench you for the first quarter of the game this weekend."

Ouch.

Ackerman's snicker turned into a low hiss. I elbowed him off the bench.

The dumb jockstrap thing had been his idea. But I was the only one who had actually ended up going through with the dare, which I considered a spectacular failure of sportsmanship on everyone else's part. The reporter's discombobulation had been entertaining, though. His eyes kept straying to the one ball hanging out of my jock—unintentional escape artistry on the part of my testicles.

That had been last season, though. I was on better behavior this year.

Fifteen minutes later, ten of us sat in the media room as the reporter—not the one who'd seen my nuts—held out his recorder to capture our responses while he asked questions.

They were garden-variety questions, and the guy seemed a little bored.

I knew I was. My thoughts kept straying to Jesse, the shower, the library, and the videos we'd made. The expression on his face when he got close to losing it, an addictive mix between pleasure and pain that I couldn't get out of my head. Was I chasing a random thrill, or was it something else? I'd analyzed the events to death, and all I really knew was that I was eager for whatever was next.

Reid stretched his arm along the back of my chair and drummed his fingers against my shoulder. "Don't be getting any ideas, Harding, I'm just stretching my arm," he teased when I slowly swiveled my head toward him.

I rolled my eyes and snapped to attention when the reporter said my name. "I'm sorry, can you repeat the question?"

"I asked you how you were feeling this season after that shoulder injury sidelined you last year?"

"I've had a lot of PT and made a solid recovery, so I'm feeling pretty good about it. We've got a strong team this year." I thwapped Reid when he pretended to snore. Maybe a little harder than I needed to. "Fuck off, I'm being good."

The reporter angled the recorder toward Reid next. "Reid, you've got draft scouts looking at you pretty closely. How's that feel?"

"Pretty damn good." The reporter chuckled along with him. "I worked really hard over the summer to be the best I can this season."

I gave him some side-eye for snoring at my answer when his was a total snoozefest, too.

"Silver Ridge is rigorous, academically speaking. Do you have any trouble balancing coursework, a social life, and football?"

"What social life?" Reid joked, then flashed one of his charming quarterback grins. "Nah. I miss seeing my boyfriend sometimes, but he's amazingly understanding."

I frowned as the reporter perked, all traces of his boredom fading. "Does your boyfriend play sports, too?"

"Nah." Reid waved a hand. "And thank goodness. We wouldn't see each other if he did."

What the fuck? I tried to maintain a neutral expression, but the whisper of movement around me suggested this was news to the rest of the team, too. I didn't know any of them to be homophobes, but Reid had gone to a lot of trouble after Jesse had dumped his ass to make sure everyone knew about all of his hookups with women.

I jabbed a finger in Reid's back as we filed out of the room after the interview ended. "I thought you were seeing that blonde girl. Jenna?"

"Not really. We used to hook up, but it wasn't serious."

"So who's the guy you're dating, then?"

Reid squinted at me. "Since when have you ever been interested in anyone I'm seeing?"

A lot more than I wanted to be lately. I mimicked his casual shrug. "I'm not. Just mildly curious. Jenna seemed into you. She was at all the games last year."

Reid tipped his head toward the reporter. "*CA* has been doing individual profiles highlighting LGBT athletes for some documentary they're making." He shrugged. "It'd be a nice extra shot of publicity." He finger gunned me and turned away as Coach barked my name.

"Did you mind your fucking manners in there?"

I made a halo over my head. "Sure did."

"Good. How's the shoulder." Coach squeezed my good one extra hard, then gave a lighter pat to my tender one. I'd come to understand that was his love language. "You need any extra PT before the scrimmage? Thought I caught you favoring the left a little earlier." He narrowed his eyes at me. "You'd let me know if you needed extra attention, right? Because I need you strong this year, even if Doc has to shoot you up with cortisone before every game."

"Yep. I'm good," I promised, ignoring the tiny twinge in my shoulder as I tossed a distracted glance in the direction Reid had gone.

I looked for Reid in the locker room again when I grabbed my duffle, but he'd vanished.

At the house, I heaved my bag toward the stairs and followed the sound of laughter into the kitchen.

Cam sat on one of the kitchen counters while Jesse bustled around among bowls, produce, and spices carpeting multiple surfaces.

I greeted them both with a nod and darted aside when Jesse swatted at me as I grabbed a stalk of celery. Crunching down on it noisily, I leaned against the fridge, trying to guess what Jesse was cooking without having to ask. "What's up?"

"Cam has Applebaum for Western Civ, remember?"

"And I got called up to the front today for one of his infamous on-the-spot pop quizzes." Cam let his head droop to one side and his tongue loll out of his mouth. "I got five out of ten right."

"Ugh," I groaned sympathetically. "Yeah, I remember you mentioning that at the cafe."

"Oh that's right, you were there."

My gaze snapped to Jesse. Had he really forgotten we'd sat across from each other for two hours and planned all kinds of sexcapades? What the hell?

The teasing smile that followed suggested he hadn't.

I narrowed my eyes at him threateningly, then turned to Cam. "Is that your desk in the front yard?"

"Yeah. We needed more manpower to get it inside, so I left it there for later."

The night after Hype, Mark had called a house meeting and we'd voted Cam in with Mark's stipulation that if there was any sign he was using again he'd be kicked out and forfeit his deposit. I wasn't much worried about that. Cam had even dropped out of Sigma because it interfered with his job and NA meetings. I hadn't seen him within breathing distance of a bottle of alcohol or any other mind-altering substance over the entire summer.

But right then I had my eye on Cam for a different reason.

He blatantly stared at Jesse's ass as Jesse nudged me aside and reached into the fridge, then grinned when he realized I was watching him, one shoulder hitching as if to say, *can you blame me?*

Jesse kicked the fridge door shut, a carton of eggs in one hand. He patted my chest with the other. "Can you move? It's like trying to work around one of those big cement columns you see in parking garages. I'm making a frittata—because I know you're going to ask. And no, I'm not sure there will be enough for you, because I know you're going to ask that, also."

Cam slid off the counter. "Can I help?"

"I can help, too," I chimed in.

Jesse fixed us both with a dramatically dubious expression. "I've lived in this house for two fucking years, and the number of times someone has offered to help is one, maybe two." He shook his head. "But no, I don't need two helpers. It's just a frittata, not beef bourguignon."

"I can chop the veggies, then." Cam shot me a smile and grabbed a knife. I guess he thought he was letting me off the hook. Wait, he *was* letting me off the hook. What the fuck? I hated cooking.

"*Sam.*" Jesse nudged me again and gestured toward the fridge. Which I was blocking. Again. "I was kidding a second ago. I'll save some for you, okay? No need to guard your share, or whatever you're doing." The way his smile curved placatingly did something weird to my insides because there was an element to it that felt intimate somehow. It was the same kind of smile he'd had on his face the other day while I struggled to come back down to earth after he'd rubbed a finger over my hole just before I came all over his fist in the library. It was the first time my knees had ever literally shaken from an orgasm.

"I'm just gonna—" I glanced around, spying a broom tucked in a corner. It'd probably been there for months. Still had the wrapper on and everything. "I thought I'd sweep up. Feels like someone spilled some cereal or something." I rubbed the sole of my foot demonstratively.

That earned another skeptical assessment from Jesse. Whatever. I knew how to sweep, and it was anyone's guess how long it'd been since someone had swept, vacuumed, or mopped in this place.

I ripped the wrapper off as Jesse cued up some music on the Bluetooth speaker. Turned out the kitchen floor was pretty damn filthy, and a few minutes in, I forgot the whole sweeping bit had been a ruse.

I pulled out chairs, sweeping under the table, in the pantry. I even scooted the fridge out so I could get in the crack between it and the cabinet, whisking the broom to the beat of a One Direction song.

I whipped around in a 180 spin, MC Hammer-style, to find Jesse and Cam leaning against each other and silently cracking up.

"Nice moves." Jesse bit his lip, and then his laughter burst free.

I made the end of the broom my microphone and leaned toward him as I mouthed the chorus.

He shoved me. "You're ridiculous."

"Wanna see me whip? Lawnmower man? The worm?" I grabbed the broom and wielded it like a staff, twirling it through the air. "Macarena? Hammer dance? I'm particularly gifted at the sprinkler."

Jesse fixed me with a challenging arch of his brows. "Tango. Bring it. "

"My specialty." I chucked the broom blindly to the side, grinning as both Jesse and Cam flinched when it clattered loudly against one of the kitchen chairs. Jesse let out a shout as I grabbed him by the waist and whirled him around, then dipped him low. "I have no idea how to tango. Does it show?" I confessed close to his ear. "Just go with it. Feels right, yeah? Pretty close?"

"Not at all close." Jesse threw his head back with a laugh, and I reveled in the sound. I'd had way too much fun trying to provoke it out of him lately, too.

As I righted him, his eyes met mine, a vivid sparkle dancing through them, a kind of glow that suffused his whole face. His lips were startlingly close to mine, and for a second I forgot Cam was right there behind us.

A crazy sensation exploded in my chest, a weird tension that crackled outward and made me warm all over. The realization dawned with the same heated thoroughness, reaching into every corner of my body: I wanted to kiss Jesse.

Not watch him jerk off, not let him jerk me off. I wanted that, too, but I wanted to know what it'd be like to kiss him without the camera and without the pretense of a video.

I must have made some kind of face, because Jesse's brows pinched together with concern. "You okay?"

"Yeah. Head rush." Two head rushes were occurring, actually. I shifted my hips and let him go so he wouldn't feel my boner strengthening like a Category 4 hurricane.

"Um, Jesse," Cam called out. "I think...do I need to stir this or something?"

"Oh shit!" Jesse rushed over to the stove and yanked the pan from the burner. He inspected the frittata and poked at it a couple of times before setting it aside and declaring, "It'll live."

I picked up the broom and returned it to the corner just as Jesse barked out another curse.

"I'm going to be late for my date. Cam, it needs to go into the oven for about seven minutes. Keep an eye on it. Just leave enough for me."

"You're going out with John tonight?" I'd assumed that ship had sailed.

"Yeah, we finally found a time that worked for both of us."

"So why are you cooking dinner, then?"

He pressed his lips together, adorably recalcitrant before he relented. "We're eating at a restaurant I'm not familiar with, and if their food sucks and I can't eat it, I want to know I've got something good waiting for me back here. Otherwise, I'll get preemptively hangry."

"Preemptively hangry," I echoed. "Only you. Plenty of good stuff waiting for you back here." It popped out of my mouth before I could stop it, and Jesse's eyes crinkled a little at the corners.

"Well yeah, but you know what I mean."

I pretended I did with a nod. "I hope you have a good time. I'm gonna go get some studying done. Cam, I'll help you with that desk in a little while."

Once in my room, I flopped on my bed and scrolled aimlessly through my phone, trying to distract myself from the slightly uneasy feeling in my stomach. I knew what it was, and I knew it didn't technically belong there, but I couldn't help it, and not even checking the bank account I'd set up for my Only-Fans earnings helped, this time.

18

JESSE

It was painfully evident before we'd even received our entrees that John and I were not a match. That shouldn't have been a problem considering the oath I'd made to bang my way through senior year. It didn't have to be a love match to hook up with someone, and in my short interactions with John, I'd gotten a similar impression, that this was a slightly classier step up from the average Grindr swipe and suck.

The problem was I couldn't muster any enthusiasm. And I hadn't been able to even before the date. I'd accepted when John asked because I thought I should, because I told myself that making sex videos with a friend *did not* fall within the goal posts I'd set for senior year. That, in fact, it worked against the goalposts no matter how much I liked hanging out with Sam and no matter how much I really, *really* looked forward to messing around with him.

I'd assumed once I'd actually gotten out of the house—read: out of sight of Sam—and around John, what I remembered of his good looks and charm would have me salivating again.

But that wasn't happening either.

John was attractive and funny, but as we sat across from one another, I had all the desire to rub up against him that I might have for a cardboard box.

We still had at least one course to get through. We'd discussed his time at the U, law school, working for the law firm, my time at the U, how much I loved cooking. I wasn't sure what was left.

"So which part of town did you say you live in again?" I asked, taking a cheerful stab at another topic.

John smiled congenially. It was the same kind of smile I'd given him, which told me we were both striving to be polite awhile secretly hoping the other one would be the first to call this date out as a bust so we could both relax. "I rent a loft in Forsythe."

"Ohhh, I love lofts." Maybe we could shift to decor and aesthetics. I looked forward to aesthetics someday when I didn't share a house with four other grimy dudes. "What kind of vibe do you have going? Sleek and minimal or cozy and lived-in?"

John considered for a moment, his gaze straying to my phone sitting at the edge of the table as the screen lit up with a notification. "The furniture was already there when I moved in. I'd say it's a renter-chic vibe." He chuckled. "Lots of beige and neutrals."

Okay, this topic was a fail. Painful. He nudged his chin toward my phone screen again. "You need to see who that is? Looks like a fireworks show going off over there."

"Sorry, that's so rude of me." The first notification was from Sam. I had no doubt the rest were, too. I clicked the screen to darken it and turned the phone over. "It's just my roommate being an idiot."

"Sam?"

"I can't wait to tell him you immediately knew which roommate I was referring to when I said 'idiot.'"

John laughed again. He had a nice easy laugh that, combined with his warm blue eyes, should've given me butterflies in my stomach, but didn't. I automatically contrasted them with Sam's and found them lacking. "He seemed cool, though, at the party. Are you two close?"

I held back a laugh. If only he knew. "We've grown closer recently. We have a class together this semester, and we both come from big families, though I think his was much more relaxed and affectionate than mine. And he's the exact same way. Probably why we get along so well." I tapered off, realizing I was blabbering. "Anyway, he's one of my favorite humans, which is kind of a feat lately. So many of them suck." That last part slipped out, as did what I suspected was a fond smile I fought to contain immediately. If I'd thought maybe I could salvage the date before, the expression on John's face now openly said we were past that point. "We have this running joke about cockblocking, so I'm sure he's blowing me up in an attempt to keep up the streak that began the night of Mark's dad's party."

"He was cockblocking you?"

"Well, inadvertently. He still insists he was providing wingman services."

"For me?" John seemed amused as I shrugged. Why not tell the truth?

"Yep."

John winced. "Okay, yeah, he's not the greatest wingman, probably. Although—" He tilted his head to one side, considering. "When I was looking for you before I had to go, he was the one who asked me to leave my number for you."

"Really?" I blinked, both intrigued and slightly dismayed to learn John hadn't left it of his own volition. Not that it mattered now.

"So maybe he wasn't a failure as a wingman after all. He seemed like a good guy. Told me you thought I was cute and that you're funny and nice. He mentioned the cooking again. Apparently you've really impressed him in that regard. He said you were one of his favorite people, too."

"Oh." Heat spread all through my chest and over my cheeks. Normally I'd be more embarrassed at what sounded like Sam trying his hardest to foist me upon John, but instead I envisioned him telling John all of that and another one of those fond smiles threatened my lips.

I was dying to know what kind of messages he'd been sending. Was he trying to *Cyrano de Bergerac* my date?

John leveled a gaze on me. "This isn't going to happen, is it. The spark is gone, yeah? It's not just me?"

I blew out a relieved breath. "It's not just you. I guess it was one of those one-night-only things?"

"Maybe." John's pensive expression broke around a smile. "So how about we just eat our meal and hang out as friends, then call it a night?"

"Sounds great."

When he excused himself to go to the restroom, I grabbed my phone and pulled up my messages.

All twenty bazillion of them.

Sam: *what's up?*
Sam: *Whazzzzzuuupppp?*
Sam: *How's your date?*
Sam: *Hope it's going well. If not, give me the signal. Blink once if you're bored out of your mind.*

Sam: *Blink twice if you need help.*
Sam: *Okay, done being obnoxious. Maybe.*
Sam: *Is this guacamole in the fridge still good?*
Sam: *Fine. I really will leave you alone now.*
Sam: *For real, though, he better be treating you nice.*

I wasn't sure where to start with all of that. I laughed as I scrolled through the messages again and imagined how pleased with himself he probably was.

Jesse: *There's no guacamole in the fridge so I hope you didn't eat whatever it was.*
Sam: *Too late. Am I going to die?*
Jesse: *Better keep a toilet handy.*
Sam: *Kidding. I sniffed it and passed. Since you're replying does that mean shit's going downhill? Need me to call and say there's an emergency? I can make something up.*
Jesse: *It's fine. No need to send a rescue squad.*
Sam: *Oh. Okay. See you later I guess. Or tomorrow.*
Sam: *Be safe or whatever.*
Sam: *Does that sound condescending? You know what I mean.*
Jesse: *No, it just sounds fatherly, which is creepy in its own way. He's coming back. GTG.*

JOHN AND I HUGGED WHEN THE UBER STOPPED OUTSIDE OF THE house. Our "date" had ended up being the equivalent of a dying campfire. Cozy and warm, but not a single flame. The upside was through the course of conversation, I discovered he had a friend who was a chef at The Golden Spoon, where I'd been dying to eat, and he promised he could get me in sometime, and with someone I actually wanted to go on a date with, which was really nice of him.

It was almost midnight and a Thursday night, so I expected everyone except Cam to be out. But when I walked in, both he and Sam were sprawled on the sectional, a nature documentary droning on the TV.

I thought they might be asleep, but both immediately jerked their heads my way when I shut the door behind me.

"How'd it go?" they both spoke at the same time.

I put my hand back on the doorknob. "I'm gonna go out and come back in again and hopefully pop us out of the twilight zone. That was creepy as hell, and I'm not sure whether it's the unison part or your mutual investment in my love life, which suggests sad things about me." I kicked my shoes off. "It was fine. Not a love connection, but maybe friends. I had a good time, I guess. What are y'all watching?"

"No clue." Sam scrutinized me carefully, but I wasn't sure what he was looking for. "Want to join, or are you heading to bed? I'm getting pretty tired, actually."

"I'll hang for a while. Can we switch to *The Great British Bake Off*, or are you both super invested in seeing this cheetah get his guts ripped out?"

Cam shifted slightly on his couch and tossed me the remote. Sam shot a look over at him before swinging his feet off part of the couch he'd claimed and making room for me.

I changed the channel and flopped down in the empty space next to Sam. "Thought you were tired," I said when he didn't make any move to go to bed.

He shrugged. "Might watch a little longer. See how this turns out."

I grabbed a handful of popcorn from the bowl on the coffee table. "Where's Ansel?"

"Said he had a date." Cam yawned.

"With who?"

"He didn't say that."

"He's such a weirdo." If one day Ansel popped up on Instagram as some running phenom who lived out of a van and just drove across the US uploading videos of himself doing yoga, running marathons, and scaling various mountains, I wouldn't have been surprised.

"A cute one, though," Cam said.

"Agreed."

Sam gave me a sideways look, and I tossed a piece of popcorn at him. "He is. It's okay. You can admit it, too."

Ten minutes later, my eyelids were drooping. When I swung a look over at Sam, though, he seemed wide-awake, his posture stiff.

"You okay?" I said quietly and craned a look back at Cam. He'd fallen quiet, too, but I wasn't sure whether or not he was asleep.

"What? Oh yeah," he whispered back. "Really nervous about this challenge."

I side-eyed him. "Not to spoil it for you, but they're all going to make something delicious and be lovely while doing it." We hadn't even reached the technical challenge yet. We were still in my favorite part, the signature challenge where contestants showed off their tried-and-true recipes.

"Well, I've become a little invested already. You cold?" Sam eyed my arms, which I'd hugged around my chest. No idea why. But before I could respond, he dragged a blanket from the back of the couch and offered it out to me.

"Gonna tuck me in, too?" I teased, then chuckled quietly as

he rolled forward, tucking the blanket tightly around my shoulders and then stretching it out over both of us.

"You would kill it on this show," Sam said, sotto voce, and I felt the warmth of his large hand close around my toes and squeeze. Somewhere in the midst of the getting comfy and blanket draping, my socked feet had naturally come to a rest against his outer thighs. I hadn't given it any thought before, but now I was on high alert.

"You've placed a lot of unearned confidence in my baking skills when I'm pretty sure I've never baked for you."

"It's the same thing as cooking, right?"

I gasped in mock horror. "You take that back right now. They're not the same thing. There are people out there who are amazing cooks and shitty bakers. And vice versa."

"Hmmm, maybe you should bake something for me, then. Let me be the judge."

"I see what you're doing." I snuck a look at him, but his focus was still drilled at the TV, his profile to me, not even a hint of a smile to suggest he was messing with me.

Okay, I'd play along.

I wiggled my toes and stifled a smile when he squeezed them tight. Something—probably his thumb—swept lightly over the top of my foot and hooked beneath the band of my sock, dragging it down slowly. I tensed. If he fucking tickled me right now while I was enjoying this cozy cocoon of *GBBO*, blankets, and beefcake jock, I'd end him.

Instead, he pulled my sock all the way to the ball of my foot, then pressed his thumb firmly into my skin, following the curve of my arch.

I couldn't help it. I moaned. It was a tiny insignificant sound that somehow managed to ring through the air like a siren. I threw another glance over my shoulder. Cam's eyes were slits.

He didn't even fucking move. Sam's face was a different story, though.

He was grinning now, though still staring at the TV while he rubbed my foot. His other fingers got in on the action, too, caressing the top of my foot, squeezing and relaxing. I'd had a foot rub exactly once in my life. A girl in eighth grade had given me one on a dare because the other classmates we were playing with weren't sure what else to do with me, I guess—I'd declared my gayness loudly and early. If her foot jobs were a prelude to other jobs she might give down the road, then I was glad to have gotten off easy. Or, rather, not gotten off at all.

Sam, however, was good at this. A maestro, even. In spite of his complaints, maybe his massage sessions with the trainer had some side benefits. The pressure and heat of his fingertips melted every bit of resistance away, and the sensation extended up the backs of my calves and thighs, all the way to my groin.

He kept messing with the bit of sock he'd left on my foot, running his thumb over the skin under it, then on top of it. By the time he inched it the rest of the way off, I swore I felt every millimeter of fabric sliding over the sensitive arches of my feet, and he might as well have been sliding my boxers down my thighs the way pleasure did a lightning bolt dance through me.

And he still wouldn't look at me either.

I tried to keep still as he freed my other foot, and had to bite down on my knuckles when he reached his other hand around, attacking the soles of my feet in tandem.

I must have made some kind of crazy blissed-out face because when he did finally look over at me, he bit back a grin. His gaze darted above my head to Cam on the other couch, then moved back to the TV.

Sam pulled both my feet into his lap and kept his left hand

on one while the right ventured from my foot to my calf with a stopover to caress my ankle gently.

"Feel good?" he said quietly, and I nodded like a bobblehead. I might as well have had drool dripping down my chin. I had no idea what was going on right now. My body was just a vast sea of sensorial endpoints rippling with Sam's every touch.

From my calf, he coasted a large hand up my thigh, leaving a wake of heat behind. I swallowed hard when I shifted my feet slightly in his lap and encountered the stiff ridge of his cock.

In a surprising response, his gaze traveled to Cam again, and then he spread his legs wider.

Any chance I could've convinced myself he wasn't actually hard melted away when his dick literally twitched against my ankle as he rubbed his thumb over one of my big toes.

Look, I'd never given feet much thought. They were handy for walking, yanno? But there was some alchemy of touch, environment, and Sam himself happening right now that made me consider the toes I wiggled against his shaft in a new light.

An intriguing and possibly highly sexy light.

Sam nestled deeper into the couch and rested his head back against it, eyes falling shut. The hand on my foot tightened, keeping me close as his hips flinched upward into the heat of my sole. Meanwhile, his other hand skated from my thigh to blanket my groin in warmth.

I arched as the heel of his palm nudged the base of my cock. Fuck, it felt insanely good, and I was so turned on I could barely see straight.

It was hard enough holding back the little whimpers and noises that kept trying to break free, but when Sam ran a finger up and down my zipper and then gave me a querying look, I almost gave myself whiplash nodding.

He peeled my zipper down slowly, and it took me a second

to catch on that he was doing the same thing on his end. Where before my feet had been rubbing up against stiff denim, they now encountered hard, hot flesh.

I gulped as Sam shifted his thighs and maneuvered his dick between my feet. He put his hand to his mouth and then brought it to my feet, slicking up my insoles. A little push and his cock glided between, warm and wet and... *holy shit*, I used to make fun of people with foot fetishes, and now I suddenly got the appeal. It was weird and kinky and sexy, and the smoothness of his cock against the sensitive arches of my feet felt amazing. I only wished there weren't a blanket obstructing my view.

Sam's lashes fluttered closed, and his jaw tensed as I cottoned on to what was happening and got into the rhythm, pressing my feet a little closer together to increase the friction. A shudder rippled over his shoulder, and then he blinked his eyes open, angling a look at me at the same time he squeezed my dick through my boxers, then pulled it out through the little panel.

"Show me?" he said softly, with another cautious glance thrown over my head toward Cam.

On TV, they were discussing red velvet cake, and I was one more of Sam's sultry whispers from frosting the outside of my jeans.

I spit in my palm, then slipped my hand beneath the covers, wetting up my dick before I wrapped Sam's fingers around my shaft and kept my grip over the top of his. Fuck me sideways if I didn't full-body shiver when he started pumping me. Gingerly at first, like he was feeling me out, then more firmly when I squeezed his hand.

We moved in subtle rhythm, Sam's watchful awareness of Cam nearby muting my instinct to buck wildly into his touch.

Something about that was insanely erotic, too, though, like a souped-up version of petting in a movie theater, with the threat of being caught a mere glance away.

The pace was hypnotic and forced me to remain completely present and focused. I felt every inch of his cock sliding between my feet. His grip tightening on my toes became an additional pleasure tacked on to the shock waves radiating through my balls.

Sam released my dick and grabbed onto my feet suddenly, his head arching back against the couch. His teeth clamped down on his lower lip as he had the quietest orgasm I'd ever witnessed. His release poured over me in thick spurts, and then he brought his slick hand back to me, wrapping me in his thick fist. Two pulses inside that perfectly lubed grip and I came, too, turning my head to the side and burying the instinct to cry out in my own shoulder as the orgasm ripped through me.

Loosening his hold on my feet, Sam glanced around, then shrugged and used the blanket to mop himself up and wipe off my feet. So that would need to be washed posthaste.

But since he'd led the way, I did the same and then let out a sigh of contentment that lasted for all of three seconds before reality checked in to say *what the fuck?*

"What the fuck?" I hissed at Sam, deciding to go with the words pinging around wildly in my brain.

He shook his head quickly and ticked it toward Cam.

"Are you two still watching this, or can I change it?"

"You can change it," Sam said at the same time I shot him a murderous look. Had Cam been awake this entire time? Had he been watching us? On a purely kinky level, that was kind of hot, but on a roommate level, no. I had to live with him for the rest of the year.

I started to sit up, but Sam reached under the covers and

smacked my leg. He pulled out his phone, typed something, and two seconds late my phone buzzed. I opened the message.

Sam: *I'm 90% sure he was asleep that whole time.*
Sam: *But don't get up.*
Jesse: *Why not?*
Sam: *He'll definitely figure it out then.*

I started to type "how," then looked down at the blanket.

Jesse: *Oh my god.*

Sam clapped a hand over his mouth as his shoulders shook with laughter.

Sam: *Just wait. Bet he'll fall back asleep again in a second and then we're home free.*

I didn't know if he did, though, because the booze I'd had at dinner and postorgasm delirium hit me all at once, and I fell asleep instead.

I BLINKED MY EYES OPEN AND STIFLED A GROAN. HELLO, headache. There also seemed to be a desert in both my eyes and throat. I rolled onto my back with a sigh, squinting against the morning light. Then stiffened as I stared at the lump next to me.

Sam was in my bed. *Holy shit*, was he in my bed. He took up three-quarters of the damn thing. He was shirtless, too, his sleep pants a little twisted and exposing more skin. His head was turned away from me, the rise and fall of his chest peacefully slow.

I rolled over on my little Manhattan Island of mattress, putting my back to him, and closed my eyes, willing myself back into dreamland. Hopefully he'd wake up soon, see his mistake, and slip out quietly.

Sure enough, a few moments later, the bed shifted as he moved, and my pounding heart slowed in relief. *Please leave.* I sent the thought out into the universe, not that it had listened to me when I'd asked for my own room at home for ten years in a row, or the time I'd fallen up the high school stairs in front of a full hallway of students and cut my chin open—since falling down them was an understandable error of mechanics and gravity where falling up signaled a special brand of idiot.

I would give it credit, though, for the time I puked on a skeez named Bobby Freedom instead of going home with him junior year, because I definitely would've regretted that the next morning.

But if Sam didn't leave, we'd probably have to address last night, and I wasn't sure I wanted to do that. I didn't want to be the one to fact-check my own personal *Penthouse Forum* letter come to life.

"You awake?" The words fell warm across the back of my neck as Sam's fingers brushed over my waist, lingering before dropping away.

Zero to hard in 2.5. It was a new record for me.

"No," I said, then rolled over with a sigh. "Why are you in here?" Shit, did that sound too accusatory? It totally did. Feeling vulnerable turned me into a defensive jerk.

Something flashed through his expression, and then he gave me an apologetic smile. "I didn't mean to be, honest. Cam got up and went to bed, and I didn't want to leave you down there by yourself, so I hauled you upstairs and kind of stumbled as I was putting you on the bed. I thought I'd just lie here for a minute—your bed is really comfortable, by the way—then I fell asleep."

I had a very vague recollection of this, I decided, two seconds before my eyes jolted wide. "The blanket!"

"It's on the floor." He chuckled, the sound of it warm and sleepy, like the lazy stretch version of a laugh, and damn, it was alluring, too. Sam in the morning was dangerous.

I put a hand over my chest and breathed deeply a couple of times before something else occurred to me. "Why doesn't the idea of getting caught bother you?"

Sam laced his fingers behind his head and shrugged. "Because we didn't. Because I try not to worry too much about something before it occurs."

"How very Zen of you. Must be nice." My baseline was an anxiety minefield, and my metal detector was constantly crapping out on me. "So, do you have a foot fetish?" Wait...*I* was bringing up last night? What kind of fuckery was that, universe? Cruel.

But there came that soft chuckle again, like a warm breeze moving cotton-soft across my cheeks. "Maybe I do now. I don't know. I've never done anything like that before. I was horny and...I don't know, your feet were touching my thigh and they were all warm, and then I started touching you and it seemed like a good idea and you seemed into it." His gaze dipped toward me. "I mean, I didn't misinterpret that, did I?"

I gave him a solemn nod. "Actually yes, that part where I was thrusting into your fist and coming all over it was a cry for help. You couldn't tell?"

He rolled his eyes "The videos and stuff that we're doing?

I'm into it. It's hot. I dunno, I guess I was curious what would happen off camera."

I digested that for a second. I knew all about the spectrum of sexuality in theory, but I didn't actually know what it was like to be anything other than what I was, which was Grade A gay.

Like, there had never been a single second of doubt for me, so my friends who had struggled to figure out their own identities, I could sympathize with them, but I couldn't *relate*, which would have been a weird thing to say aloud, probably. So my best understanding was that when a guy was fooling around with another guy but also claiming to be straight, it was smart to take him at face value because he was probably thinking in terms of orgasms, not long term.

Sam shifted on the bed, facing me. "I like you."

He said it so casually that I had a hard time determining what kind of like he meant. I mean, I could Venn diagram it with last night's foot incident in the middle and arrive at a hypothesis, sure. But that didn't mean I believed it. "Well, stop it." I hoped it came out somewhere halfway between a tease and caution. Then I caught a glance at the alarm clock and bolted upright. "Shit, my little brother is going to be here in five seconds." Or half an hour. Same thing.

"Yeah? Which one?" Sam rolled upright slowly, not getting the five-alarm memo. He stretched his arms overhead, every human muscle known to man putting itself on rigorous and artful display. I sighed internally.

"Matt." It was visitors' weekend, and even though he'd already applied to the U early decision, he craved time out of our crazy house, too. Of all my brothers and sisters, we were probably closest even if just by default in the birth order.

"My brother's coming, too. But not until later this afternoon."

"Does he play any sports?"

"Ha. Nope." Sam rubbed his lower lip thoughtfully. "There's a Sigma party Saturday night, though. You should bring Matt if you're not working. Give him a taste of the Greek life."

I beaned him with my pillow.

"What?" He laughed.

"On a scale of one to I-don't-even-need-to-ask, how hard did you have to exert yourself holding back something about *me* tasting the Greek life?"

Sam lurched forward, lips brushing over mine before I could react. It was so quick, it was hardly more than the sensation of crackling static. A little zing of electricity and then gone, but boy did it have a lasting impact on my heartrate and my ability to breathe properly.

My mouth fell open, and I waited for words to follow. An admonishment or joke or…something. But nope. My throat had ceased working, too.

Sam slid from the edge of the bed and stood for another languid stretch, this time exhibiting his back muscles. God, all that was missing was a fan of peacock plumes bursting from his ass.

He glanced over his shoulder at me, gaze dropping to his own asscheeks and then lifting to meet my eyes. His lips split in a smug grin as he flexed each cheek individually.

"Smug isn't cute on you," I pointed out, and he laughed as he strolled to my door. He peered out through the crack, then opened it wider, which I took to mean Cam had already left for work.

"Think about that party, though, for real. It'd be fun." He started through the door and then swiveled around to face me. "John's loss, by the way. I didn't think he was a good match for you, if you want my honest opinion. You'd have been bored of watching *Law & Order: SVU* with him in a month."

I exhaled a gusty sigh because he wasn't wrong. But I didn't know what to do about my pounding heart or the fact that it had absolutely nothing to do with John.

19

SAM

Kimpton U had us running all the fuck over the field Friday night. I was drenched a half hour in and at the hour mark, actively hurting.

"Harding, get some water for fuck's sake," Coach hollered at me during half-time.

"Gladly," I muttered under my breath and trotted off to the cooler, scanning the student section in search of Jesse. I found him sitting with his brother and mine, as well as Mark, Chet, and Cam, color high in his cheeks, pom-poms in his hands that he and his brother kept bopping each other with. He was wearing a football jersey that'd been cropped above his belly button, and Jesus, was it distracting.

A tingle ran over my lips as I thought back to this morning. I hadn't wanted to get out of that bed, and I was bummed I wouldn't see him the rest of the night since I'd promised my brother we'd have a night out with the football guys after he claimed it was the closest he'd ever be getting to football.

"What're you staring at?" Reid's voice came from behind me.

"Just checking out the stands." I said, affecting a casual tone.

Reid squinted in that direction, his lips parting slightly. "That must be Jesse's brother. Wow, Jesse wasn't lying when he said he was bigger. Jesus."

I frowned. "When were you talking to Jesse about his brother?" I thought Reid had long since turned in the pass that allowed him to have that kind of familiar conversation with Jesse, even if he had tried to make amends recently.

"I don't know. Freshman year, probably." He shrugged. "Hey, are they coming out with us tonight, Jesse and his brother, I mean?"

I stared at him. "I don't think so."

I didn't want to get in the middle, but shit, I started wondering if Reid was up to what I thought he was. If so, I didn't like it.

When he caught me watching, he cocked a brow in question, and I finished off the rest of my water before tossing the bottle back on the bench and heading back out onto the field without answering.

Reid stepped under the showerhead next to me after the game, soaping himself up vigorously. A current of tension ran between us, but I wasn't sure if it was just me until Reid gave me that same assessing look he'd given me on the field earlier.

"What's up with you and Jesse?"

All right, more blunt than I expected.

I scrubbed shampoo through my hair. "How do you mean?"

"Are you close friends?"

"He's my roommate, obviously, and I suppose I'd say we've grown pretty close, yeah." I wouldn't mention the part about how the shit that had gone down on the couch last night had effectively reset my barometer on sexual fantasies. I didn't have a foot fetish, I didn't think, but I wasn't sure when I'd last gotten off so hard. No, that was a lie. It'd been with Jesse. Again. Every encounter kept topping the one previous, and my OnlyFans subscribers were growing like kudzu thanks to him. *This is insane*, he'd said last week, when I'd handed him an envelope with five hundred dollars in it—his half of the profits. He wasn't wrong, but lately it wasn't the only reason I wanted to keep going.

"Is he seeing anyone?"

I snorted. "Seems like that's something you could ask him yourself."

"I think he's probably still pissed at me."

"Do you blame him?"

Reid turned a scrutinizing look upon me, like he was trying to peer behind the guardedness that arose in me anytime Jesse came up lately. "I apologized to him the other day. Like, a heartfelt one. And I meant it."

"Doesn't mean he has to accept it."

Reid narrowed his eyes. "He *is* seeing someone."

"You're out of control, dude. Let it go."

He sighed. "All right, fine. But what would you do? How would you get someone back?"

Fuck me.

"I wouldn't have cheated on someone in the first place."

"It was more complex than that."

"Not really," I argued, frustration creeping into my voice.

"No, it was. He was so damn...sweet. I didn't know what to do with it after a while. I mean, we were both younger, and he was pretty inexperienced—"

Reid gaped at me as I chortled. I couldn't help it because, once again, I was thinking back to last night and then to the numerous other encounters Jesse and I had had. A mean little part of me wanted to say Jesse had apparently gained plenty of experience after their breakup.

"What's he into lately? You live with him, so you probably know, right? What's he watching on TV? He used to like *Top Chef*. Does he still?"

I could tell Reid about how into his job as a sous chef at Fuego he was, that his favorite video game lately was Northern Nights, that he loved *Once Upon a Time in Hollywood*, hated *Joker*, and was on the fence about *Little Women*. That he was completely addicted to *Bake Off*, all of which made me grin because *huh*, I hadn't realized that I'd picked up on all these things about him over the past couple of months.

What I did realize, though, was that my mean streak ran deeper than I thought, because I said, "He's not really into that anymore. He's all about *Hell's Kitchen*." He hated that show with a passion. "Ask him about that next time. But if you're really smart, you'll leave him alone."

Twisting off the tap, I stepped out of the shower and left him behind, low-key dreading what promised to be an exhausting night ahead of partying with the football team when I would've been perfectly happy to go home and lie on the couch again with Jesse.

20

JESSE

I sucked noisily at my mimosa and nudged my shades up my nose. Less than thirty yards from our cheap foldout lawn chairs was a skin feast and hot dude buffet the likes of which I rarely saw outside of a phone or computer screen.

Sam, Mark, and Nate's fraternity was doing a charity car wash for visitors' weekend, and I was inwardly berating myself for not having taken advantage of this occasion the last three years.

Seriously, when else was it acceptable to sit in a lawn chair and stare at a bunch of half-naked guys soaping up cars and themselves in the process? Never mind that I seemed to be fixated on one in particular. I watched with undisguised delight as Sam blasted himself with a hose, then shook his wet hair out with a grin. Was that not somehow illegal?

"We should all have restraining orders taken out on us," I said.

Eric lowered his shades and gave me a salacious wink

before toasting me with his glass. "Speak for yourself. I'm only interested in one guy out there, and he loves it when I watch."

"You know, you and your brother look absolutely nothing alike," Joel piped up from next to Eric, thankfully interrupting a line of conversation that could have only gone scandalously downhill.

I peered around Eric at him. "Thank you so much, Joel. I have never *ever* been told that before. I wonder if I was adopted," I said with mock horror.

"Does anyone else in your family have red hair?"

Eric burst into a laugh and swatted Joel lightly. "He was messing with you, man."

"I know, but I'm curious."

"You realize you're one to talk, right?" Joel was almost half Sam's size in both width and height.

"Unfortunately." Joel nodded solemnly. "I love Sam and all, but him graduating and going off to college so I no longer have to stand beside him looking like a pipe cleaner next to a fucking bridge pylon has been the best thing that ever happened for my ego. One of our sisters is huge, too, but the rest of us are small to average size."

"My mom has flaming red hair and my second youngest sis, too, but I got the wishy-washy genes," I confessed.

Joel cocked his head appraisingly at me. "I kinda like it like that. You really see the gold highlights in the sun." He angled another glance at my brother, who was currently horsing around with Sam. Not many cars were getting washed. No one seemed to care. The view was still spectacular, though. The group of moms standing a dozen feet away seemed to agree.

My gaze lingered and I forgot what we'd been talking about when Sam looked up and tossed a wave in our direction, water still dripping down his chest like he'd be posing for a swimsuit calendar any second, and his trademark crooked grins hooking one corner of his mouth.

I must have made some sort of noise because I caught Eric's gaze shoot over at me from the corner of my eye.

I cleared my throat. "Really nice day for a charity car wash, huh? Guess you could say the weather was feeling...charitable."

Eric lifted an amused brow. "You could, yes." He added on a mocking air *ba-dum-tss* high-hat tap.

I straightened in my chair as Sam trotted toward us. He feinted left and hauled Joel from his seat in spite of his protests. "You're next," Sam warned me with playfully narrowed eyes, unperturbed by Joel's fists hammering at his back. I could totally see why Joel had been glad for Sam's absence. He really did look tiny next to him. I supposed I did, too, but instead of being annoyed by the idea, I found it a mega turn-on. Feeling Eric's gaze on the side of my face, I tried to temper my goofy grin.

Sam pointed at Eric. "I'm not messing with you. Nate'll have my ass if I even breathe too close to you."

"Good call," Eric agreed.

Sam trotted off with Joel still flailing, and I sucked down more of my mimosa to the blissful sight of grown men roughhousing. "They should make car washing a sport."

"Wouldn't disagree with that." Eric's gaze practically prowled over Nate, staying glued to him as he moved around the wash area with a bucket and a sponge, possessive and adoring at once.

"Aren't you ever scared Nate will change his mind and decide he misses women?" I blurted.

Eric set his mimosa down and laced his fingers over his waistband, head cocking as he watched Nate another intent moment before angling a look over at me. "No more scared than I am that he'll decide he wants someone else altogether, woman or man. Just because he's into both doesn't mean he feels like he's missing out because he's with one over the other."

I swirled the dregs of my mimosa. "What about when you were first with him, though? Before he'd figured stuff out, back when you were just fooling around."

Eric gave me a longer stare. "Early on? Yeah, that was nerve-racking." He scrubbed a hand over the back of his neck thoughtfully. "I kept waiting for the other shoe to drop. For him to say he was done or wasn't into it. I thought about calling it off a lot at first." He paused, then continued when I prompted him with a look. "But I couldn't. And then when I tried to, it lasted all of a few weeks before he called me out. They were the most miserable three weeks of my life, and I do not recommend that tactic." His gaze moved Nate-ward again, drawn like a magnet. "Being with him was different than with anyone else I'd ever been with. From the very first moment. Sounds crazy, right?"

"No," I said softly, "sounds nice." And I absolutely wasn't thinking of lying in bed with Sam the other morning and how for the five brief seconds that I'd allowed the sensation to creep in, the solidity of his weight, and the sense of him surrounding me and his warm, sleepy laugh had felt better than any insignificant hookup I'd had in the last three years.

Eric cut me a sidelong glance that turned suspicious. "I thought you didn't mess with baby bi's anyway. That's been your trumpeting call since I've known you."

I didn't even try to act surprised that Eric had seen through my question. He was perceptive that way. But I also appreciated that he didn't call me out specifically. "I'm not. I mean, I'm not sure he's bi, technically. I'm not sure…shit, he kind of defies labels." I accidentally smiled at the thought and then rubbed it away with a groan. "Ugh. I'm just setting myself up for disappointment, and it's extra annoying because I *know* I'm doing it and I'm still doing it anyway. At least when I walked in on Reid and that girl, I was legitimately surprised. That one wasn't my fault. But this was supposed to just be sex videos, and now it's like I actually look forward to the company, too, even when—"

Eric spit out a mouthful of his drink. "Come again? Could you repeat what you just said?"

I sealed my lips around my drink straw, and Eric yanked the glass away, leaning closer.

"Did you say you're making *sex* videos with him? With Sam Harding? The two of you?"

"Which part of that is it that you're having the most trouble believing?" I demanded, growing a little defensive at his incredulity.

Eric put his hands up placatingly. "Easy. Don't get defensive when you're the one hurling the bombshells. Why the hell are you making sex tapes?"

"It's a long story and...*fuck*, I should've stopped at one mimosa. I hope he doesn't kill me. If he does, will you avenge my death by—"

"No. Focus." Eric stared at me, and I shook my head vehemently.

"I really can't tell you, but I can share that it's consensual, and there's a reason for it, and...god, for such a happy, no-worries kind of guy, he's got me all confused."

Eric was still frowning. "Nate and I haven't even made sex videos yet."

"How would you? Judging by what I've heard in the past, neither of you would be able to concentrate long enough to hit Record once you got started."

He sniffed. "Please."

"Anyway, moving on. The point is, when you see a fire and

then deliberately stick your hand in the middle of it, that's just stupid."

Eric smiled. "You know, some people gradually inch closer to the fire, enjoying the warmth, stepping back if necessary, assessing according to their comfort level. Some manage to not get burned. Imagine that."

"Did you?"

Eric upended his glass. "No. I mean, I tried. I think it looked like I was standing fireside, but I had my...*hot dog* right smack-dab in the middle. It got a bit crispy at points, I suppose." He eyed his empty glass, then me, and exhaled a self-deprecating chuckle. "Right. Think I'm done with mimosas for now." He set it aside and stretched out his legs. "It worked out, though, in the end. So maybe don't be so afraid of the what-ifs. Because the what-ifs are worse than regrets, if you ask me."

"What's your per-hour rate?" I joked, even though I was wondering over what he'd said. He wasn't wrong, but I'd gotten really good at justifying ways to keep my heart from getting rototilled like it had freshman year.

"This one's on the house. Although"—Eric wiggled his brows—"next time you make pot roast, you might let me know. I miss your cooking. Nate and I are absolutely shit at it. If it was just Nate, he'd eat steamed chicken breasts and rice with broccoli all the time. If it was just me, I'd eat frozen meals. So we live in a gustatory purgatory of trying to meet halfway, usually with stir-fry. We eat a *lot* of fucking stir-fry."

"Buy an Instant Pot. Live it, love it."

"Instant Pot, all right," Eric echoed, and we both glanced up as Sam came barreling toward us.

Truth to tell, 280 pounds of muscle combined with his wild-eyed grin wasn't the worst I'd ever had speeding recklessly toward me. When I was sixteen, my whole leg was violently sexually assaulted by a horny St. Bernard named Paul when he got out of our neighbor's backyard. The idea of a violently horny Sam, however, wasn't unappealing at all.

I threw my hands up as an ineffective shield when he dipped low and scooped me out of the chair into a fireman carry.

"You can't just manhandle me because I'm fun-size." I smacked his back.

"I can and I will," he rumbled.

Underneath the jokey exterior, the low timbre of his voice hit me in the pit of my stomach.

He set me down on a patch of grass, clamped his hands on my shoulders, and turned me around. "Hit it," he called, and just as I started to issue a strongly worded threat, my brother aimed the water hose at me and blasted it.

"You fuckers," I howled, squirming in Sam's grip as the icy deluge doused me.

Matt dropped the hose and leapt, wrestling me to the ground. We'd done this all through high school, too, usually resulting in me pinned and giving the mercy yell. I alternated between crowing with laughter, cursing him, and throwing elbows as we rolled. Then Sam turned the hose on both of us. Matt relented, and I rose up onto my elbows, sopping wet, muddy, and exhilarated—a sensation that was only heightened when Sam extended a hand to pull me up.

I let him yank me to my feet.

"This is all your fault."

"I'm very sorry," he said in a way that wasn't with a football field's distance of contrition. His grin faded as his gaze moved down my body and back up. My tee was plastered to my torso, my nipples torpedoing the wet cotton as a shiver racked my shoulders. Sam glanced over his shoulder at a water fight that had broken out near a white SUV, then back at me, little drops of water spiking his eyelashes.

I had a sudden urge to gently run my thumb along the fan of them.

"Can I?" Sam reached out, hovering a knuckle near my cheek. "You've got a little bit of mud—actually, you're covered in it..." He trailed off, and I nodded.

He rubbed my cheek lightly, and then, gaze darting over my shoulder at something I couldn't see behind me, he let his hand fall back to his side and licked his lips, calling my attention to the plump center point of his mouth. God, his lips were like a cherry-red ribbon wrapped around one of the most spectacular smiles I'd ever seen.

"I had an idea for a scene that maybe we could discuss later. Or tonight at the party?"

"What party?" I asked like a dimwit, still stuck on his smile.

"The kegger."

"Oh, no, we're not going to that. The heyday of me and frat boy keggers has come and gone."

"C'mon, it'll be fun." Sam raked his teeth over his lower lip, and I wondered if he knew what kind of effect it had on those with wimpy willpower such as myself. "I want you to."

And sunk. Ugh.

I jumped as Matt slung an arm around me from behind. "What are we going to?"

"The kegger tonight at Sigma."

"Fuck yeah." My brother reached over my shoulder and bumped fists with Sam before ruffling my hair. "I'm starving, Jess. Can we go grab a bite?"

"Yeah, sure."

The wattage on Sam's grin cranked higher as he rocked a

step back. "So I'll see you tonight, then. *Jess.* Don't worry. I'll make sure you have a good time."

I didn't even know how the fuck to interpret the wink that accompanied that statement. But my dick didn't seem to have any trouble.

21

SAM

I was still trying to recover from Friday night's game and the car wash earlier today when we headed out for the Sigma kegger, but I wanted to show Joel a good time.

Judging by the way he was bopping around with his Solo cup in the air, I'd accomplished that mission. I glanced at my watch. Another hour and I could probably convince him to bail.

I grabbed the cup out of his hand and swallowed some of the punch. "Don't drink too much of this shit or you'll be hugging a toilet later."

Joel cackled. "You act like I've never been to a party before." He snatched the cup back. "Oh my god, this is the best kind of torture. Look at that guy over there. Do you know him?"

"Hayes? Yeah. He's cool."

"I don't care if he's cool. Is he gay?" Joel waggled his brows.

I laughed. "I don't think so, no. And even if he was, he wouldn't hook up with you tonight—no one here would—because they know I'd kick their ass."

"Ugh. The patriarchy is so gross."

I shoved him. "That's not patriarchy, that's big brotherhood."

"Right." Joel rolled his eyes. "Why do you keep glancing toward the porch? Waiting on someone?"

"No," I lied and tried to sneak a look at my watch. Jesse and his brother were going for dinner earlier, just them, but it was almost ten. How fucking long did dinner take?

"You are the most unsubtle person I know."

I stared at Joel, slightly affronted. "No I'm not. What do you mean?" Fuck, had I come on too strong with Jesse? Was I scaring him off when I didn't even really know what I was doing in the first place?

Joel snickered. "You get the dopiest face around Jesse. That's him, right, the twink you were bending my ear about a while back?"

I dragged a hand down my face. "Is it really that obvious?"

"I don't think it is to him, but it is to me." Joel shrugged. "He's cute. But his brother? Dayum. He's a meat and four. Speaking of..." He nudged my shoulder, and I cast a glance at the porch for the fiftieth time, but this time was rewarded by the sight of Jesse and his brother stepping outside and hovering near the wall.

"C'mon." I didn't want Jesse to feel awkward or uncomfortable or regret coming, so I lifted a hand to him and started in that direction. The look of relief that crossed his face when he spotted us gave me more of a buzz than all the punch I'd had.

"Glad you found your way here after all." I handed him my cup as he wrinkled his nose. "Here, have some shitty punch."

Matt and Joel quickly vanished toward the kegs, leaving me and Jesse alone on the periphery of the party. "Want to see something?" I asked on a whim.

Jesse flashed me a smile I read as guarded interest. "Is it something the general population can see?"

"Nope." I ticked my head toward the back door of the frat house. "C'mon. Upstairs."

"Mmmm, sounds like half the dreams I had in high school of what college was going to be like."

I chuckled and snagged a pair of beers for us on the way inside.

The interior of the house was packed, and I was prepared to use my size to clear a path if necessary to keep Jesse out of the way of arms and elbows, but he did just fine on his own, slender figure cutting through the crowd with ease or brushing people out of the way with a charming smile and "excuse me" if he couldn't slide between.

I wasn't sure what it was about watching him walk through a crowd that did it for me, but suddenly I felt that same strange mixture of desire, possessiveness, and pride in my chest I'd felt on a few previous occasions.

Swallowing against it, I moved with him up the stairs and pointed to a third staircase. At the end of the third-floor hallway, I lifted onto the balls of my feet and yanked on a panel in the ceiling.

"You're taking me into an attic?"

"Just go, smartass." I stuck one beer in my back pocket and held the other one as I followed him up, and once we were on the plywood landing, led him over to a window before shoving it open and crawling out. The porch was about twelve feet wide with a brick surround and some broken-down porch furniture. The place mostly got used for smoking weed during the week, but we kept it closed during parties.

I plunked down on a rickety bench and sank back, closing my eyes. There was a nice breeze going, and the noise of the party sounded far away. I let out a contented sigh and cracked an eye. Jesse stood at the railing, but his head was tipped back looking at the stars. "What do you think?"

"It's not a bad view for being in the city," he said with a squint. "I can at least pick out the handle of the Big Dipper." He held out his hand, and I tossed him a beer, then eased from the bench and leaned against the wall alongside him.

I cracked the tab and took a swallow of icy brew. "What are you like on a date?" I'd been wondering ever since his date with John.

Jesse sputtered around a mouthful of beer, swiping his mouth with the back of his hand before barking out a laugh.

"I don't know. I haven't been on many actual dates in a while."

"You went out with John the other night, but you didn't tell me the whole story, just that it was a bust. Do you get nervous?" Was he picky with a menu since he had such high standards when it came to food? The thought made me grin.

I couldn't tell whether the musing smile that followed was because he could see right through me or just because he found me ridiculous. "Sometimes, yeah. But John was my first real date in at least six months. The last couple of years have been mostly hookups. What are you like? Is this where you bring your victims…errrr, dates"—he shot me a wink—"to seal the deal? Show them the stars, then show them the brightest star of all?" He snorted softly to himself.

"I've never tried it before. Is it working?"

His gaze sharpened on me. "Is this…did you want to do a scene up here or something? Was that the idea you mentioned earlier?"

"Nope. That was a poorly thought-out ruse to try to entice you into coming here." I set my beer can aside. Jesse's gaze lifted warily to meet mine as I took a step closer. "I need to kiss you again. For real this time."

"You do?" He squinted at me as I cupped his jaw and nodded. "Okay. I mean…wait. Why?"

"I need to see something."

His shoulders relaxed incrementally as I tilted his chin up, and when I brushed my lips over his, I felt him rise onto his toes to meet the soft sweep of my mouth. A tingle danced over the nape of my neck and slid down my spine. *There.* There it was.

Jesse's hands landed lightly on my shoulders and squeezed, which I took as permission to trace the tip of my tongue over the seam of his lips and open him up to my exploration. His grip tightened and his body pressed closer to mine, a soft *mmph* escaping him as our tongues moved together, smooth and slow and so damn sensual, like neither of us had anyplace else we wanted to be.

And just like the other morning in bed—although on a greatly expanded scale—it was comfortable. Not alien, not weird. That was the thing that'd struck me most. I'd wanted to know whether it was a fluke or not.

Now I did.

And it wasn't.

I ran my hands along his sides and then tentatively cupped his ass until the resulting moan made me bolder, and I squeezed the handful of it I had in each hand.

"Fuck." He tore his mouth from mine, and we rested cheek to cheek, panting. "What did you need to see?"

"If kissing you again would feel as good now as it did the other day."

"Oh." The cool tip of his nose ran along my jaw. "Did it?"

"Uh-huh. But I think we should do it some more just to be certain."

Jesse leaned back a little to meet my eyes. "Are we doing this? You sure?"

"Hell ye—" I didn't get to finish my sentence before his mouth was back on mine, just where I wanted it.

I squeezed his ass again, and this time he properly translated the extra emphasis I put in my grip and jumped up, wrapping his legs around my waist. I braced him against the ledge of the porch, keeping a tight grip on him with one hand while the other slid under his shirt. His skin was so fucking smooth and warm, his breath causing his stomach to rise and fall quickly under my touch.

"Shit," he moaned as I grazed his nipple with a thumbnail the way I'd wanted to earlier in the day at the car wash when his shirt had been plastered to his body.

I'd still been uncomfortably hard a half hour after he left, and so much shit was becoming clear to me. I wanted Jesse in a way I'd never wanted anyone else before, and I sensed that we were both dancing around the edge of acknowledgment, watching our steps, each wary for different reasons. And maybe it was ridiculous, but I didn't want to chance messing up whatever it was we were dancing around.

I just wanted it to keep going.

Jesse cursed again as I shoved his shirt up and bent my head, licking down the sleek slope of his neck and nipping his collarbone before sucking his nipple into my mouth. It was small and tight, and I derived a ridiculous amount of satisfaction from the way he arched into the circles I licked around it and how I could feel goose bumps pebbling his skin beneath my hand.

"*Sam.*" His voice was quiet but strained.

When I brought my mouth back to his, he groaned into it and my cock twitched hard for the unique sensation. Girlish moans, yes, I'd had those. But this was hoarse and gravelly with a desperation I could almost taste, and I fucking wanted more of it.

Jesse's arms tightened around my neck and I fumbled toward his fly, wanting to taste him. He reached a hand down, too, when I fumbled his zipper and yanked it open. I dived a hand behind the fabric panel, grunting in satisfaction when I reached his dick.

"Fuck yeah, that's good." He moaned as I squeezed and pulled him out. I rested my forehead against his, and we both looked down at his rigid cock poking up between us, my hand wrapped around it. I swiped my thumb over the bead of precum that oozed from his slit and lifted it, touching the tip of my tongue to it and tasting the hint of salt before Jesse surprised me by sucking my thumb into his mouth.

The suction and heat of his lips transmitted directly to my dick, and I whispered a curse, yanking him closer. I wanted to do the shit I'd seen in the gay porn I'd been watching recently, where the guys rubbed their dicks together. Frottage. I wasn't sure if you were supposed to ask for it, though, and that sounded kinda fucking weird in my head, so I planned to just go for it.

The dazed look in Jesse's eye as I got a hold of my zipper suggested he might be on board.

"*Samson!*"

It was loud enough that we both stopped.

Jesse peered over his shoulder. "Shit," he muttered and slid from the ledge, messing with his zipper. "Your brother."

"Wha—" I leaned around him to peer down at the party below. "You've got to be fucking kidding me."

"Yep, let's go."

We raced downstairs, and by the time we got to the porch, Joel was twirling stark-ass naked near the band with a Solo cup in his hand, his jeans tied around his neck like the world's most pitiful denim cape.

I threw an arm around him, which tightened into a headlock—brotherly, of course— when he tried to wriggle free. "Your dancing days are over for now, baby bro. You lost privs."

"I'm just getting started!" Joel crowed in a slur even as I guided him toward the door.

"We'll walk with you." Jesse fell in step beside us. "I grabbed the rest of his clothes."

Matt came around to Joel's other side and helped guide Joel along. He looked like Mickey Mouse stuck between two bears.

We progressed slowly and had to stop once so Joel could hurl in some bushes. Once we got back to our house and got Joel into the upstairs bathroom, I went into the kitchen, got some bottled water, and wet some washcloths, which I carried with me upstairs.

Jesse's brother sat on the bathroom floor with his back against the cabinet while Joel hugged the toilet. The sounds coming from him were disturbingly harsh.

"Ugh, don't miss that kind of drunk," I muttered. Matt made a grab for the water and washcloths, laying the cloth over the back of Joel's neck and twisting the cap off the water before handing it to him. "You and Jesse are both the caretaking type, huh?"

Matt shrugged with a faint smile. "I suppose, yeah. I learned it from Jesse. He was always looking out for us. Sometimes he was more of a parent than our parents." He cleared his throat and inclined his chin toward Joel. "I like him, he's nice. You should've let him keep dancing. He was having good time and wasn't hurting anyone."

"Uh-huh, and if we'd left him alone, about three minutes hence he'd have been spewing all over the crowd."

"Yeah, yeah. Maybe so." Matt cast another glance at Joel as he pitifully gulped air. "I'll sit with him for a little while."

I left him there and headed toward my room, where I found Jesse smoothing over the sheets on the bed. He'd placed a trash bin near the bedside table.

"I wasn't sure if he'd sleep on the floor or the bed."

"I'll probably let him have the bed." I offered a grateful smile that faltered when Jesse opened his mouth and promptly snapped it shut again. Had he been about to...? No, that was crazy. It was ridiculous for me to think he'd been about to offer me space in his bed. Especially when his brother was here, too. "My mom's going to be so pissed at me."

"Aww, nah, he should be all right tomorrow. He's not comatose." Jesse leaned against the doorframe. "There's a secret stash of electrolyte powders in an old spaghetti box in the pantry. Ansel hid them after Nate kept stealing them. He thinks no one knows about them. One tonight and one tomorrow and I'll bet he's fine. I should've grabbed them while I was down earlier. I'll go—"

"I'll grab them in a sec. Don't worry about it." I dropped a pillow on top of the mattress and sat down on the edge. "About earlier on the roof. You're not..."

Jesse waved a hand. "Oh yeah, no, that was fine. Don't even worry about it."

"That wasn't what I was going to say. But okay." I frowned.

"Oh shit, I insulted you." Jesse smacked his forehead. "Fuck. No. Wait. Back up. I didn't mean to insult you. I just meant I didn't have any expectations out of it."

I mustered a thin smile. "I get it. I promise. I just thought you should know that I liked kissing you. And the other stuff that happened...I liked that, too. That's all. Doesn't have to be anything more or less than that."

"I know. I'm trying not to swoon over it."

"Do you swoon?"

"Oh yeah. Freshman year a guy could've told me a bird shit on my head and I'd have swooned that he'd gone to the trouble to tell me. Nowadays it takes a little more." He cut me a coy sidelong look. "Like a guy telling me I've got a pretty pucker."

"I've never said the word 'pucker.' I wouldn't say that."

"I know. But you could. I'd be into it." His grin faded. "The thing is, I already know this story. This is what I do. I get a crush. I dive into something headlong. I don't think about what's right for me. I don't think at all. I don't come up for air, and then all of the sudden I'm thirty feet deep, alone with no air." He cocked his head. "That's pretty dark. Let me rephrase in a much less poetic fashion: I let myself get too attached too fast and then am heartbroken when the other person with a heart that functions at normal human speed decides that I'm not a good match for them and they want to move on."

"How long does that usually take?"

"A few days." He chuckled when I turned a concerned look on him. "I'm kidding, but still faster than the average human. Reid and I were confessing love after two days. I pop crushes like a fourteen-year-old dude pops boners. So I just have a little bit of trouble trusting my instincts sometimes." He met my eyes. "Even if certain things seem...really nice."

"You don't want to get hurt."

"I don't want to get hurt."

"You don't want to jinx it."

"I really don't want to jinx it." He nodded, his voice quiet.

"So maybe we could just keep on doing exactly what we're doing for a while without trying to...to define it."

I didn't understand it. Not fully, but I understood that the fear was real to him, and I understood not wanting to get hurt. I didn't want to get hurt either. "Okay. No jinxing, then."

Jesse stared at me for a long moment and then nodded before pushing off the doorframe as Matt guided Joel into my room.

Shortly after I turned out the light, my phone buzzed. My brother was already snoring on the floor at the foot of my bed. I opened the message, a grin forming the second I saw the *J* in his name.

Jesse: *I liked it, too. I mean, for the record.*
Sam: *Was also gonna tell you you're a really good kisser but then figured you'd get all cocky about it.*
Jesse: *So what if I did?*
Sam: *Well then I would've wanted to kiss you again right there next to the trashcan Joel is currently hugging like a teddy bear and you were too busy silently freaking out.*
Jesse: *I wasn't freaking out. I was just...digesting.*
Sam: *You were freaking. You still are. It's okay, I kinda am too.*

22

SAM

Jesse picked up his laptop, scooted his chair back in, and came around the other side of the library table where I was sitting as we did homework. Or tried to. I'd read one page of trigger point therapies in the last ten minutes because we kept getting sidetracked. Most recently because Jesse turned his laptop in my direction and pointed at two recipes on screen, one for a red velvet cake and one for angel food cake. That had devolved into a whispered discussion about a recent episode of *GBBO* and why angel food cake sucked, in my opinion. Except I had no business weighing in on baking matters in the first place. If I walked into our house and there was an angel food cake sitting out on the counter, I would eat it with gusto. Cake was cake at the end of the day. But for the sake of argument—because Jesse was especially sexy when he got indignant over baked goods—I picked a side.

"Hi," he said, plopping down next to me with a grin that made me suspicious.

I eyed it warily. "What..." I trailed off as he closed a hand over the top of my thigh, his palm warm and the gentle squeeze he gave my quad oddly provocative.

He planted an elbow on the table and angled toward me. "Trust me?"

I swallowed as he squeezed again. "Kind of. I'm at about 80 percent and dropping. Is this about angel food cake? I can change teams and go to bat for it. Apparently that's something I do lately." That last part came out under my breath.

"Eighty percent is good enough for me. Put your phone under the table and hit Record."

Oh. So we weren't going to be discussing baked goods anymore. "*Jesse.*" He moved his hand higher, gripping my nuts through my pants, and in spite of my misgivings, they were clearly on board. I sucked in a slow breath as he flicked my button open and lowered my zipper.

"Look around," he said softly. "What do you see? Is anyone paying us any attention?"

There were a couple of solo studiers at a bank of study carrels that weren't paying us any mind. Another wide table with lamps on top like the one we were sitting at was filled with what looked like a study group. And there was a cluster of armchairs a dozen yards from us where one guy was sleeping and a girl sat with her laptop perched on her knees and earbuds plugged into her ears.

"Not really?"

"Exactly." Jesse stroked his fingers over my crown and then traced his thumb in a firm touch up the thick vein that ran the length of my cock. I held back a shudder. Jesse followed my sightline to the study group.

"They're not looking." He pressed his thumb to my slit. "God you've got a fantastic cock." He grinned. "The rest of you is all right, too, I guess."

"Jesse..." I didn't know where I was going with that sentence, and then it didn't matter anyway because Jesse did the crazy-making thing where he twisted his fist down my shaft and the rest of the breath in my lungs exited with a quiet whoosh.

"Not gonna be able to do the full onslaught—too much shoulder movement might catch someone's eye—but..."

"This is good." I bit back a groan as he twisted over my head. "*Fuck*. This is fine."

"Yeah?"

I nodded slowly, nerve endings singing with pleasure, and my whole body strained with effort to keep still and not buck into his hand. "You were right. You've truly nailed the dry jerk." This was my second go round with it, and it was every bit as good as the first.

"Told you it was an art form." He flashed me a saucy little wink that made my dick jump in his grip, then squeezed tightly, and I let out a groan. I couldn't help it. My eyes widened in alarm, and I glanced over my shoulder again as Jesse chuckled softly.

"No one's looking. It's all good. Relax. Damn, you're leaking like crazy now. I got this idea from a vintage video where this guy gets a beer in a restaurant surrounded by people."

"I think you need to stop talking."

"I think I need to keep talking—it's clearly having a positive effect. Think you can come over my fist in under five minutes?"

"Definitely," I gasped. "If you keep doing that." He concentrated on my head again, doing some combo with his palm and thumb that made me want to arch out of my seat. My balls tingled. "Fuck, maybe under three. How do you *do* that?"

"Many years of practice. Jesus, I wore the wrong underwear for this. Again."

Jesse removed his hand briefly to adjust, and I bit my lip to see the tip of his cock peeking out just behind his waistband.

"No," I hissed when he started to pull his shirt down over it. "Leave it like that. Let me see it."

His tip was glazed with precum, and as I spoke, another drop of the clear fluid emerged from his slit. He shifted around, head rubbing against the denim, and let out a slow breath.

"Fuck, I think I might actually come like this."

"Tighter," I urged him and winced with pleasure as he did as I'd requested. My gaze traveled upward from the juice leaking from his cock to his eyes. His hair was disheveled, and his lips were wet and parted, his eyes glazed. "You're so sexy." It came out unbidden, but it was true. Reid had been an idiot to cheat on him. I didn't even understand how anyone could. Jesse was funny and sweet and hot, and fuck me did he know how to give a hand job. Everything, really. He was good at everything.

"Really?"

I nodded. "Yeah, I wanna see you come really badly."

"If you come, I will. I promise. You got a big load in there for me?"

"Uh-huh," I said dully. It was all I had. Pleasure saturated me, and I stopped worrying about the people around us. Forgot about them, in fact.

"Wish I could lean over right now and suck you into my mouth. I want you filling it. So big and smooth, that fat head bumping the back of my throat. All that precum coating my tongue. Actually...hang on."

"*Jesse*," I hissed as he glanced around and then ducked under the table.

23

JESSE

I bumped my head on one of the crossbars under the table but recovered quickly and pushed Sam's knees wide as he gripped the top of his thigh with one hand and tried to keep the camera steady with the other.

I fucking loved giving head, and my only regret as I closed my fingers around Sam's thick base and sampled the supersized drop of juice glazing his tip was that I wouldn't be treated to those throaty moans of his I'd come to absolutely fucking adore.

But the way his thighs shook when I took him deep was a good second runner-up. His fingers tangled in my hair and took root, tightening as he got closer to coming apart.

The combination of hard-core deep-throat action and my fist working his base was what finally did it. And though it was quiet enough that I was sure I was the only one to hear it, the sexiest little growl rumbled in his throat as he slid to the edge of his seat, thrusting so deep that my watering eyes spilled over as he lost it. I swallowed twice and then used the rest of his jizz to bring myself to a quick, gut-zinging orgasm.

With my cheek resting against the inside of his knee, I stroked us both slowly through the comedown, having discovered after our third video that Sam absolutely loved a post-O slowstroke, and that I absolutely loved the blissfully dopey smile that resulted. I honestly couldn't think of another person I'd enjoyed getting off so much. Giving Sam pleasure was truly a pleasure, and as he stroked my hair gently, in the back of my mind it occurred to me there could be a time when that stopped and I'd have to be okay with it.

I pushed the thought aside because that was for some other Jesse to worry about. Not present Jesse, who still had the delightful taste of Sam in his mouth and spunk all over his boxers.

"I have no idea what that video's going to look like," Sam said quietly when I emerged from under the table and we began packing our stuff up. "Trying to stay quiet made me all shaky. I'm not even sure I got the money shot, and I know I accidentally got your full face in there at least once."

"Most of that money shot hit the back of my throat, anyway. The rest can be edited. But I'll bet it'll be a hit. The public shit always is. Everyone wants to watch it; few actually want to do it." I double-checked under the table and on the chairs to make sure we hadn't left any unwanted DNA surprises for the next table guests, and then we headed outside.

"I'm gonna have to tell Coach I did a big leg day yesterday when he asks me why I'm running like shit. My thighs are toast from the straining. Jesus. Worth it, though."

"I don't have work tonight, so when you get home I'll give you a massage if you want." I waggled my brows invitingly. "Technically we haven't tackled straight-boy massage yet."

"I've been thinking about that, actually."

"Ohhhh, you have? This sounds promising." I'd only been half-serious. I mean, obviously I would've jumped at the chance to play out the massage fantasy for Sam's OnlyFans page, but I equally liked the idea of splaying him out on my bed and rubbing him until his muscles were Jell-O just because his body probably needed it, and I bet he'd love being pampered. I didn't care if he had a team trainer; there was no way Pat would put as much dedication and care into it as I would.

"I think we've probably recorded enough jerks and blowjobs." Sam's gaze lingered on me sidelong, and my stomach swooped before a pit the size of Montana opened up. He was going to tell me he'd met some quota, that we'd banked enough videos and my services were no longer required. A sour taste filled the back of my throat as Sam stopped in front of the stairs to the Life Sciences building and faced me.

His brows pinched in concern. "Are you okay? Shit, you look pale." He grabbed my shoulders like he was afraid I was about to keel over even though I put a hand up in protest.

"I'm good. I got light-headed for a minute there," I lied, because who the fuck wanted to admit they'd had an anxiety spike over potentially not being able to film a guy jerking off anymore. My mother would be so proud.

"Here, sit for a second," Sam insisted, turning me around and guiding me to a nearby bench. "Low blood sugar is nothing to mess around with. If you passed out, you could crack your head on the pavement."

"Says the guy who regularly takes a beating on the field. What are you looking for?" I asked as he dug through his backpack.

"This." Sam produced a granola bar with a triumphant flourish and handed it to me. "Eat it. My youngest brother has hypoglycemia, so I got used to always having something tucked away. He knocked his front tooth out once when he passed out in our kitchen, and then my mom almost passed out because of all the blood. Our dog, Teddy, ran through the blood and tracked it through the house and…yeah. Big fiasco."

"What a charming family story to relive at the holidays," I said as I nibbled a corner of the bar.

He dropped down onto the bench beside me. "We've got many just like that. My sister—not the one with the blood disorder—is a reflexive puker. If she even hears someone gag or cough the wrong way, she hurls. I'm sure you can imagine what that was like when a stomach bug ran through the house."

I laughed, even though it sounded awful, because he told the story with the kind of brotherly fondness that lit up his face.

"I'm sure you have stories like that, though, too, huh?"

"Some, yeah. I don't know, every time I think of my family, I just think of chaos and noise. And sometimes it was lovable, and sometimes it was overwhelming." It turned out that granola bar was pretty tasty, and the chocolate chips in it fortified me enough to tackle the topic Sam had been alluding to earlier. "So what were you saying a few minutes ago, about filming?"

"Oh, right." Sam stretched an arm out over the bench behind me and twisted his back one way and then the other. "I was wondering how you'd feel about moving on to something different." He chuckled. "Fuck, I don't know why I'm suddenly nervous. Anyway, maybe tackling some of those other requests we've been getting in the comments. Like for um"—his chin dipped low as he met my gaze sidelong—"penetration?"

"Who did you have in mind for the recipient?" There'd been requests going both ways. I swallowed hard, and it felt like one of those cartoon-style swallows where you could literally see the blob going down the character's throat. I couldn't help it, though. It was like I'd opened the door and found the Publishers Clearinghouse prize patrol on my doorstep, except instead of a big fat check, it was a big fat cock up for grabs, and it remained to be seen whether I'd use my winnings wisely or end up broke and cooking meth in a trailer park.

I needed another granola bar.

Sam considered for a moment. "Oh. Well, whoever, I guess. Shit, I've never even asked you if you're a top or a bottom or…"

"I'm a whatever-gets-the-job-done but with a preference for bottom. I can't imagine that's surprising."

"I didn't want to assume," he said, and then came a prompting arch of his brows. "So what do you think? Is that too far for you?"

I burst into laughter. I was so relieved he wasn't telling me he wanted to stop filming, and so ecstatic and simultaneously nervous as hell about riding the monster in his pants, that I probably sounded a little hysterical. I pulled myself together and cleared my throat. "Yes. I think we're ready to graduate to the next level."

"Good." Sam's grin beamed as bright as if I'd told him he'd just been awarded my Rotel dip for life, and then he glanced down at his phone and stood. "I'm about to be late for class, but we can discuss how we want to do it tonight?"

Naked and immediately, preferably.

I nodded, and he started to turn away, then spun back around. "Shit, I know you said you were feeling better, but are you sure? I can bail on this class if you want me to walk back to the house with you."

He was ridiculous. And adorable. And… *Simmer down, Jesse.* "I'm perfectly fine now. You're right, that granola bar did the trick. I'll see you tonight."

He gave me another assessing up and down and then, apparently satisfied, nudged the toe of his shoe against my calf in what I guessed was a goodbye? Affection? Friendship? All three? And loped across the grass, leaving me light-headed for real.

I tossed the granola wrapper in the trash and headed toward the house, walking on air. I was so high on Sam's BDE that when I passed by Reid standing in a cluster of people chatting and he waved, I waved back.

Wrong move.

Reid detached from his group and trotted over toward me. "Hey."

"Hey," I returned cautiously, waiting to see what he wanted.

"What class do you have next?"

"None. Just heading home."

"Ah." Silence stretched, and from the corner of my eye I could see him drumming restlessly on his backpack straps as we walked. "So is any of your family coming for Homecoming?"

"Nah, not this year." They had freshman year, but it'd kinda lost its luster after that, and it was hard for my parents to get away from work.

"You coming to the game?"

"Maybe. I'm not sure yet."

"You should. Last Homecoming ever? Come on." Reid nudged me with a smile, and since he didn't seem to want anything from me aside from small talk, I returned it and then listened to him chatter about senior year, football, and his hopes for the draft all the way until I had to divert to get to my street.

As we said goodbye, I decided maybe I didn't hate him as much as I used to. So either the prospect of what I was pretty sure was going to be great sex with Sam had some restorative properties, or Reid's apology in the cafeteria had provided a more powerful sense of closure than I'd expected.

Maybe it was a bit of both.

When I got back to the house, I stood alone in the kitchen grinning like an idiot for a solid minute as I thought about Sam giving me his granola bar, then for an additional minute thinking about bottoming for Sam. And finally, I did what one naturally did when wanting to express their extreme gratitude and reluctantly growing affection: I made a big ol' batch of Rotel and put it in the fridge with a sticky note plunked on top that read, *For Sam only!*

24

SAM

The next Thursday was unseasonably warm, so when I got done with my weight lifting session early, Mark, Nate, and I picked up a case of beer and a few $15 plastic kiddie pools that we dragged into the backyard of the house and filled. We each occupied one and set the cooler full of beer in the middle.

"Damn, I love senior year." Nate tilted his head back to catch the sun on his face. "This is the life."

Mark and I lifted our beer cans in solidarity.

"You and Eric figured out where you're going after graduation?" Mark asked.

"Probably DC. Makes the most sense. Lots of job ops for us there, and Eric already has a line on some engineering firm he's been talking with. What about you and Chet, or is that even up for discussion yet?"

Chet and Mark had been on the down low for a while due to some drama surrounding Mark's family.

Mark hedged. "We'll definitely be in DC for the summer

because Chet has a law internship waiting on him. But I don't know what I'm gonna do."

"Trouble already?"

"With Chet, you mean?" Mark laughed. "Fuck no. I'll be with that asshole for the rest of my life, probably." The goofy grin on his face was smitten, and between him and Nate, I couldn't help feeling a little like they were part of some couples' club I'd been left out of. "I just mean with my life. I changed my major to pre-law, pretty much hated the internship I just finished and…" Mark dismissed the subject with a wave of his hand. "Never mind. I'll figure it out. Beer me?"

I nudged the cooler open with my toe, leaned forward just enough to swipe a fresh can, and lobbed it at Mark before dropping back into the pool. "My plan is to go to Vegas, spend a shit ton of money in a strip club, and hopefully wake up married. Thanks for asking."

Mark cocked his head and tsked me. "Awww, feeling left out?"

"A little bit, actually."

"I saw that girl Natalie all over you a while back. Nothing came of that?"

I laughed. "That was months ago. And nah. I wasn't into it." I hesitated. On the one hand, if there was anyone who'd get my situation, it was Nate and Mark. On the other hand, I wasn't ready to be up-front about my videos, so more than half the story would be missing, and Jesse was an even more complex subject.

I took a fortifying sip of beer. "So, anal sex."

Nate spluttered on his beer.

Mark whipped his head toward me. "What?"

"With guys," I elaborated.

Mark's eyes narrowed, and he and Nate exchanged a glance.

"What about it? You want to have it? You want us to tell you about it? This is...what the hell is happening?"

"Tell me about it."

"It's the same as with girls, dude. Just prep it and poke it."

Mark wrinkled his nose at Nate. "Oh, is that how it goes down for you, Mr. Know-it-all?"

"More or less. What, are you and Chet doing rituals to call down the rain beforehand? It's not rocket science."

"I've never done anal with *anyone*," I admitted, and the weight of both their eyes on me made my cheeks heat.

"Actually, that's not surprising," Nate said. "I'd be hesitant to let that monster in, too."

"Great, thanks. Super helpful."

Mark raised a hand. "Are we going to talk about the bigger picture here? Are you questioning things? Wanting to do anal with a guy?"

"Ummm, both?" I liked how Mark said "questioning," though, instead of outright asking me if I was gay or bi, because I was still trying to figure that part out. I just knew straight was no longer the right fit for me. "I've kind of got a crush. And it kinda happened by accident." I scratched my head. "Maybe?"

Nate and Mark exchanged a look. "So are you gonna tell us who it is or what?"

"Jesse."

"Are you shitting me?" Mark crowed and then fell back laughing. "You're such a dickhead."

Nate threw his empty beer can at me, and I wasn't really sure where to go with that because I hadn't thought it through.

I'd just assumed they'd automatically believe me.

"I hate to be the bearer of heartbreak, but Jesse's not all that keen on you."

I blinked. "What? He likes me."

Nate tipped his head back against the edge of the pool, another laugh bubbling up.

"It drives him batshit that you eat everything in the fridge. He bitched all summer about the wet towels you left on the bathroom floor. He calls you *meatbutt*." Mark delivered that last bit in a dramatically low voice.

"Meatbutt?"

"That might actually be a compliment," Nate interjected. "Not 100 percent sure, though."

"Soooo...this crush. Did it involve a dare and someone's dick getting sucked?" Mark joked, which, all things considered, wasn't that far off the mark.

But I knew at that second I wasn't going to confess anything more about how it'd come about. I didn't know how to without going back to the beginning, and I hadn't talked to Jesse about it either.

"It probably won't amount to anything. It's just...I didn't know if it was maybe a little weird for me to even be interested in a guy because of what I said about sucking off that other guy and not being into it."

Mark sat up abruptly, water sloshing over the side of the pool. "Oh shit, you're serious." He narrowed his eyes again. "Wait. Are you serious?"

"Yeah." I nodded. "I'm really into him." That wasn't a lie; it just didn't expand on what all we'd been doing together.

Nate shrugged. "Fuck if I know. Sexuality shit still confuses me sometimes. Love's easier, I think. You love who you love, and regardless of how that fits into the spectrum of sexuality, I'm pretty sure it's one of those things that when you know, you know."

I got that funny feeling in my stomach again.

We all startled as the back door banged open. Jesse leaned

in the doorway, staring at us with a puzzled expression. "Is this a meeting of the American Society of Rejects? I'll let Ansel know when he gets home."

"Yes. And you're now dis-invited." Mark flipped him the bird.

"I'm wounded. There's a pizza guy here. Want me to put it on the counter? Or shall I just set it in the middle of your...hobro camp?" Jesse's gaze landed on me, moving up my calves and torso, and finally met my eyes. His lips quirked before he moved on, a tinge of color in his cheeks.

"Do you call me meatbutt behind my back?" I spread my arms over the back of the pool and widened my legs a little, smirking when Jesse's eyes zipped down between my legs before he focused resolutely on my face.

I slid a hand between my thighs for a quick adjustment that made his Adam's apple bob in a hard swallow. The tinge of color in his cheeks became a full-on scarlet flush.

"*Meat*...um...oh yeah. It might've crossed my lips a time or two. Maybe five or ten or a hundred." Jesse jabbed an accusing finger in Mark's direction when he snorted. "Traitor! That's against the roommate handbook."

"Right, but the American Society of Rejects operates by a different set of rules. We're all morally bankrupt."

"Right." Jesse rolled his eyes. "Anyway, I'm leaving the pizza on the counter."

"Have some if you want," I offered. "There's plenty."

He wrinkled his nose sourly. "Madzo's oversalts their crust. It's atrocious."

"I think you mean, 'Thanks for the offer, but I'll decline.'"

"Wasn't that what I just said?" He smiled sweetly at me and then, with a quick glance at Nate and Mark, stepped back inside and let the door shut behind him.

Silence stretched for an awkwardly long time, and then Mark busted out laughing. "I honestly don't think I've ever seen you flirt with someone before. That was a trip."

"That was flirting?" Nate looked bewildered.

"Oh, it was definitely flirting. Shit, I'd put money on some hard-core frottage within a week."

God, I wondered what he'd say if he knew what had gone down in the library the other day. Not to mention everything that had come before.

After we killed the pizza, Nate and Mark split to meet up with their respective others, and I was left with a rare moment of having nothing to do. Jesse's keys were still on the counter, but he wasn't downstairs. I flung myself on the couch, flipped through the channels restlessly for a while, then turned off the TV and climbed the stairs, standing outside Jesse's door for a handful of seconds trying to come up with a good excuse before I decided fuck it.

A muffled *yeah* came when I knocked on the door. I pushed it open. It was cool and dark inside, and I assumed the lump under the covers was Jesse.

"Late nap?" I asked.

"Mmmmph. Yeah. Tazla wants to go to some drag show that doesn't start until eleven, so plenty of time."

A nap sounded pretty good. The pizza and beer had made me drowsy, and we had an away game we were leaving for tomorrow, so I wasn't going anywhere else tonight.

I pulled off my shirt and tossed it on the floor, then closed the door behind me and dive-bombed the bed.

Jesse's tousled strawberry blond head popped up from beneath the covers. "What're you doing?"

"Taking a nap with you."

He stared at me. "Just like that?"

"Yeah. Why not?" I pulled the covers back and nudged his thigh. "You inspired me."

Jesse laughed. It was a sound light with humor and maybe a tinge of disbelief. "You're ridiculously simple at times and incredibly complex at others. I can't pin you at all."

"Well—"

"No, don't explain it. I kind of like that about you."

I was tempted to tell him he was similar. Strikingly direct at one moment and unreadable the next. And that I liked that, too.

I pulled the covers up, and Jesse exhaled a quiet hum of contentment as I curled around him, draping an arm over his shoulder.

"Mark once told me you were a cuddler. I didn't believe it."

"Yep. Unapologetic about it, too." I ducked my nose into the clean scent of hair curling at the base of his neck and spread my palm over his sternum, feeling his heartbeat beneath. The rise and fall of his chest was lulling. "I can't believe you call me meatbutt behind my back."

"It started as…not exactly insult, but then—"

"Don't even try to explain."

"No, let me. It's kind of a compliment, though, if you think about it. You do have an ass that won't quit."

"Yeah?" I slid my hand from his chest across his rib cage and then lower to cup his rear. I'd had the opportunity to do it a few times, and just like the others, the firm contact crackled through me and woke my nerves endings up. "Yours is pretty slammin', too." I kissed his shoulder, then the back of his neck, and rose up on one elbow to capture his mouth when he angled toward me.

Jesse closed his fingers around my wrist and guided my hand to his erection, rubbing against the heat of my palm with a soft moan. "Do you have your phone with you?" he asked as I snagged the waistband of his pajama pants and dragged them down.

"Mm-hmm. Got something in mind?" I trailed a touch over the curve of his ass and slid my hand between until I reached his balls.

"Sure do—*shit, that feels good.* Whip it out—phone *and* dick," he added with a grin as he rolled and slung a leg over my hips before crawling astride me. "There are a couple of other things your fans have been asking for that we haven't tackled yet."

A low, hissing curse poured from my lips as Jesse slid his bare ass back and forth over my trapped cock. "What are these things?"

He grabbed the phone from my hand. "To start with, you're gonna roll on your stomach and let me eat your ass, then we'll see what's what from there."

If he thought I was going to put up an argument, he was dead wrong.

Afterward we sprawled in sedate, exhausted satisfaction among the muddled covers. On my phone was forty-five minutes of Jesse wrecking me with his tongue and then demanding that I get up on all fours whereupon he pulled my dick back between my legs and drained it as efficiently as a fucking milkmaid. He straddled me and finished himself off by coming all over my softening dick before collapsing on my chest.

There were definitely some lines blurring between us, but I'd never been so consistently satisfied in my life.

With his head still on my chest, Jesse scrolled through Twitter on my phone and we checked out preview clips posted by other OnlyFans performers. This usually devolved into Jesse making narrative voice-over and stylistic comments that left my stomach aching with laughter. But a lot of times, he was insightful, too. He truly had an eye for this stuff.

"Have you ever considered doing the filming stuff professionally. Or styling? That's a thing, isn't it?" I didn't like what happened to my blood pressure when I imagined that scenario, though.

Jesse laughed softly and tossed the phone aside. "Styling is a thing, yeah. And filming, too."

His voice was a drowsy murmur that tickled the side of my shoulder. "It sounds fun in theory, but honestly? I don't think I want a wild life like that."

"What do you want?"

"Simple, I guess. I want to cook. Have my own place. Eventually have someone I love who loves me back. You? I don't think I've ever asked."

"Same."

He rubbed the scruff on his chin against my skin and laughed. "You want to cook, too? You've been holding out on me, asshole."

I thumped him on the crown of his head. "You can keep the cooking. I'll stand by with a weight loss plan and gym routine."

"Mmmm, that doesn't sound too bad. Maybe your gym can be near my restaurant. We can have an understanding. Special discounts. You scratch my back, I'll scratch yours. That type of thing. Speaking of...how about you—*yeahhhhhh*. That's what I'm talking about."

25

SAM

I'd watched twenty-seven "stuck-in-a-dryer" scenes in preparation for ours, and Jesse had been right: there was one for every pairing possible.

But regardless of how prepared I thought I was, I still almost dropped the laundry basket I was carrying under one arm when I pushed open the door to our laundry room and found Jesse on his knees with his arms and head inside the dryer.

"I hear you snickering." His petulant accusation made me grin. "Did you already hit Record?"

"I did. I can edit this out." I cracked up when he waggled his ass at me. "You're gonna have to stop that, though." His chuckle echoed through the dryer as I set down the laundry basket and aimed the camera at his backside. "What'd I tell you about sticking your head in dark holes?"

"*Godammit, Sam.*" Jesse snaked an arm out of the dryer to flip me off.

I caught it and bent over to bite the tip of his finger. "All right, all right," I relented. "Let's start again." I backed up a couple of steps. "You look like you need a little help there, huh?" I drawled. I'd noticed recently that our on-camera back-and-forth had felt a lot more natural. We still had a basic idea of where we were going, but otherwise we played off each other a lot, which ended up being way sexier to me than trying to stick tightly to a script. Subscribers had noticed and appreciated it, too.

"I was trying to get this sock that was stuck, and then I got stuck, too!" Jesse sounded so convincingly offended by his predicament that I almost started laughing all over again.

"Uh-huh, you're in a real pickle." I panned the camera down his body to his perky little ass poking up in the air, then shifted the camera to the bulge in my jeans that'd formed the second he'd shaken his rump in my direction. Some things were just instinctive by now.

"So you think you could help me get out? I'd owe you big."

"Owe me big, huh? What do you have in mind?" I fiddled with the legs on our bendable tripod and got it set up so the camera would catch Jesse from his waist down.

I pointed the other handheld camera we'd gotten a while back down at my crotch as I rubbed the heel of my palm up and down my erection, resenting the cameras a little bit, honestly, because I was really fucking turned on and didn't necessarily want to think about camera angles and focusing issues; I just wanted to indulge in this fantasy with Jesse.

But then again, if it weren't for the cameras, I supposed he wouldn't be here in the first place.

"Whatever you want. Is there something you want?" Jesse's voice took on a breathy quality that could've been for show, but I didn't care. It was definitely working. "You help me out of here, and then I'll give you whatever you want."

A harsh intake of breath sounded as I reached down and

dipped my fingers just inside the waistband of his jeans, skimming along the top of his ass and loving the goose bumps that lifted on his skin as a result. "I think I've got a better idea." I snapped the waistband of his underwear against him lightly. "I think I'm gonna take what I want first, and then I'll help you out. How does that sound?"

He cursed softly as I caressed a hand over his ass, but his voice came out firm. "I think we should stick with the original plan. You wouldn't take advantage of me when I'm so helpless, would you? What kind of roommate would that make you?"

Reaching around, I flicked open the button on his fly and lowered the zipper. He whimpered when I squeezed his erection. "This hard dick says you like my idea better, so I think we'll stick with that. It's not taking advantage if it's something you want, is it?" I gave his ass a smack when he didn't answer immediately.

I'd grabbed ahold of the top of his jeans and started to drag them down to mid-thigh when a flash of bright pink stopped me in my tracks.

"Fuck," I whispered and blindly reached out to set the camera in my hand on the top of the washer, not even caring when I almost knocked it off.

I'd assumed the waistband I'd been feeling seconds ago was attached to standard issue briefs.

It wasn't.

Jesse had on a jockstrap. A hot pink jockstrap with stripes and lace detailing, and never in all the days of my life did I for one moment think I'd be into something like that, but holy shit was I.

I blew out a measured breath, my pulse pounding in my throat at the sight of his ass as I tugged his jeans the rest of the way down.

"Say something," he whispered, and then louder, but so hesitantly it made me ache, he added, "I was all out of clean underwear. I can...you can take it off me if you don't like it."

Fuck, I'd made him self-conscious. "Shh. I love it," I murmured and hoped he could hear the sincerity in it inside that metal drum.

I dropped down to a crouch just behind his ass, running my fingertips up the inside of one knee, a thigh, and over the curve of his bottom until he shivered.

When I made it to the seam of his ass and caressed lightly over his hole, Jesse jolted, banging something inside the dryer.

"Sa—*Jake*, whatever your name is, that's not—"

I spread his cheeks and buried my face between, flicking my tongue lightly over his entrance. I'd done it to girls before, but it was a hundred times sexier tasting Jesse. He moaned and wiggled, and I grabbed him by the waist and held him still, thrilling in the size difference between us. I got the appeal now.

"*Wait*," he cried, and I froze. "This wasn't part of the scene, you don't have to—" The needy wiggle of his ass came in defiance of what he'd just said.

"You want me to stop?" I rubbed my thumb against the muscle until it gave the tiniest bit, and a harsh intake of air sounded from inside the machine. I kissed his left asscheek, then swept my lips lightly over his entrance and gave it a kiss, too. "You just tell me and I'll stop. But otherwise, I'm gonna keep licking and sucking this pretty hole until it's ready to be filled with my cock. That sound all right to you?"

"*Jesusfuck.* Y-yes? I mean yes. *Yes.*"

"Good." I rubbed soothing circles over one plump cheek and then the other. "I was hoping you'd say that."

"Oh fuck. *Oh fuck.*" Jesse started up with a chorus of curses as I got back to work lapping and sucking every bit of skin I came across with the same kind of focus I'd dedicated to studying the football team's playbook. Except his moans and gasps were even more rewarding than a completed pass or touchdown. I tried to read the shifts and twitches of his body and adjust accordingly to maximize the pleasure.

Reaching beneath him, I found the front of his jock soaking. I stroked him lightly over the fabric until he writhed in his attempts to chase the friction of my touch, and I was forced to pause and yank my own zipper down to give my aching dick some breathing room.

Sliding a hand beneath the fabric, I popped his dick out as I tugged his balls with the other. "I'm trying to be patient and take care of you first, but you've got me so fucking turned on right now I can hardly bear it."

"*Please*," Jesse moaned. "Just do it. I want it so fucking bad. I've wanted it for so long."

It was all mixed up in my head now, what had been in our plan for this scene and what hadn't. I knew I'd gone off track a few minutes back, let slip out the things I'd never said to another human in my life and probably never would, but they'd been right on the tip of my tongue as I knelt behind him, and all I'd had to do was just open my mouth and let myself have exactly the kind of crazy fantasy sex I wanted with him.

But even in light of all that, the plea in Jesse's voice when he told me how bad he wanted me buried inside him rippled through my body and rang through my mind like the percussion wave of a gong being struck.

I jammed a hand in my pocket so fast the friction from the denim almost singed my thumb. After fishing out one of the packets of lube I'd stuffed in there, I shoved my jeans lower on my thighs and sank back on my heels, then tore open the packet too eagerly and spilled half the lube on the floor. The rest coated my hand, which shook a little as I pressed between Jesse's cheeks and smeared it around his hole.

I needed to stretch him, I remembered that much. I circled my thumb around his rim and had to grab the base of my dick to keep it in check over the way his muscle contracted and pinched with my touch. And when I finally pressed inside and got my first hit of searing heat clamping down hard on my thumb, I was the one to groan.

Jesse rocked himself on my thumb, then the two fingers I inserted while I watched, mesmerized and anticipating that same intense heat sealed around my prick.

"*Sammm*," Jesse wailed, and I didn't need any more encouragement. I smoothed a hand up his gorgeous back and positioned my tip at his entrance after getting it nice and wet by running it up and down his crack. My dick was as charged as a lightning bolt and in dire need of something to strike.

That first inch inside Jesse was a kind of ecstasy I'd never experienced before. I had a big dick, that was just straight-up fact, and it had never, ever been inside something as small and tight as the ass in front of me. Perfect heat cinched around my crown, and I stuttered out a lust-dazed cross between a curse and a moan. My eyes would've rolled back in my head if they weren't so mesmerized by watching how I disappeared inside him.

Keeping a hand on his ass to prevent him from sinking down on me all at once like he seemed inclined to, I pushed deeper slowly, reveling in the liquid fire that coated my shaft until his cheeks were flush against my abdomen.

"Oh fuck yes," Jesse whispered when I eased out halfway and gathered up a jockstrap in each hand. "Use me just like that."

Fuck.

I snapped forward, driving into him, letting his cries become my focus and guide my tempo. Otherwise I'd have lost it in seconds. He didn't seem to be having too much trouble handling me, which was a huge relief. So to speak.

I'd kind of mapped out in my head what I'd expected to happen, and what I thought fucking him would feel like. Pleasure? Yeah, I'd anticipated heaps of that, but what I hadn't counted on was it expanding beyond my cock and becoming a full-body experience.

All of it—the affection I had for Jesse and the desire, the way he made me feel when he smiled at me, and the deep, pupil-blowing lust I felt when I looked down at him, along with the pleasure unfurling in tremor-inducing tendrils that reached the deepest parts inside me—had me dizzy and overwhelmed.

And just when I thought I was going to lose it, I pressed my splayed hand into his lower back, halting him as he rocked back to meet my thrust.

Before Jesse could question my momentary pause, I was on my feet and hauling him from inside the dryer to plant him on top of it instead.

"Wha—" he started, and I cut him off with a kiss. His warm palms came up to cup my jaw on either side, and his tongue moved with mine like he'd been ready and waiting for the invasion. Craving it, even.

I fumbled with his jeans, tugging them the rest of the way off without breaking the kiss, and then squeezed between his thighs. He let me tilt his head back and kiss down one side of his neck and up the other until I made my way back to his lips.

"I know this isn't what we planned, but I didn't want to end like that," I murmured against his mouth. "Wanted to be able to see you, kiss you while fucking you."

"The video..."

"Fuck the video."

Jesse nodded mutely, lips softly parted as he braced his palms on the dryer and spread his legs wider, exposing himself to me as I leaned back.

I pulled him off the edge of the dryer, cupped his asscheeks, and lowered him onto my cock. There was no denying the rush I got out of seeing his tiny ass impaled on my dick, that tight ring of muscle stretched wide around it and the flare of heat in his eyes every time I thrust.

He looped his arms around me, our mouths and teeth by turns clashing and caressing as we writhed against each other, chasing the friction in every place we touched.

Jesse cinched his arms and legs tighter, harsh breaths puffing close to my ear and mixed with these little growls and encouragements and endearments that made me feel drugged.

"Sam!" The warning squeeze came suddenly, and I froze mid-thrust as Jesse whispered in my ear, "Someone's here."

We'd accounted for the whereabouts of all our roommates, but that didn't mean they stayed where they were supposed to. We held still, listening to movement in the kitchen and Mark and Chet's voices.

"They probably won't stay long." The words were hardly even a whisper. I nodded to show I'd heard.

My dick didn't understand our intermission, though. It throbbed insistently inside Jesse's tight passage, and I couldn't help a tiny little thrust that made him dig his fingers into my shoulders. His gaze shot up to mine, eyes wide and lips kiss-swollen and tempting.

Carefully, I swiveled us around and propped him against the wall adjacent to the door. Through the crack, I could see Mark and Chet moving around in the kitchen making a snack as they chatted idly.

Jesse clamped around my dick, and a shudder ran through me, the pleasure intensified by my attempts to hold back.

I mouthed a curse, then put a finger to Jesse's lips as I pulled out and drove back into him, slow and deep.

His body melted against me, and he sucked on the tip of my finger, back arching from the wall as I gripped his hips tighter and changed the angle. One of his hands flew up, clapping over his own mouth, and my finger within it, as he exhaled noisily through his nose.

I shot another gauging glance into the kitchen before moving inside him again. Mark and Chet seemed plenty preoccupied, though, and I couldn't wait. Resting my forehead against his, I slid my grip to the back of his thighs and held him open for the hard, shallow thrusts I unleashed.

My lips brushed the back of the hand he had clapped over his mouth, and he let it fall away to drape around my shoulder once more. His mouth brushed incidentally over mine as we both fought to keep our breaths quiet, and somehow the exchange of breath that came along with it was more intimate than a kiss, more intimate than my dick inside him and his body wrapped around mine. A thunderhead of pleasure gathered inside me and let loose all at once. I probably bruised the backs of his thighs squeezing them in place of crying out as I shattered.

I hated that I couldn't make any noise, that he couldn't hear how wrecked I was, but maybe he could see it on my face.

When the last tremor of orgasm had faded, I slid free of him and kept right on going down to my knees. His mouth opened —maybe to protest, maybe to make demands—but a shake of my head reminded him to be quiet.

Gripping him by the base and examining the rosy hues and

thick veins, I stretched my tongue out to capture a drop of fluid from his tip.

The contrast in feeling between sucking Jesse's cock and what I'd done on a dare years before was so vastly different it almost seemed like I'd been two different people. Maybe I had been. Or maybe *then* and *now* were in constant flux along a greater timeline of experience. Maybe both experiences could live alongside each other, valid in spite of their differences— maybe even *because* of their differences. Maybe there was more to my sexuality than a one-off blowjob, and I could be both the guy who hadn't enjoyed it back then and the guy who was currently living for the way Jesse's fingers knotted in my hair as I sucked him.

Maybe I *was* the kind of guy who needed some time for a bond to form. Or maybe Jesse was unique on his own.

I didn't know for sure, but I was absolutely certain that what we were doing together felt right. Felt good. Felt *true* for me in a way nothing else had. And I didn't want it to end.

I lifted my eyes to find Jesse's, and he quivered in my hands, clenching the roots of my hair so hard it stung before he flooded my tongue with his seed.

My head rested heavily against his abdomen, buoyed up and down by his breaths, and his hand splayed hot on the top of my hair. My breath slowed, and then my pulse. When Jesse touched my elbow lightly, I accepted the hand he extended and pulled myself up, then slid my hands along his jaw and kissed him again, still dazed.

The water turned off in the kitchen, and we held still as Chet spoke. "You need to tell your roommates not to leave stuff in the dryer when no one's here. That shit's a fire hazard."

"Know what else is a fire hazard?"

"Think I've got an idea. Good thing one of us has a big hose."

Jesse met my eyes and rolled his, and we both held our laughter until I nodded a confirmation that they'd left the room. Then we collapsed onto the laundry room floor and let it out quietly, just the grounding moment I needed after an orgasm that'd had me orbiting the sun.

Jesse shoved himself up and leaned back against the dryer, eyeing the bendable tripod on top of the washer and then looking around until he found the other handheld that'd fallen on the floor. "God only knows what's on this video."

That was the least of my worries. As far as I was concerned, this one had been for him and me.

I rolled upright with a grin. "I guess if it's a bust, we'll just have to do it again."

26

SAM

I stared at the ingredients spread all over the kitchen island, then consulted the recipe on my phone screen. A recipe was basically a playbook, and I had hundreds of plays memorized that I was able to execute with no problem, so this shouldn't be any trouble. But maybe it would've been wiser to pick something easy for my first go rather than chicken cordon bleu. Since I couldn't ask Jesse and didn't trust any of my other roommates, I'd googled "fancy" chicken recipes and picked the one that sounded the most delicious. Plus, it was a French dish, which I figured was promising.

Ansel banged through the back door, stopped and stared for a moment, then immediately made a grab for the cheese.

I swatted his hand away. "Fuck off, I'm making something."

He managed to grab a carrot before I could stop him. Now I knew how Jesse felt.

"Why?" He sounded bewildered.

"Just…because." I realized I didn't have a good answer. At least not one I wanted to give him.

"Did you get a damage deposit from Sam?" Ansel asked Mark as he came in from the front. "He says he's cooking."

"Oh fuck. I probably should've doubled it in that case." Mark poked around my groceries. "Are you making enough for everyone?" That was always the fucking question in this house. Once again, I felt Jesse's pain. The answer was no, but it didn't feel safe to reveal that yet.

"I need to get past the first step to begin with, which I can't when you assholes are messing with my stuff."

"Step one: call for takeout instead." Mark smirked.

I ignored them and unwrapped the chicken, set it on the cutting board, then washed my hands and flicked my screen awake to read the recipe again.

"It's like watching a caveman trying to figure out how to read a pictogram," Ansel joked.

"*The primitive man examines his stores after a long day of hunting and gathering,*" Mark said in a Morgan Freeman-style narrator voice as I picked up the cheese and then put it down again. "*Unsure of what certain food items are, he might be better off sticking to grilling small vermin over the fire.*" I picked up a knife. "*Ahh, he wields a rudimentary instrument with which he will...he willllllll....*" Mark paused dramatically, waiting to see what I was going to do next.

"With which he will murder his roommate if he doesn't quit fucking distracting him," I warned as I swiveled toward him and stabbed the knife in the air.

He and Ansel burst into laughter. The front door opened and shut, and Jesse appeared in the kitchen a second later. So there was my element of surprise ruined. "Great, the gang's all here," I deadpanned.

"We're watching Sam cook."

"Attempting to cook," Ansel corrected.

"What's on tap?" Jesse glanced at the mess on the counter. The sideways smile he gave me made me tingle from the top of my head to my toes. "Chicken cordon bleu?"

"I'm thinking of downgrading to chicken nuggets," I confessed.

"Way better idea. Save me some." Mark clapped a hand on my shoulder and then headed out of the kitchen.

"Me too." Ansel stole another carrot and darted out of the kitchen, narrowly missing the one I threw at him.

Jesse dropped his backpack near the table. "What's the occasion?"

"Uhhhh..." *Not helping the caveman analogies.* But I couldn't seem to make my mouth form the simple combination Y-O-U.

"Hmmm." Jesse furrowed his brow. "Usually for those special *uhhhhhhhh* kind of occasions, I'd go for a filet, medium rare. Classic, simple, timeless." He winked and nudged me with his shoulder. "Chicken cordon bleu is one of those deceptive dishes. Sounds fancy and complicated, but it's not too bad. Want me to help you?"

"I thought you had a study group tonight?" In my head, he arrived home and I had the whole thing finished and ready to plate.

"Got canceled. This is a way better use of time anyway. I'm starving."

I thought Jesse would just take over the cooking, but we ended up going through the recipe together, him guiding me through the steps and making me do everything when I knew he could've done it himself ten times faster.

He didn't seem to mind at all, and we joked back and forth as we did it, teasing each other like we often did now. Flirting, I guess Mark would've called it. Whatever it was, it was nice. We put the chicken and veggies in the oven to cook and then tackled all the dishes we'd dirtied, Jesse drying while I washed.

"It was supposed to be for you," I admitted, handing over a bowl. I loved how he had such an array of smiles, the one that formed for my confession just a teeny, tiny twist of his mouth that you had to look close to see.

The oven chimed a second later, and we pulled out the chicken. Jesse poked at it with a fork before declaring it perfect. Not three minutes after that, Ansel, Mark, and Cam all showed up in the kitchen like a pack of wild dogs, suddenly hungry and wondering if there was anything to eat.

"You should've just said no. You're too nice." Jesse lifted his head from the crook of his arm where he was sprawled next to me on my bed and gave me a stern look. "Now what will you eat for lunch tomorrow?"

I fought back a smile at his concern. That had been the plan for the extra chicken I'd bought, but none of that mattered after Ansel, Mark, and Cam had come sniffing around. I'd ended up giving them the extra servings. "You would've done the same thing. Don't pretend like you wouldn't have."

"I would have." His sigh of agreement turned into a rumbling purr when I reached out to fiddle with a strand of his hair.

I'd meant to move it away from his cheek, but that pleased sound had me sinking my fingers through the red-gold strands and rolling closer, drawn like a magnet when his eyes fluttered shut.

"You really were cooking for me?" he murmured into the kiss I brushed over his lips.

I made a noise of assent as he clutched the front of my shirt, keeping our mouths sealed. I loved the warmth of his kiss, how he gave himself over to it like it was the most important thing we were doing. Maybe it was. It felt like that a lot more lately. I'd noticed it even when we were shooting videos for OnlyFans, too. One or both of us would get lost in the moment, forget what we'd planned to do, forget to be conscious of the camera and the angles. Sometimes I wasn't even forgetting. Sometimes I suspected Jesse wasn't either. I had no plans to call attention to it, though.

His body moved against mine as the kiss deepened, and I was glad to hear his moans as I let my hands roam over him. I'd learned they told me how he wanted to be touched. The low timbre of these suggested gently, so I moved with care.

"No one has ever touched me like you do." He peeled back, eyes bright and avid on me as I helped him out of his shirt and then stripped mine.

Our pants came next.

"How do I touch you?" I bit back a groan as the heat of his naked body seared over my skin and his cock slotted next to mine, but I couldn't help the quiet curse that escaped.

"Like you're listening. Like you hear me. Like you're paying attention."

"I am." I groaned again as Jesse began stroking us both, my cock leaking all over the place because I just reacted that strongly to him now. "You do the same," I managed, arching my back as he closed around my head and squeezed.

"Because I am, too." His lips found mine once more, my hands found his hips, and eventually he slid a leg over my torso and my eyes rolled back in my head as he guided me inside him. I didn't know when lube had happened and didn't care. I just knew the heat of him around me was the best thing I'd felt in my life, and the way his breath spilled raggedly over my lips suggested he felt similarly.

No cameras, no discussion of angles, no script.

Just us.

27

JESSE

Cam had been jiggling his knee for the past ten minutes while I finished cooking my omelet and plating it. First I could ignore it, because it was just this tiny movement in my periphery, so I just angled my head a little bit as I continued cooking. But then when I'd glance over, he'd still be going, and it was like I could feel the vibrations even though I was no longer looking.

I set my plate on the kitchen table and dropped into a seat next to him. "What's up."

Cam's startled gaze cut toward me. "Huh?" I ticked my chin toward his knee. "Oh." He forced himself to be still. "Nothing. I'm good."

I studied him. "Are you having a...craving or something?" I didn't know what the NA terminology was, and I sure as shit didn't know how to support him if he was, but I'd try.

He shook his head. "Nah. Just got a lot on my mind. I'm not thinking about using, though," he added quickly. "Promise. I've got a sponsor to call for that. And I haven't had to call in months. I'm good, I swear." He let out a slow breath. "I feel like that's all I keep saying: I'm good, I'm fine. Blah, blah, blah. But I am."

"So what's on your mind, then?"

"Are you and Sam together?"

Fuck, was not prepared for that. Should've been but wasn't. After all, Cam was the only one in the house not distracted by sports, booze, or currently punch-drunk on love, and Sam and I *had* gotten off eight feet from his head a few weeks ago. "Um, no?" Wait, that wasn't supposed to have a question mark. Lee from statistics was rubbing off on me.

"So...you're just hooking up, then?"

Double-wide trailer of fucks.

I squinted at Cam. When in doubt, stay quiet. That was challenging, though, because I wasn't the quiet type. My tongue liked to flap even when my brain was on standby. "I...um...no. We're not. We're just—" I tapered off to regroup and organize. "What?" That worked while I prepared to apologize for our couch antics.

He chuckled softly. "When he came in here earlier to grab breakfast. You offered him some of your omelet." When I didn't bite—even though he was making a very good point because I was a selfish bastard who never offered my food to anyone—he continued, "And then he just stood there and watched you cook with this expression like he was watching Namath and the Jets win the '69 Superbowl."

I didn't get the reference, but I sort of got the gist. "Oh. Well. We just blow off steam together sometimes. It's not a thing." I felt bad about lying outright, but fudging a little bit was okay.

"Really?"

"Yeah, no. It's just some fun. But maybe you could not mention it to anyone?" Eww, no, even fudging it felt kind of wrong. I kept thinking of the stupor I'd walked around in for seventy-two hours after Sam and I had hooked up in the laundry room. The initial high had lasted a solid twenty-four hours, then it'd been re-upped when we decided to do an impromptu video the next day of Sam railing the hell out of me over his desk. And then twenty-four hours after that, I got home late from Fuego and saw light coming from underneath his door and figured I'd say hello. Except when I opened the door he was wearing some dorky-adorable clear plastic-framed glasses because he couldn't find his other pair, and somehow in helping him look for them around his room, I ended up riding his cock.

We'd forgotten the camera that time, too.

"I'll keep it to myself, sure. I was just curious." Cam propped his chin on his fist, bright eyes roaming my face. "For the record: if you ever find yourself in need of someone else to blow off steam with, I think you're pretty great. You're really hot, and we get along well. I'm not clingy or weird about shit." He ran a hand over his mouth and shook his head. "I guess I'm probably off-limits for all kinds of reasons—probably really good ones. But I promise my head isn't as much of a mess as it used to be, and I'm good at keeping things on the down low if that's what you like."

I nodded mutely, feeling like I'd walked into the twilight zone. Not in a bad way; I liked Cam just fine. We'd been friendly for months and hung out together more now that he moved in, but I hadn't necessarily gotten the vibe he was interested. I wondered if this was how Eric had felt around me when I was crushing on him? Then decided probably not, because I'd never told Eric. Nate probably had, though, because I'd gotten all fumey with jealousy at first when I'd found out they were hooking up.

"Thank you," I said, then laughed self-consciously. "That's a really weird thing to say thank you to, I guess."

Cam burst into laughter, too. "You totally just did the verbal equivalent of a left swipe. Ouch."

"I did." I buried my face in my hands. "God, now I feel like an asshole. Damn, you're so direct. It caught me off guard."

"Sorry, side effect of rehab and NA. I don't dance around things much anymore. Staying honest with myself and everyone else is the best shot I have at staying sober. Don't feel bad, though—I just think you're cool, so I figured I'd tell you. No harm, no foul." He stood from the table and carried his cereal bowl to the sink. "And I won't mention anything about you and Sam. Not my business."

We both glanced at the back door as Sam slammed back through it. "Forgot my phone." He glanced around and spotted it on the counter near the toaster.

"I'm out. Catch you later," Cam said and thundered upstairs whistling.

Sam tucked his phone in his back pocket and eyed me. "Everything okay? You're doing your uncomfortable smile." His gaze strayed to the door as he frowned. "Did Cam say something?"

"No. Not at all. What's this uncomfortable smile you're talking about?"

"The one that looks like you picked it up off a dirty Walmart aisle, dusted it off, and slapped it on your face."

"Wow, vivid."

"There's your real one. Way better." Sam grinned. "I meant to mention earlier my parents will be here for homecoming, and I'm getting a bunch of really good seats for them and some of the other guys. Would you come? My brothers and sisters will be there, too." He sucked on his lower lip, brows furrowed like he wasn't sure what I'd say.

"You want me to meet your family?"

"I mean, in a no-pressure way because I know we're casual and stuff, and they don't exactly know what's been going on, but—"

"Sure." I pressed up onto my toes and smeared a clumsy kiss along his jaw before Sam caught me by the elbows to keep me steady. I'd never met another guy's parents before. I mean, on purpose. There'd been a few unfortunate morning-after meetings in my past, which had not been my finest hour. But despite the nervous butterflies that erupted in my stomach over the prospect, Sam's resulting smile made me decide I'd chosen the correct response.

He let me go. "I'm gonna be late. See you in statistics, yeah?"

28

JESSE

The game was tied at the half, and when the third quarter started, I was on the edge of my seat.

"Watching this live is twenty times more stressful than watching it on TV," I complained.

Mark chuckled. "What you meant to say was, 'watching this live is twenty times more *awesome* than watching it on TV.' Look at these fucking seats! I can see the edges of the jockstraps beneath the tights!"

Chet smacked him lightly on the back of the head. "Watch it."

Mark wasn't wrong, though. I should've been enjoying it. Or, at least enjoying the visuals, because Sam dressed out in his football gear made my knees weak. He looked like he could eat me for breakfast. I wished he *had* eaten me for breakfast, but he'd had to be at the stadium early. Every down, every tackle, every time someone raced toward him or vice versa, I broke out in a fresh wave of nervous sweat, afraid he was going to injure his shoulder again. I could tell it was bothering him by the way he was leading with the other one, but he was doing his best to play it down so he could stay on the field.

A whooshing cheer went up as Sam scored a first down, racing toward the goal line with the ball tucked under his arm. He looked big and powerful, a tree I wanted to climb and make a fort in and never leave. Everyone around me rose from their seats, and I joined, whooping and hollering until the opposing defense swarmed Sam, trying to keep him from scoring.

The din died down with a hush as the ref blew his whistle, and the players untangled themselves, leaving behind a single guy who didn't move.

My heart shot into my throat as I stood on my tiptoes trying to see, but I was too fucking short. I caught a glimpse of the U's colors, though, and my heart reversed course and plummeted from my throat to my toes.

"Hey." Nate squeezed my shoulder reassuringly. "It's not him."

"You sure?"

He nodded. "It's Mischka. Looks like a broken ankle."

"God." I exhaled a long breath. I didn't know who Mischka was and didn't care. He wasn't Sam. That was all that mattered. "I need a tranquilizer to watch this shit."

Nate chuckled and threw an arm around me. "Sam is big, quick, and sturdy as hell. He's gonna be fine."

"Yeah, I'm sure everyone says that until they're laid out on the field with their tibia sticking out of their leg. Wait." I swiveled toward Nate. "How did you..." I narrowed my eyes at Eric, though he was leaned over chatting with one of Sam's brothers. "Eric sold me out."

Everyone sat as Mischka was hauled off the field. The players milled around waiting on the refs. Sam glanced over in our direction and that alone made me catch my breath. A loopy smile curled on my lips.

Nate nudged me. "That right there; you're selling yourself out. Eric only mentioned you had a crush on a baby bi. So does Sam know how stupid you are for him?"

"Sort of. I don't know. We're just keeping it casual and stuff."

"Uh-huh. Casual works great until it doesn't." The knowing roll of Nate's eyes flustered me.

"Plenty of people do casual long term and it's just fine." I didn't sound remotely convincing.

"Uh-huh."

"Shhh, I'm trying to concentrate."

By the fourth quarter the U was leading by seven, and they shut out Southerland as the clock wound down for a solid Homecoming win.

I had to admit that even if it was nerve-racking being so close to the edge of the field, the rush of winning and the energetic charge of the crowd made me understand why people got addicted to this game. It also helped that Sam had made it through the game without getting hurt.

"C'mon," Nate urged as people spilled onto the field. "Let's go celebrate."

I hesitated until he yanked me after him.

Sam's family walked en masse toward where he stood talking to a reporter holding out his phone for Sam to speak into, and the anxious tickling feeling in my stomach started up all over again. His parents had gotten delayed when one of Sam's sisters had broken her arm after falling off a piece of gym equipment right before they were about to leave. They'd gotten to their seats just before the anthem was sung. My introduction had been a brief wave and then a short conversation during half-time. They seemed really nice, but I really wanted to make a good impression and I was afraid I'd say or do something dumb. It had me on edge.

As we walked onto the field, Nate and Eric got sidetracked when they spotted Amanda. I waved to her as I tried to figure out what I was supposed to be doing, stuck in some kind of weird social limbo among several different circles.

I offered Reid a polite smile when he tipped me an acknowledging nod, relieved to have closure with him and no longer actively stoking an inferno of hatred inside me. Now it was just the tiniest flicker of a flame.

He waved me over, but I shook my head, my smile faltering as he trotted toward me.

"I'm so glad you came," he said, out of breath. "This is actually perfect."

He didn't think I'd come for him, did he? I frowned as I thumbed behind me. "Sam got all of us seats."

"Pros of having a player for a roomie, right?" He slung an arm over my shoulder, and it caught me so off guard that even when he started navigating me across the grass, I didn't immediately shrug him off. He leaned too close, speaking confidentially. "Okay, listen. I need the hugest favor ever, and you're literally one of the nicest guys I've ever known and the only one I can ask to do this. I'll even pay you if you want."

"Hold up." I slowed my steps, but he kept urging us forward. "Do what?"

"I need you to be my boyfriend again for, like, five minutes. Just five minutes. I just need to introduce you to this reporter, and then you can walk away. I mean, I'd take you for my boyfriend for longer than that, but you already said—"

"What the fuck?"

Reid gestured toward something—I wasn't sure what—and

turned to me, his eyes pleading. "Five minutes. It could mean my future."

"But why? No, wait, just no—"

"Five hundred dollars. C'mon. Five minutes. That's nothing."

"There he is!" A tall guy with a swoopy brown coif, holding a microphone, rushed forward and stopped in front of us. "Great game, Reid. That play-action pass in the third quarter really showed the speed gains you've made." I tried to slide from beneath Reid's arm, but he gripped me tighter. The reporter looked me over, his smile gleaming. "Might this be the mysterious boyfriend we've heard so much about?"

No. No fucking way.

Reid's desperation was telegraphed to me on its own fucking wavelength as he said, "Yes," and leaned in to kiss my cheek.

"No." I leaned back at the same time, and his lips smushed awkwardly over my jaw.

"We're having a bit of a…a disagreement, actually." That was Reid; in for a penny, in for a pound.

When the reporter cocked his head, I nodded emphatically. "He's right. We are."

Three years I'd stewed over the things I wished I'd said to Reid the day I caught him cheating. Three years I'd been polite, always made way for him and others like him. I didn't stir up shit, I listened when people needed an ear, I fed people when they were hungry. I cooked and cleaned and fucking took care of people, and I was *happy* to do it for the most part because I was good at it, and because, sure, a certain part of me liked feeling needed and useful. And nine times out of ten, people were grateful and didn't take advantage of me.

In the back of my mind, I could admit I'd always hoped that

at some point maybe the same would happen to me in return. That karma would reward my good behavior and mete out the punishment guys like Reid deserved. But the second I'd felt Reid's desperate gaze on my face and the *yes* slipped out of his mouth, so confident that I, once again, would look out for *his* best interests, I finally fucking got it. There was only so much you could do for a person who was only capable of taking.

Sometimes karma needed a helping hand to balance the scales.

I stood a little taller. "See, three years ago, when I was a naive little freshman, a naive, romance-loving gay boy ecstatic about freshman year of college, I met Reid here." Reid cocked his head, brows pensive like he wasn't sure whether this was going to go well for him or not. I smiled at him, and the confusion evaporated as his shoulders slumped. Guess he wasn't confused anymore. I swatted him away when he made a grab for my arm. "I met him the second week of school. My first-ever boyfriend, and it was everything high school Jesse had dreamed about. We were madly in love. He told me daily. Even hours before I walked in on him with someone else. So my argument falls heavily on the 'I'm not the mysterious boyfriend' end, considering we haven't been together in years—though he did offer me money to pretend."

"You're lying." Reid exhaled a noisy, frustrated sigh.

"What the fuck?" Sam's voice boomed from behind. "Did you just say you're with Jesse?" He shoved Reid's shoulder.

Reid staggered back a step before rebounding with a glare. "What's your problem, Harding? You've been a dick to me all semester. Is this roommate loyalty bullshit, or are you changing teams late in the game?" he smirked at his own wit.

"Stop," I cried, trying to step between them, but Sam was already lunging forward to shove Reid again, this time with more fervor.

"What if I did? You have a problem if he's with me?"

Reid took a menacing step forward and then stopped, his mouth falling open as he looked between the two of us, though it was Sam he addressed. "*Are* you with him?"

"I. We—" His gaze darted over to me and then over his shoulder at his family behind him before shooting back to me. There was a plea in his eyes, but I wasn't sure how to read it. The old scripts kicked in and my heart turned itself inside out. *This is why you don't mess with baby bi's,* an insidious voice in the back of my head insisted, even as I tried to mute it.

I was hyperaware of all the eyes on me. So much for making a good impression. Heat flooded my face as Sam's dad's brows furrowed and his mom's pinched together with what looked like concern. The voice inside my head got louder.

"He's a great piece of ass, but I'm sure—"

Whatever Reid had been about to say next was lost to the breeze, possibly along with a tooth or two as Sam's fist connected with his jaw. Chaos erupted and I got jostled and shoved as teammates, coaching assistants, and a ref surged forward to break them up.

I stumbled backward, the spots of heat in my cheeks becoming a lake of fire.

Something bumped against the side of my face, and I whipped a look aside to find the reporter, his mic an inch from my lips. His smile was falsely apologetic even as he asked, "Any comment?"

"Fuck off," I said, and then stepped around him and fought my way through the crowd as I sped toward the other side of the field, desperate to get away from everyone's stares. The logical part of my brain said that none of this was my fault, but the other half, the larger one said I'd made a scene. Sadly, another thing I'd learned over the years was that you could run away from a lot, but it was impossible to outrun your own humiliation. That didn't mean I wouldn't give it the ol' college try.

29

SAM

Right after the clock ran down at the end of the game, I'd started toward Jesse as he streamed onto the field with everyone else. Then I'd gotten sideswiped in a tackle by my brother Tanner. Despite being half a foot shorter than me, he tried to noogie me as he wrestled me to the ground.

"Stop, dude, stop. I have to—"

"Samson." My dad's voice boomed out, pride heaped in his tone. "Looking strong."

"Th—"

My mom was right on his heels. "I brought your favorite brownies."

"Oh gr—"

"Can I run around the field?" Tanner shouted.

"*No!*" came a chorus of three voices, including mine.

This was what a big family was like: speaking in short bursts because inevitably someone would interrupt. I'd had grand plans to introduce my folks to Jesse in a less boisterous setting earlier as a prelude to hopefully introducing him as my boyfriend at some point, but the fresh new cast on Cassie's arm had thrown a wrench in that.

Suddenly I was surrounded by all of my family members, which was usually great and supportive and all, except when I was trying to get to the guy who'd given me such a huge, sweet smile in the third quarter that I'd almost fumbled a pass with the realization that I really needed him to know, for better or worse, that I'd fallen for him.

"I have to—"

"And I've got fried chicken. Enough for all your roommates, too. I left it in the car. I figured we'd drive over and get it all set up while you wrap up," Mom droned, and I nodded absently, looking around to see where Jesse had gone.

From the corner of my eye, I spotted Reid with his arm around Jesse.

Oh hell no. The same infusion of adrenaline that'd fueled me through multiple pile-ups, three completed receptions, and a half dozen first downs during the game earlier surged through me with renewed force, filling me with the irrepressible desire to punt Reid in the direction of the goalposts.

"I'm in love with my roommate, and I have to go make sure he understands that," I said barked out. "Make way." I shouldered through my two brothers and started after Jesse.

Later I'd have time to appreciate how utterly still and quiet everyone got at once for literally the first time since I'd been alive.

"We love you, honey!" my mom called from behind me.

"Is he gay?" I heard Tanner ask as I trotted off.

And then everything had gone sideways.

Coach's scowling face was suddenly in mine as I was hauled from the ground, Reid next to me.

"Whose fault is it?" Coach shouted between us. "Never mind, I don't give a good goddamn whose fault it is. We still have games left and if you two don't pull your heads out of your asses and act right, I'll bench both of you for the rest of the season."

No way he'd bench Reid, but I wasn't about to say that. Me, it was 50/50 either way.

"Apologize to each other," Coach demanded.

We did so in a begrudging mumble that wasn't convincing to anyone. I imagined we were in for the extended uncut version when we got to the locker room.

I grimaced, rubbing my shoulder, and glanced out over the field at Jesse moving away. Every shrinking inch of him twisted the knife in my heart harder.

He hated feeling like a fool, hated looking like one even worse. Just like I'd fumbled on the field earlier when he'd smiled at me, I'd fumbled as I'd walked toward him and Reid. I'd made a scene and put Jesse in the middle of it, and then I'd verbally flailed when Reid asked us if we were together because I wasn't sure if Jesse wanted me to say anything. The look in his eyes had answered the question well enough, though.

The team headed toward the locker room, but another look at Jesse's clipped movements had me peeling off in his direction. It couldn't wait until later.

Jesse cast a glance over his shoulder at me, nostrils flaring, and then he sped up, too. "Go away, Sam. I have terrible resolve, and I'm bad at articulating properly when I'm upset."

"Okay, all of that last part makes it sound like a pretty good time to approach you, honestly."

"God, I'm so embarrassed right now."

"You shouldn't be. Reid's the one who looks like a dumbass. You were just setting the record straight."

Jesse huffed out a sigh. "I just can't believe he blindsided me once again. I *hate* being caught off guard. I *hate* looking like a dumbass. Especially on a repeat basis. And *especially* in front of your parents. And then there was that whole awkward moment where you didn't know what to say about us and..." He shook his head.

"I know," I said breathlessly. "Could you slow down a little?"

"No. Use your big-ass redwood quads to keep up."

"I like *GBBO*. I was kind of skeptical at first, but I'm a fan now. And I like watching it with you. I don't want to watch it by myself."

"Okay, well, you didn't have to do any of that shit back there for that to continue."

"I checked out *Thrice Bound by Oath* from the library, too." I grimaced. "I actually didn't like those, but I can see why you did. All the characters have their own code of ethics, even when they're shitty ones and you love them even when they make mistakes and do questionable shit constantly."

"Okay, again not seeing the point."

I sped around Jesse and dropped to one knee in front of him.

He pulled up short, eyes flaring wide. "What on earth are you doing?"

"I don't know." I threw up my hands in desperation. "It's an oath of fealty or something. I'm trying to get you to stop and actually listen to me."

The corners of Jesse's mouth twitched briefly. "An oath of fealty? Holy shit, you *did* read the books."

"Yeah, and Damian was a total horse's ass in all of book

eight, and it really fucking pissed me off. He didn't deserve Landon. Not that Landon was any fucking prize for the first half of the book, anyway. When he pulled that shit with—" I shook my head. "Anyway. Yeah, I read every single one. Now please listen to my...moment for a minute. Fuck." I squeezed my eyes shut. "I really wish I had a better plan or, like, a boom box or something."

"Would it play Peter Gabriel?"

"That was a good song. But nah, probably I'd pick that one you love by the Jonas Brothers. 'Only Human'? *Goddammit.* See." I pointed an accusing finger up at him. "This is you doing your Jesse thing. You're deflecting. Classic defense. You're really fucking good at it, and honestly, it's kind of one of the things I like about you." I frowned. That had slipped in there. Whatever. "Like really, really like. Like...*love* about you, actually." I peered up at him, unnerved by how absolutely awful I was at anything approaching romance. Maybe I should just cut to the chase. "I want you to be mine. My partner, my boyfriend, whatever you want to call it. Call me traditional, but I want it to be official. I don't want there to be any fucking doubt who you're with. I don't want to have to look to you and try to figure out how to answer. I want it to be well-known. I'm sorry for causing more of a scene with Reid, but I saw him next to you and it pissed me off and I reacted impulsively. The idea of you with *anyone* else turns my stomach."

"It does?"

I nodded. "You're the first person I look for in any room. I hear you louder than anyone else. Even when you're quiet. Sometimes *especially* when you're quiet. I've never wanted to be with someone else as much as I want to be with you. Making you happy makes *me* happy. I've never felt that with someone else either. Everything about you makes me feel impulsive and excitable, and it's both scary and exhilarating as hell."

Jesse's lips formed a soft O, and I couldn't tell whether or not that was a good thing. But when in doubt, offense. "So here's what I know is true. One, this is definitely the worst love declaration ever, and I'm sorry about that. I'll try to think of something better and we can have a redo if you'll let me. Two, I want to watch *GBBO* with you every day. I want to study with you and be with you and cuddle with you, and sleep in your bed and do...*fuck*...do all the really sexy things we've been doing together that I had no idea I was missing until I met you. You have the softest lips, and even kissing you is hotter that any sex I've ever had." I swept a hand back through my hair, and it came away damp with nervous sweat. "You told me not to fall in love with you, and I failed. I usually hate failing anything. But I'm not sorry this time."

"You love me?" Jesse whispered, and I nodded, starting to rise. "Don't get up yet!"

"Okay." I waited, dimly aware of the crowd still on the field behind Jesse, and my family, along with Nate, Eric, Reid, Mark, and Chet staring at us.

"Say that part about my lips being soft again. And then tell me who killed Elspeth in book six."

"Your lips are soft, and you're a really good kisser. The best. You're also great at cooking, which I've always said. You're smart, and funny, and being around you makes me feel really good, like everything will be all right. You're a great cuddler, and you're not a pushover, though I know you think you are sometimes. That's because you're a genuinely fucking nice person who cares about other people, and that's not a defect, it's a fucking asset, Jesse." I sucked in a breath. "Heinrich killed Elspeth in book six, which also pissed me off, and since we're being brutally honest, I really wanted to quit then, but I had this whole game plan about how I was going to finish the entire series and then casually drop spoilers into conversation one day and impress you."

"That would've been impressive. But this isn't bad either." Jesse grabbed my jersey and tugged, urging me upright and looping his arms around my neck. His warm hands cupped my sweaty cheeks, and his magnetic eyes snared my gaze as he lifted onto the balls of his feet.

I felt the kiss he brushed over lips all the way to the marrow of my bones.

"I'm totally going to cry now," he whispered and tipped his head toward the sky, but I angled his face right back down and then gently swiped my thumbs over his tears.

He buried his face against my chest, and we stood like that for a few minutes with our arms wrapped around each other before he lifted his gaze to mine. "I love you, too. And for the record, I need to confess that I didn't want to go on that date with John, I just told myself I should because I was scared. And there's never been a chance in hell that I would now or *ever* have gotten back together with Reid, but if either of those things made you even a tiny bit jealous, I'm not going to complain, because I really wanted you to be mine, too. I'd convinced myself I couldn't have you."

"I'm yours," I promised, and saying the words out loud made my heart swell in my chest with the *rightness* of them.

"Guys like me typically only get guys like you in the movies, you realize," he said softly.

"Technically we've made a lot of movies together," I reminded him. I kissed him again through his laughter and then glanced over his shoulder as someone whooped. Half the crowd was huddled en masse facing us like a human satellite dish. In the distance, Joel lifted one hand, flashing me a thumbs-up.

Jesse dragged the tip of his nose over my neck, his breath warm on my skin. "Everyone's looking at us, aren't they?"

"Yeah, but it's okay. I promise."

A squawk of feedback had us both reeling as Coach stepped forward with a megaphone in one hand while he waved his clipboard in the other. "Wrap it up, Harding. We ain't done here yet."

Jesse pecked me once more on the lips. "Go. I'll see you back at the house."

"Fuck, okay." I wished we could just turn around and walk home right now, crawl in his bed, and shut out the world.

I left him behind reluctantly and trotted back across the grass.

When I stopped in front of my family, they all fell silent. "Wow. I had no idea it was possible to get everyone to be quiet at once." Joel chuckled, and my dad reached out and gave me a solid smack on the arm. I fumbled over what to say. "Am I supposed to say something meaningful here? Because I'm kinda out of gas." I thumbed over my shoulder. "That's my roommate Jesse. He's feeling embarrassed right now over some shit that's not his fault, so when you get back to the house, can you be really fucking nice to him? Because he's also the guy I'm in love with, and it'd mean a lot to me. I had a different plan for how that intro was gonna go, but it didn't work out, so..."

My mom swooped her arms around me and squeezed me so tight I struggled to breathe. "Of course, sweetheart." She cupped my cheeks in her warm hands and smiled up at me. "You make me so proud for so many reasons."

"*Harding!*" Coach hollered through the megaphone again, and my mom released me.

"Go, we'll be at your place setting up for dinner."

I loped toward the locker rooms with one last glance over my shoulder at my family's smiling faces, and not even the prospect of being reamed out by Coach and probably having to apologize to Reid again could take away the happiness bubbling inside me.

30

JESSE

I swear Sam's dad took up two-thirds of our kitchen just standing in front of the stove heating something on top of it that I couldn't see. Meanwhile, Sam's mom, Carla, bustled around pulling foil from the tops of dishes and barking orders at the other kids, instantly making herself at home. She had the same warm vibe Sam had, and I was instantly drawn to her.

"Can I help with anything?" I offered, and she smiled kindly to me, brown eyes twinkling. Her smile reminded me of Sam's.

I'd gotten home before they arrived and had just enough time to get to my room, have a cross between a breakdown and the kind of hysterical fit of excitement usually reserved for Harry Styles—because, let's face it, Sam was my own version of Harry Styles—then pulled myself together and went back downstairs as the doorbell rang. All of them had clustered at the front door, each with a dish in their hand, Carla leading the charge. The gratitude I felt when not a damn one of them said anything about what had happened on the football field was so great that I almost burst into tears of joy on the spot.

"Nah. We've got a system down pat. Don't mind us taking over the kitchen."

"No one's going to complain."

"I hear you're quite the cook. Sam says you taught him how to make chicken cordon bleu."

I laughed at the memory, even as my cheeks heated for what had come afterward. "Yeah, sort of."

She looked me over more carefully. "I can tell he's over the moon for you, you know. All through high school, he was more into sports and his friends than getting around with girls. But he talks about you all the time. Jesse this, Jesse that." Her smile widened. "Oh, you're a blusher. Well, you'll get over that quick enough with us."

She laughed as I rubbed my cheeks dramatically, and then my smile faltered. "I feel like I should say something about what happened on the field, because I don't want you to have this awful first impression of me. It's a really long story, but—" I stopped as she laid a hand on my shoulder.

"Do you care for my son?"

I swallowed and nodded. "Very much. He's like…like all the birthday wishes I made but never got, stored up and rolled into one big gift I received at a time when I needed it most."

"Then that's all I need to know. The rest is between the two of you." She winked at me. "The only thing I'm going to hold against you is that he says you make Rotel better than mine."

"Oh, well, I can share the secret to that easy."

"Then I'd say we're golden."

"I didn't mean to eat that much." Chet groaned and collapsed onto one of the couches next to Mark and slumped against his shoulder.

"You say that at least once a day. You think you'd learn."

"Glutton for punishment. I wouldn't be with you, otherwise."

"You'll regret that."

"Now or later?"

Chet's smile took on a wicked curve. "Later."

I made a half-hearted grab for the TV remote and when I missed, gave up and collapsed back on the other couch. "I'm still trying to figure out which of you is the bigger asshole in this pairing."

Predictably, they both pointed at each other.

"Mark, definitely," Nate said, a drumstick in his hand as he and Eric wandered in from the kitchen. How he was still eating was beyond me.

Mark seesawed his hand, and I broke into a stupid grin as Sam appeared behind Nate and Eric.

"Your family is so nice." I made room for him as he approached, dropped onto the couch next to me, and wrapped me in his arms, my own human cocoon. I loved it. "They want you to come over Christmas if you can." He rubbed his lips back and forth over the crown of my head and then pecked me on the temple.

"Wow. When you two are in, you're in." Nate gaped at us.

"Could've seen that one coming." Ansel smirked.

Sam and I both looked over at him. "How?" I asked. "You're hardly ever here in the first place. Have you ever even seen us hanging out together? Until tonight, the last time I saw you was a week ago when you forgot your extra pair of running shoes."

Ansel twisted the cap off his beer and flicked it at Sam, then indulged in a leisurely swallow of his beer, evidently enjoying our rapt attention. "Freshman year. The two of you."

"I hardly knew him freshman year," I countered. "I knew him by face only, because he was friends with Nate." I wasn't going to bring up waving a dildo in front of him shortly before collapsing into my pity party.

"That may be what you remember, but it's not the full story."

"Quit being cryptic, dude." Sam's voice dipped low the way it tended to when he was starting to get agitated.

Ansel waved the mouth of his beer bottle back and forth between us. "You two were making out one night like the world was about to end."

I glanced at Sam. "Pretty sure we'd remember that. Sam, any recollection?"

"None."

"Same."

Ansel laughed. "I don't know about Sam, but Jesse, you told me to forget what I'd seen and to never ever, ever speak of it again. I couldn't tell if you were really upset or really excited, but you were definitely really drunk. It was outside one of the frat houses. I didn't know who you were back then, but Sam I recognized from the football team."

I squinted at him. "And you witnessed this how?"

"I was taking a run."

"What time was it?"

"I don't know, four in the morning?"

"Who the fuck goes for a run at four in the morning?"

"Someone who wants to get some miles in before practice at five?"

"What frat house?" Nate asked.

I shook my finger at him. "Don't feed the troll, Sanders."

Ansel's cackle was remarkably troll-like. "I can't remember. The one that's near the greenway. Kappa maybe?"

"Wait, was this early fall?" Nate again, sounding thoughtful this time.

"Yep."

"Holy shit." Nate turned to Sam. "Remember that Kappa party when I found you passed out cuddling a tree—incidentally, quite close to the running trails? You were still hammered when we woke you up. Mark helped me lug you back to your dorm, and you kept talking about making out with someone, but you were hardly speaking English by that point. *And—*" Nate turned toward me next. "—this was the same night after you and Reid broke up. You got absolutely blitzed at that same party. You were so hungover you didn't make it to any classes the next day, remember? You went through a whole sixer of Gatorade I brought you. It was the same night you wrote all that random shit on Reid's door."

"Oh my god." I squinted, trying to dredge up any memory of Sam and coming up empty. Still, I couldn't discount it as a logical possibility.

The skepticism in Sam's expression vanished. "Holy shit. The one random memory fragment I have of that night was of writing on a door with Sharpie marker." He cut a look at me. "Do you remember this?"

"I have a vague impression of kissing someone. Like, their lips. And something about Reid's door. Of taping the dildo there. But it's really blurry." I covered my face. "I thought it was a girl I kissed, though. I don't even know why. And I don't remember anyone with me at Reid's dorm. You don't remember at all?"

Sam shook his head. "Not even a little. That's fucking wild. And kinda scary."

I frowned at Ansel. "Why did I ask you not to tell anyone?"

"Beats the fuck out of me." He shrugged. "At the time, I figured maybe one or both of you were in the closet, so of course I didn't say anything. I didn't want to be responsible for outing someone. And then you never mentioned it again, so neither did I. So you two have been hooking up since then?"

"What? No!"

"Only since early this fall," Sam said and wrapped his arms around my shoulders.

Mark spluttered. "Are you kidding me? That long? I was thinking a couple of weeks."

"*Aha!* Now you know what it feels like to be completely blindsided by your roomies like I was when I walked into the kitchen to find you and Chet." I smirked and craned my neck to glance up at Sam with a grin. "That's kinda where it all started, isn't it?"

"Shower," he amended

"Shower," I echoed, wiggling my shoulders against the rumble in his chest.

"Holy shit." Mark's bewildered exclamation had all of us cracking up. "This house has some kind of mystical power, I guess. Chet and I are the outliers. Does that mean Cam and Ansel are next?"

Cam raised his hands. "Leave me out of this one." He gestured across his forehead. "Pretty sure 'hot mess' is written right there."

"You're not a hot mess. You've cleaned up well enough in my opinion." I swatted him.

"The person I'm hooking up with doesn't go to the U, so I think it's safe to say the curse...or blessing, as it were, ends with you two." Ansel took another swallow of his beer and set it aside. "What? You think I don't have a social life? What do you think I do all the time?" he asked when we all stared flatly at him.

"Run?" I suggested.

"Bury bodies in the woods," Mark offered.

"Jerk off with your own tears?" Nate's contribution.

"He probably has a harem somewhere." That was Eric's deduction. "I get that kind of vibe."

"I keep my business to myself." Ansel lifted one shoulder and maintained his cryptic smile even when Nate shoved him.

"It bothers me that I don't remember kissing you," Sam said as we brushed our teeth and got ready for bed later. "Though the first time we kissed, which I guess was technically our second kiss, something felt familiar. I got the tiniest sense of déjà vu. I couldn't place it, I just knew I liked it. Did you have the same feeling?"

I tore off a piece of dental floss, handed it to him, and he murmured a *thanks, baby* that went right to my fucking heart and melted it from the inside. I loved that he just slid into the endearment and fully embraced it. "I wish I did, but I don't. At all."

"Maybe we weren't standing up." Sam waggled his brows at me.

"You could be right. Nate said something about you hugging a tree. Maybe we were sitting against it. Which reminds me"—I untwisted the floss from my finger and tossed it in the trash—"we need to do some more outside stuff, probably. I mean, assuming you still want to make videos?"

"Fuck yeah I want to, unless you don't want to." Sam paused

in his flossing, eyes cutting to mine in the mirror. "Then we won't."

I shook my head rapidly. "I still want to do them. I love doing them with you." I loved exploring fantasies with him and the thrill that doing so on camera provided.

Sam smiled shyly. "Okay, good. Because I really like doing them with you, too."

"Do you think we did anything else that night we kissed?" I asked a second later. The thought had been circling around my mind.

"Considering we were both that slammed, I'm not sure how...functional either of us were."

"The spirit may have been willing, but the flesh was very definitely—"

"Flaccid."

I curled my lip. "Gross. Never say that word again. It belongs in the retch closet with all the other words we do not ever speak."

"Like what?"

"Like moist. And lickety split. Snatch. Broth." I ticked them off on my fingers and made a gagging sound as I shuddered.

Sam spit out the water he was swishing with and grinned shamelessly. "I thought moist was a good thing. I like getting certain parts of you really moist."

"Please don't force me to break up with you before we've really gotten started."

Sam pulled me in close and pushed a hand down the back of my pants, fingers following the curve of my ass. If he spread his fingers, he could probably grip the whole thing. The thought had me rubbing needily against him. "Maybe we just need to retrain your brain. Replace the current association with a much more pleasant one." He laid a string of sucking kisses up the side of my neck as he pressed a finger between my cheeks, and my head fell back like rag doll's. Then he licked a spot just under my earlobe, and my entire body broke out in goose bumps the way a peacock's feathers suddenly shot up.

"Okay," I said faintly, already convinced he'd change my mind in under five minutes.

But I'd make him work for it.

EPILOGUE
JESSE

"How we doing?" Sam charged into our tiny galley kitchen with a towel thrown over his shoulder and came to a stop behind me, peering around me into the various pots I had on the stove. "You need me to get anything? Table is set, I got out all those fancy dishes you wanted. Oh, and I went ahead and did a load of laundry and put it away. I found that sock you'd been looking for, too. The one with the stripe. It fell behind the washer. Shit, I need to put that beer and wine in the fridge, I for—*mpppph*."

He melted into the kiss I twisted around and laid on him, and I could feel his heart speeding up beneath the bit of his shirt I'd clutched in my hand to bring him down to my level.

The only reason I had no regrets about cutting the kiss short was because it meant I got to see that goofy grin spread over his face afterward like sunlight creeping across a forest floor, warming everything in its path.

"What was that for?"

"Because I love it when you get more keyed up than me."

"It's our first Friendsgiving. Chet's Mr. Fancy Law Student. Eric designs fucking bridges or whatever. Nate's working for a senator, and Mark...well, Mark has a big fat trust fund, even if he is going to be a teacher. I design workouts and meal plans."

"Your competitive streak comes out at the strangest times." It was especially fun when it came out in the bedroom, but Sam did have his keeping up with the Joneses moments where he felt like he was low man on the ladder of life achievements—which was both ridiculous and ridiculously endearing to me. "You don't just design workout plans. Remember that guy who lost a hundred pounds? You help people become stronger and healthier. You help them build or rebuild confidence. That's not nothing. And, you should totally show everyone the blueprints for Fuel."

Sam was opening his first gym in the spring with some of our OnlyFans earnings and had spent the past year prepping for it, meeting with architects to design the interior of the warehouse space he'd rented, building his own workout programs, and tapping his old football buddies at the U for marketing help here and there. I was certain it would be an amazing success, but the closer we got to it, the more anxious Sam got.

"Show them, they'll love it." I kissed him again, softer, when he hedged. "It's going to be great." And then I had to turn away because my eyes were brimming the way they sometimes did when my heart got too full too fast. It was the love version of brain freeze where I got bowled over by all that I had now: by the man standing behind me, our small but cozy apartment with a view of City Park below, the best coffee roasters ever on the first floor, a job I loved, and cooking classes I loved even more.

But mostly because of the man standing behind me.

Sam folded me into his arms, his words rumbling close next to my ear. "You doing that thing where you tear up, baby?"

"Maybe." I stuck a spatula in the mashed potatoes and stirred them with a sigh. "You take such good care of me, and I'm such a fucking sucker for it."

His lips moved over my neck. "I love taking care of you. Love making you feel good." My eyes fluttered shut as he slid a hand down the back of my pajama pants and cupped my ass. "Love everything about you, including this tight little ass."

"You're doing that on purpose." I tapered off on a moan as I pushed back against him.

"Maybe." He swatted my asscheek with a chuckle. "All right, let's get this show on the road."

MARK AND CHET ARRIVED FIRST. SAM LET THEM IN AND FIXED them up with a drink while I finished dealing with a turkey. I'd long learned one didn't just cook a turkey, one *dealt* with turkey. It was probably dumb to cook a whole bird for a bunch of heathens like us, especially when we'd all be eating plenty over the next few days, but between our crazy schedules, Sam and I didn't do a lot of entertaining at our place or have people over, so it was nice to do it for once.

"That smells amazing." Mark appeared in the doorway nursing a beer. "Sam must have cooked it."

"You're funny."

He winked.

"Sam does all right, though, as long as it's clean eating. If it's something delicious and savory, forget about it." I stirred the gravy on the stove and then turned the burner off.

"What's the status of the restaurant?"

"Pushed until summer because of a delay on some materials, but it's still happening. And that's actually better because I'll have officially graduated from culinary school by then." I'd kept my job as sous chef at Fuego for the rest of senior year and beyond when I started culinary school. I'd gotten really tight with the owner, and when he decided to open a new restaurant, he'd asked me to be part of the team doing it. I wasn't executive chef yet, but I took it as a sign that I was heading in that direction. I wanted to get enough hands-on training, and then I hoped to eventually open my own restaurant. Only Sam knew that, though. I was too afraid to speak it aloud to anyone else, yet, but we'd started putting our savings together for it, too.

"Keep us posted on the opening. Chet and I are definitely coming, even if I have to drag him out of the law library."

"I will," I promised and dried my hands on a towel as the doorbell rang again, and I heard the boom of Nate's voice as he came in.

Mark grabbed his beer as I checked the turkey one more time, then trailed him into the living room.

Sam grabbed Nate and Eric's coats and tossed them over the couch.

"Sorry we're late," Eric said. "Guess who doesn't know how to change a tire?"

"You?" Chet laughed.

Eric clenched Nate's shoulder. "Nope, this guy right here. Mr. Apple Pie and Baseball. Mr. All American Boy Next Door can't change a tire."

I squinted at Nate. "You helped me change my tire sophomore year after I ran over a nail. Or did I hallucinate that?"

"That was me." Nate's smirk morphed into a full-on grin and then laughter as Eric's grip on his shoulders tightened.

"You motherfucker. You were lying?"

Nate shrugged. "It's cold outside and the pants you're wearing dip nice and low when you bend over to do something like, say, change a tire."

Eric opened, then closed his mouth again and shook his head. "Well played, frat boy. That's next-level right there."

"Learned from a pro." Nate's laugh was shameless.

"Y'all hungry? The turkey's already ready, so we can go ahead and eat."

Everyone looked my way, and then Mark broke into a grin. "It's so weird for you to actually offer us food instead of bitch about us asking for it."

"One day only. Take advantage."

"Let's go for a walk," Sam suggested after we closed the door behind Nate and Eric. They'd stayed an hour after Mark and Chet had to get back on the road. There'd been talk of a ski trip over the holidays either this year or next.

I sagged back against the door with utter contentment. Everything had been a success. Tomorrow we'd go to Sam's house for actual Thanksgiving, and then mine for the day after Thanksgiving.

But Sam's suggestion made me suspicious. "Since when do you waste time walking when you could be running? And there's all those dishes to take care of."

"Since I can't convince you to run with me. It's a nice day out. Not too cold. C'mon. The dishes will wait." He opened the door, grabbed our jackets, and yanked me out with him whether I was ready or not.

We took the elevator down and walked outside our apartment building, the fall air nipping at our cheeks. But he was right; it wasn't too cold, and the leaves were gorgeous.

We walked down Main, and then Sam cut us down a side street, heading toward campus, seeming to have a destination in mind despite our leisurely pace.

Spring of senior year, we'd decided it made the most sense for us to stay in Silver Ridge because college students would be a boon to Sam's personal training and gym ventures, and I'd already established a solid rapport with Alexei from Fuego, who'd also written my recommendation letter for the culinary school forty-five minutes away. I'd had no trouble getting in.

So at first it had been a practical decision, but as we walked along the outskirts of campus, with its pretty brick edifices, green lawn, and clock tower, I was reminded of how much I'd fallen in love with the vibe of Silver Ridge as well.

I laced my fingers with Sam's, and he brushed a kiss over my temple as we walked alongside the gates surrounding the baseball team's practice field.

At the main gate leading onto the field, Sam stopped and pulled out a key.

I grabbed his wrist. "Where'd you get that? What are we doing?"

"So happens I've got a really good client who's the assistant coach." Sam bounced his brows at me. "What do you say we take a look inside?"

Sam unlocked the gate, and I waited just inside, gazing at the diamond and the dugout, as he locked up behind us. "It's a nice baseball diamond for sure."

"Forget the baseball diamond." Sam tugged my hand. "Check out those bleachers."

I stared at him sidelong, my blood catching fire. "Are we gonna..."

"We're absolutely gonna. Top five fantasy, right?"

"Oh my god." I clapped my hands to my cheeks, then turned to him and kissed him. "This is the best Thanksgiving ever."

He steered me underneath the bleachers, and then I felt his lips brushing the back of my neck as he reached around me and pointed out a bag. "Our gear."

"Gear?" I craned a backward look at him.

"Think I'm gonna skimp on the experience by not having the right outfits?"

My mouth dropped open as I approached the laundry-style bag and uncinched the top to reveal a bunch of football gear inside. "This is amazing," I breathed, my cock already half-hard just looking at the football tights.

"My old uniforms. *And* I stuck in something that could pass for coach gear, complete with a whistle and clipboard. So what's your pleasure, baby?"

"Two football players, easy. Oh god, I'm so fucking horny already. I'm going to come in two seconds." I tossed Sam his football gear. "Let's do this already."

Sam had even gotten me a smaller pair of football pants. "When did you do all of this?" I asked as I yanked them up my legs. Behind me, the rustle of fabric said he was doing the same.

"I've been thinking about it for a while. Found the pants you've got on sale when I was at a sporting goods store the other day. Figured it was a sign." The jacket he'd been wearing, along with his shirt, dropped with a whoosh to the ground beside me. "When I told you I was going for a run this morning, I dropped everything off."

"Very sneaky of you."

"Mm-hmm. Okay, you ready to turn around yet?"

"Yep. Count of three?"

On the three, we both turned around, my eyes immediately

zooming to the eggplant Sam's football pants were doing an absolute shit job of constraining.

Sam, in return, stared at me, then shook his head. "Goddamn, I..." He paused, then took a step back and looked me slowly up and down. "I kinda had a picture in my head of how you'd look, but wow."

Warmth spread over my cheeks. The good kind, though, that was more desire than self-consciousness. I stood still as Sam walked in a circle around me and stopped in front of me again.

I ran a finger along his waistband and traced along the rigid outline of his cock. "Now you know a fraction of what it was like watching you on the field." Or doing anything remotely athletic, really. Even the dingiest sweatpants were elevated to erotic art on Sam. "Thank goodness we didn't get together until senior year."

"Technically..."

"Good point. Maybe that was what was wrong with me until senior year. No one could hold a candle to our tryst outside Kappa."

"That neither of us could remember."

"Shhh." I gave him a little squeeze that made him curse. "So, being the smaller one, does that mean I'm the quarterback?"

"God yes. Which means you call the plays." Sam cursed again as I gave him a little squeeze. "Fuck, I think I'm already halfway to orgasm," he said with a sigh and then skimmed his hands over my ass.

I could tell this was going to go on our sexual replays and greatest-hits list and would no doubt be recorded for our OnlyFans at some point. But I was glad not to have to think about cameras today, because Sam coming undone before my eyes over me wearing football tights was enough to wreck me.

"First play," I started but didn't get the rest out before Sam kissed me, hard and aggressive. He backed us toward one of the bleacher supports until my spine met the metal, his arms coming up on either side to cling to the framing as his hips rolled and his hard cock rubbed insistently against mine.

"Fuck." I let out an undignified whimper at the friction and pushed up his football jersey, finding his nipples already pebbled from the cold. He loved when I played with them.

Sam licked the side of my neck, my throat, and sucked on my earlobe, every confident pass of his tongue breaking me out in shivers. Three years and he knew every single spot on my body, which combinations of hands and mouth would have me writhing and which he could use to draw me out, and I knew the same for him. That kind of intimacy was the most powerful aphrodisiac I'd ever experienced, and I was an absolute slave to it as much as Sam was. When I thought about all my bold talk senior year about how I'd just wanted to get laid, I realized Sam had been right back then. I hadn't just wanted to get laid. I'd wanted to feel known and understood and loved inside out the way Sam made me feel.

I tilted my head to the side, giving him full access, and he took the invitation, hot mouth stitching fiery kisses over my cool skin. "I interrupted you. I'm sorry," he muttered. "Got too excited. Wanna try again? What's the first play you're gonna call? Where do you want me?"

"On your knees," I whispered and had another one of those moments of utter blissed-out wonder when Sam dropped down immediately. Even on his knees he was big, rising well above my waist, and when he gazed up at me while rubbing his chin over the fabric covering my erection, I swallowed against the pleasure saturating my body. It took me a moment to get the words out coherently. "Suck me."

Keeping his gaze pinned to mine, he lowered the waistband on my tights until just the head of my cock peeked out, trapped for the torment he unleashed on my crown by sucking and licking around it. I was panting and clinging to the post above my head in seconds.

"I couldn't stop looking at you during the game," he said, inching my pants a little lower, and I thought about how our gazes had caught over the dining table earlier. The warmth in his eyes and how it tinged his smile. It was another one of those subtle intoxicants, the one I'd envied most years before when I'd catch it happening between Nate and Eric or Chet and Mark.

A tingle raced up my spine as Sam sucked along the side of my shaft. "Me too—*oh, god.*" I buried my fingers in his hair as he sank lower, taking me deeper, lips moving in an expert glide, teasing my tip and moving lower to my balls. "I've been thinking about this since the locker room this morning. When you were stretching." I'd gotten out of the shower and walked into our bedroom to find him doing his post-run stretches in nothing but briefs, one leg hiked up on our dresser to loosen his hamstrings, his ass a perfect peach. But since we had company coming, I didn't have time to follow my instincts and bury my face between his cheeks. My patience was paying far better dividends than I'd anticipated, though. "I wanted you to find me after that...that *game* and—" I gasped sharply as Sam swallowed me to the root, the sudden heat and suction pulling a shudder from me.

"And?" He slid a wet finger behind my sac and teased over my hole.

"And fuck me," I managed to finish, then whimpered out his name as a plea when he nudged his finger just inside me.

Sam rested back on his heels, one hand working my cock,

the other opening me up. "How do you want to be fucked? You want me to bend you over and split that sweet little ass open, or you want it the other way, your legs wrapped around my waist and my tongue in your mouth."

These were impossible choices. "Y-you pick," I stuttered, squeezing my eyes shut in ecstasy as he sucked me into his mouth again. He worked me over slowly and patiently until I was whining and thrusting in his throat without a care for the needy sounds coming from me.

When he could tell I was about to lose it, he held my thigh and jacked me off onto his tongue, knowing how much I loved seeing him swallow my release. Once my thighs quit quaking, he stood up and kissed me nice and deep before turning me around, lifting my hands and curling them over the risers above me.

"Hold on right there, okay?" he said, kissing the nape of my neck as I nodded mutely. "Don't let go."

Cool air moved over my hot skin like a balm as Sam yanked my pants down my knees and left me exposed. I felt the weight of his gaze on me, taking in my spread legs, my ass, probably red with his handprints where he'd clutched me, and I thrilled in all of it. Even when he was silent, I could feel the perfect transmission of his love and desire for me.

I could never get enough of that first second when Sam entered me. The sting of intrusion, and then the way my body melted around him, gave way, and swallowed him. A multitude of sensations occurred at once, twining pleasure and the briefest bite of pain together into an aphrodisiac that made my head spin. Sam's moan—familiar and particular to this one instance when it was laced with a sense of a relief and release, like he'd been waiting so long and this moment was his reward—always got to me.

"Fuck me," I whispered, and his hand came to the nape of my neck, thumb tilting my chin, his kiss a hot smear along my jaw and finally to my lips. His tongue speared inside my mouth in a mimicry of his thrusts. Slow at first, which meant he was watching, enjoying seeing his big dick disappear inside me, and then with more power, picking up speed, his hands tight and possessive on me just the way I loved it. His grunts and panted breaths got me worked up all over again.

This was exactly what I'd always envisioned, my hands clinging to the bleacher above me, Sam clutching my hip, his fingers curled and his grip tight like he was just as desperate. My body swayed with every thrust, full of him and feeling every inch. His other hand splayed and roamed over my skin, fire in every caress. And finally, finally his touch trickled down my spine and pressed at the base, deepening the arch in my back.

He wrapped one arm around my chest, pulling me to him, the other one sliding behind my thigh and lifting my leg so he could go deeper.

"Oh fuck," I moaned when he tagged my prostate and then pulled out and did it again. He slammed into me over and over, his breaths going ragged and strained with effort. I unraveled from the inside out, fraying threads of ecstasy spinning loose from my toes to the top of my head, everything a sensation of suspension.

Then came the crash, sudden and intense, rushing in from the corners of my vision and taking me over, head to toe. "*Sam,*" I cried out, my hips bucking the air. He wrapped a big fist around me just in time and squeezed the back of my thigh tighter, his thick cock pulsing hotly inside me as he fell apart, too.

His cries landed across my back, heating my skin beneath the warring mix of kisses and nips of his teeth.

He slid his arms up my forearms, hands closing over mine where they clung for dear life on the risers, and he bore my weight easily as I rested back against him. We swayed together as we caught our breath.

"Was it as good as you'd hoped it be?"

"Even better." I sighed happily. "Why the hell did we wait so long?"

"Lack of optimal setting. Though we did do it in that dugout that one time."

"Mmmm, the U's stadium. Fuck, that was a really good one." Spring of senior year. Another time we'd tried to film something and had forgotten about the camera halfway through. We'd published it to the site anyway, and it remained one of our most popular videos.

Sam hummed his agreement against my temple and then kissed down the side of my face. He relaxed his grip on me, sliding a hand down my torso and then folding me into my arms, his penchant for postorgasm affection kicking in full force.

"This is my favorite feeling in the world," I admitted drowsily.

"It is?"

"Mmm-hmm."

"Good." I could hear the smile in his voice. "Because it's mine, too."

Too lazy to change back into our street clothes, we threw our jackets on over our football gear and headed home hand in hand.

"What's next?" Sam asked, nodding politely as someone passed us on the sidewalk.

"I was thinking a dog."

He laughed. "I meant more immediately."

"Me too." I winked, then swung our hands gently. "Cooking shows and naps?"

"At the same time?"

"Definitely."

A drowsy contentment settled in my bones and wrapped around me as we walked, warmer even than the coat I was wearing. It remained the rest of the walk and even as we changed and cleaned up ourselves and the apartment.

It was still there when we dove onto the couch and I burrowed into Sam's arms, listening to the patterns of his breaths slow as he dozed off not five minutes into a pound cake challenge, my head pillowed on his bicep, fingers of one hand still laced with his. I thought about freshman-year Jesse and how he'd convinced himself that romance and true love lived in big moments. In showy, extravagant gestures and loud declarations. I thought about how naive he'd been, and also how lucky to find someone who'd shown him the truth. That the deepest and most abiding love was tucked into the ordinary moments like these.

I snuggled deeper into Sam's warmth and drifted off to the familiar sounds of cake battles and Sam's soft snore, perfectly, completely content.

—End—

What happens when Sam and Jesse try to film a massage scene for their OnlyFans? Click HERE to grab that special bonus scene. Curious about what the rest of the EA crew has been up to? Join Neve's reader group on Facebook, Wilder's Wild Ones, for random sightings of Nate, Eric, Jesse, Sam, Chet, and Mark.

AVAILABLE NOW: DEDICATED

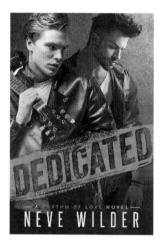

"Our greatest hit is a love song I wrote for my bandmate. And he has no idea."

Two rockers, a handful of secrets, and a publicity nightmare tossed in a remote cabin. Shaken and stirred with snark, angst, and a shit ton of sexual tension. Kaboom, y'all. A friends-to-lovers rockstar romance.

smarturl.it/GetDedicated

This needs to go right to the top of your TBR pile. It is MAGIC. If friends to lovers is AT ALL your thing, then look no further. This is the best one I've ever read. The characters are magnetic throughout and the story progresses in a wonderfully meaningful (and sometimes rocky) way. Ends with a HEA that is so, so satisfying.

—Amazon Reviewer

So many adjectives I could use for this book; soulful, dirty, gripping, honest and most of all, it's full of heart and it brought every emotion to the fore. I'm stone cold in love with this author's writing and desperate for more.

—OMG Reads

Sparks fly, banter is slung, gut-punch moments had me sucking in a deep breath as the emotions resonated within me, and the sexual tension was off the charts smoking hot. Their relationship was real and raw, even with all the duplicity surrounding them.

Not going to lie, I spent the entire day with my nose buried in my Kindle, eagerly tapping the pages and ignoring life, from page one until the end.

—Wicked Reads

MORE BY NEVE WILDER

Rhythm of Love Series

(Contemporary Romance)

Dedicated

Bend (Novella)

Resonance

Extracurricular Activities Series

(new adult/college)

Want Me

Try Me

Show Me

Nook Island Series

(Contemporary Romance)

Center of Gravity

Sightlines (Novella)

Ace's Wild Series

(multi author series)

Reunion (Novella)

Wages of Sin Series

(Romantic action adventure and suspense, co-written with Only James)

Bad Habits

Play Dirty

OH, HI!

Looking for a little more from me? You should definitely sign up for my newsletter at:

www.nevewilder.com/subscribe

As a thank you for subscribing, you'll receive a link to Study Hard, a bonus scene between Nate and Eric from Want Me, and a link to Ru and Quinn's story, a steamy novella-length prequel to the Rhythm of Love World.

I'd love to have you in my very lively Facebook reader group, Wilder's Wild Ones.

ABOUT NEVE WILDER

Neve Wilder lives in the South, where the summers are hot and the winters are...sometimes cold.

She reads promiscuously, across multiple genres, but her favorite stories always contain an element of romance. Incidentally, this is also what she likes to write. Slow-burners with delicious tension? Yes. Whiplash-inducing page-turners, also yes. Down and dirty scorchers? Yes. And every flavor in between.

She believes David Bowie was the sexiest musician to ever live, and she's always game to nerd out on anything from music to writing.

And finally, she believes that love conquers all. Except the heat index in July. Nothing can conquer that bastard.

Join her for daily shenanigans in her FB group:
Wilder's Wild Ones

facebook.com/nevewilderwrites
instagram.com/nevewilder
bookbub.com/authors/neve-wilder
amazon.com/author/nevewilder

Printed in Great Britain
by Amazon